The Thief Prince's Wife

Noor Juman grew up daydreaming about fictional characters falling in love. An avid watcher of rom-coms and reader of all things romance, she began writing her own to cheer herself up during COVID-19 lockdowns. Her other books include, *A Summer Lesson in Romance* (Noor Juman Books, 2021), and *An Autumn Guest Checks In* (Noor Juman Books, 2024).

For the latest updates, visit www.noorjuman.com. You can also follow Noor on Twitter (X if you must) at the handle: @noor_juman.

NOOR JUMAN

The Thief Prince's Wife

Published by Westland Books, a division of Nasadiya Technologies Private Limited, in 2025

No. 269/2B, First Floor, 'Irai Arul', Vimalraj Street, Nethaji Nagar, Alapakkam Main Road, Maduravoyal, Chennai 600095

Westland and the Westland logo are the trademarks of Nasadiya Technologies Private Limited, or its affiliates.

ISBN: 9789360456597

10 9 8 7 6 5 4 3 2 1

Typeset by Mukul Chand

Printed at Thomson Press (India) Ltd

One

PAYAL HAD NEVER BEEN ONE TO TELL LIES. It wasn't right. But doing the right thing was what got her into this mess in the first place.

To come up with a lie . . . no, a whole assortment of lies for every possible line of inquiry—that too to convince a hardened criminal to marry her—was a tall order indeed.

The irony of the whole situation would have reduced her to bellyaching fits of laughter if it didn't scare the living shit out of her. Growing up, she'd always believed being born American, having liberal desi parents, a top-notch education and a lucrative career would save her from the antiquated tradition of arranged marriage. Never in twenty-nine years did she imagine she'd wholeheartedly agree to a match brokered by her father.

Not that there was anything remotely 'traditional' about this match. No one—not the family elders, not even her own mother—approved of it. The family she was marrying into didn't have the right ancestry, or observe the right religion. Hell, they didn't even live on the right side of the law.

They were bratva. Ukrainian mafia, to be exact.

Suffice to say, the condensation coating her Mediterranean Mule's copper mug wasn't the only reason her hands were clammy. Eyes trained on the bar's entrance, Payal's heart jumped every time someone entered. She'd chosen a table at the back of the dimly lit establishment to give herself a tiny window of time to compose herself when her intended arrived. The last thing she wanted was for a mountainous, prominent-veined gangster man walking up behind her and taking her by complete surprise.

It was only once she'd drained half her Mule when she realised that her choice of table had left her no place to run in case of an ambush. Her breathing shallowed. A violent pounding in her ears drowned out the hushed chatter of the other patrons. She hunched over the table, struggling against an overwhelming urge to curl up into a ball. Wincing at how the fabric of her top scraped the coarse skin of her abdomen, her eyes darted around the bar for another table—one that could alert her of her future husband's approach, and also allow her a clean escape.

You're being paranoid.

She was. She knew she was. But thinking the thought didn't make it any easier to calm down.

She kept looking. The other tables with a decent vantage of the entrance were taken. That was good, though. In a way. Even though it was early in the evening, there were still enough people at the bar and individual tables—*enough eyewitnesses*—to convince her she wouldn't be harmed. Besides, her family's chauffeur Nasir was on speed dial and parked a block away if she needed rescuing.

This was what her life had been reduced to. Payal Lohani, once a tough, go-getter New Yorker, was now too afraid to step out of her parents' Scarsdale home and use public transport on her own.

A year and a half. She'd had enough of this bullshit. If a deal with the devil was what it took to buy her old life, her freedom and her safety back, then so be it. She had to put on a brave face. She could not chicken out of this.

Emptying her mug, shaking off her inhibitions along with the buzz from the vodka, she sat up straight, steadied her breath and resumed watching the door intently.

She had no idea what to expect. Oleksiy Karmazin was not on any social media. The websites for his fitness centre and security firm didn't have any photos of him either. The fact that he owned and ran an establishment called Channel Fitness gave her a few ideas though. She imagined Ivan Drago from *Rocky 4*, all blond and muscly; wearing a permanent scowl. Or maybe he resembled a Bond villain from the nineties, his head shaved, a crimson gash across a clouded eye the only colour on his sickly pale face.

Payal had never seen the appeal of the proverbial bad boy. She was too smart to harbour any fantasies about 'fixing' a man. Rage, violence, abandonment, mommy issues—that stuff was for therapists, not girlfriends. And she most definitely did not have the time or patience to be near men who lived dangerously. Her past boyfriends had all been of the boy-next-door variety. Fresh-faced, suitably polite, charming, highly educated, career-minded, with a liking for cable-knit sweaters.

Not far off, in fact, from the tall, dark-haired man who had just strode in and ordered a Brooklyn Lager at the bar, mused Payal.

On second thought, none of her exes had ever been *this* handsome.

Dressed casually in a long-sleeved Henley, the sleeves rolled up to show off a large watch strapped to a correspondingly large wrist, he perched himself on the edge of a bar stool as though he had no intention of getting comfortable and took a tentative sip of his beer. His features seemed chiseled with the utmost care: high at the cheekbones, straight up the nose's bridge, jaw perfectly squared and proportioned so it didn't splay out past his cheeks. His beard, neatly trimmed, somehow made his features appear more angular and blunted at the same time.

Despite his height and athletic frame, his easy-going demeanor, which Payal thought bordered on boyish sweetness, put the bartender in a chatty mood. How cruel the universe was, dangling this prime specimen in front of her when her fate was as good as sealed to a demon from the underworld.

A year and a half ago, she would've kept looking at him till their gazes met. Maybe bought him a drink as an invitation to her table. She might have even been brazen enough to walk up to the bar and take the seat next to him.

But that was a lifetime ago. She was getting distracted. Oleksiy Karmazin. *He* was the only item on her agenda tonight. Tearing her gaze off the handsome man, she rested her chin on her knuckles and projected all her focus onto the entrance, willing the gangster to arrive faster so she could get this over with.

The corner of her eye caught movement. Still perched on the bar stool, the handsome man was engrossed by the beer bottle he rolled in his palm but the rest of his body was angled towards her. A fraction of a second later, his eyes found hers.

Shit. Payal looked away. She swirled the ice cubes in her otherwise empty mug, trying her best to look oblivious. Uninterested.

His attention returned to his beer for a beat, fingers strumming against the brown glass in grave deliberation. Then, threading the bottle's neck through his long, slender fingers, he was on his feet, advancing toward her like a panther going in for the kill. Gone was the boyish sweetness he'd shown the bartender. His pitch-dark eyes gauged her with a barely contained ferocity. Which could be interpreted as attraction, of course. The really intense, instinctive kind. But it could also be malice.

It occurred to Payal that she might have to do more than turn him away.

She might have to make a run for it.

Shifting uneasily in her seat, Payal's hand edged towards her phone. She felt him getting closer. Her chest hurt from her heart's violent stammering.

There are too many eyewitnesses, she reminded herself.

Where the hell was Oleksiy Karmazin?

Maybe he'd change his mind and leave her alone if she looked like she was doing something important on her phone.

Hands trembling, her thumb stilled over her phone's screen as a shadow darkened her table.

'You Payal?' he asked hesitantly.

Oh.

A muscle at the back of Payal's neck smarted as her head snapped up. The way his Henley clung to his lean, well-defined chest and shoulders snagged her attention before she could go high enough to look him in the face. 'O-Ole-eksiy?'

His eyes narrowed in his study of her, glinting with something resembling amusement that unsettled Payal. He chewed his bottom lip before pointing his beer at himself. 'Yeah, that's me.'

Payal struggled to keep her head above the paralysis taking hold of her. 'Please,' she said, motioning to the seat opposite to her, begging her self-control to return. Involuntary salivation was not something she was prepared to deal with in front of this man. Not tonight. Not ever.

Planting the beer on the table between them, he settled into his seat. Payal found herself slumping under the intensity of his piercing scrutiny. Head tilted sideways, his lips pulled up in an incredulous, lopsided sneer.

'You're, uh—' He looked away, chuckled under his breath with a slight shake of the head. Payal didn't take it personally. This must have been as absurd for him as it was for her. He found his words in a thick Brooklyn accent. 'When my father said you were an accountant—I wasn't expecting you.'

For the blink of an eye, Payal thought he could see through her. Not just her clothes, but her secrets as well. Her hand reflexively shot up to her abdomen, making her breath hitch as it passed over the sensitive skin across her ribcage.

That was impossible, of course. Oleksiy was only saying what every other man said to her when they first met.

'Well, you're not exactly what I was expecting either,' she said, mustering what little of her past self's flirtatiousness she could. 'I was on the lookout for Ivan Drago.'

His brows lifted in an unamused arch. The corner of his mouth curled with barely-contained contempt as he combed his thick hair back with a sharp tug. 'Yeah, well. Sorry to disappoint.'

Immediately realising her gaffe, Payal bit her tongue. Not only had she made the egregious mistake of lumping Ukrainian and Russian people together, but her mental picture of him—that of a light-haired, light-eyed brutish thug who spoke in monosyllables—was moulded entirely on ignorant cultural stereotypes. The man sitting before her had attended the Stern School of Business, for God's sake! She'd be irritated too if every stranger expected to see Priyanka Chopra when they met her.

She opened her mouth to apologise. To tell him how far from disappointed . . . how relieved she was that *he* was Oleksiy Karmazin. That the glossy hair he ran his fingers through, the stark black of it, complemented his complexion wonderfully and looked enticingly soft. That she had an unexplainable desire to feel the bristled tips of his beard against the sensitive, most secret expanses of her skin.

Stunned by the trajectory of her own thoughts, the apology slipped her mind. By the time she remembered, the moment had passed. Gulping down the saliva pooling in her mouth, she raised her glass to signal the bartender for another.

'You want anything else?' she asked Oleksiy, trying to appear nonchalant.

'I'm good.' He shifted in his seat, looping his right shoulder ever so slightly like he had a kink in his neck. His fingertips traced a line down the misted bottle.

Payal bided the ensuing silence watching his teeth drag across his lower lip before he sucked it in and rolled it out. She was vaguely aware her jaw had gone slack. What was she so apprehensive about, again? For the life of her, she couldn't remember. How bad would it really be to have those puckered lips pressed against her own? How bad could it be to have the burn of that beard seared around her mouth, down the column of her neck, on her collarbone, around her . . .

Clearing her throat, she forced herself to meet his eyes. 'Is this sort of thing normal in your circles? Arranged marriages, I mean.'

Laughter glinted in Oleksiy's black eyes. 'Marriage isn't exactly normal in my circles,' he said, his voice soft but gravelly.

Payal's heart stilled. He was trying to scare her. She refused to take the bait. Unblinking, she waited for more.

'But yeah, when it's sanctioned, it's usually arranged. Loyalties are pledged. Assets change hands. Stuffa real fairy tales.' He took a shallow swig of his beer.

Payal brushed off the note of resentment in his tone. Arranged marriages weren't anyone's first choice. It certainly wasn't hers. But life had a way of throwing curveballs your way. 'And are these marriages usually arranged within the umm … community?'

'Not a lotta Indian brides, if that's what you're asking.'

'What, so no support groups for foreign brides of the bratva?' she joked.

'You'll never fit in,' he said coolly.

Payal's pulse raced. She'd assumed the arrangement was a done deal. That the purpose of their meeting here was more to get acquainted before the big day. She hadn't realised that the final decision was still pending. This was a job interview, one that could very well end in a rejection.

'I'm very personable,' she found her voice.

'It doesn't matter. The community's inherently insular. Distrustful of outsiders for obvious reasons.'

A waitress arrived with Payal's second Mule.

'That may be the case,' Payal replied after thanking the waitress as levelly as she was able. She leaned forward. 'But your father trusts mine. He wouldn't have agreed to this if he suspected we posed a threat of any kind to the family business.'

Oleksiy's eyes darkened, his jaw hard. Through gritted teeth, he said, 'My father might know what's right for the family business, but he doesn't get to decide what's right for me. I'm not *in* the family business. Or did he forget to mention that?'

Payal's father certainly hadn't mentioned it. When he said Oleksiy ran a fitness centre and a security firm, she'd assumed they were bratva fronts to launder dirty money.

'Then why're you here?' Payal asked, flushed with panic and frustration.

His face softened. 'To ask you to say you can't go through with it.'

The hell I will. 'But I have no objections.'

'You don't want to marry a guy who's in love with somebody else.' He believed he'd won. The corners of his eyes creased with his smirk. 'No woman in her right mind would.'

'Oh.' Payal's shoulders drooped. She hadn't factored in matters of the heart. It wasn't a priority for her, not with everything else gone to hell in her life. And she most definitely didn't anticipate a man from a criminal background to turn down her father's money on such . . . sentimental grounds.

She took a long sip of her drink, her thoughts racing. Of course, it was wrong to deny someone the opportunity to be with who they wanted to be with. Where, then, would that leave her? No security. No Columbia in the fall. Wasting the prime of her life holed up in Scarsdale, with tax season being the only thing worth looking forward to.

She'd pinned all her hopes on this arrangement. On him. She needed him for life to return to some semblance of normalcy.

And he needed her to refuse the match.

Because he couldn't do it himself.

'And do you plan to marry this person?' Payal asked, arching her brow in challenge.

Eyes narrowed, he answered, 'Like I said, marriages in my circle have to be sanctioned by the vor zakone.'

So he'll have an illicit paramour. Payal could live with that. Was she disappointed that this gorgeous man would never reciprocate the desire she felt for him a second ago? Sure. Was she crestfallen that she would be bound to a husband who'd never love her? Not really. She was, of course, familiar with the idea of marriage as a glorified business contract. Besides, what was one man's love compared with the freedom to live her life as she pleased?

He needed to know she had no qualms with his having a lover on the side. 'But you are in a committed relationship?'

Something she said hit a raw nerve. Tersely, he said, 'I'm committed to not marrying anyone else.'

'I don't expect loyalty from you.'

'And I don't think it's fair for either of us to be trapped in a loveless marriage.'

Payal suppressed a groan. This was aggravating. 'Love's got nothing to do with it.'

'For fuck's sake,' Oleksiy hissed under his breath. He turned his head away so the full force of his sneer didn't burn a hole in her. 'What's a career girl like you even doing here?'

'Actually, I'm unemployed.'

'And heading to grad school this fall, if memory serves,' he snarled. 'You're smart, you're beautiful, you come from money. You can have your pick of men. Why this? Why me?'

Because I don't want to die.

'Because I have a duty to my family.' The lies she'd been so apprehensive about telling came easier now she knew she wouldn't have to seduce the man, or put on the airs of a blushing, deliriously happy bride. This marriage would be a marriage in name only. A business contract. Once the papers were signed and the terms of agreement met, they would carry on with their own lives, independent of one another. No feelings involved meant no feelings got hurt. 'I have to look out for my family's interests—what my father deems best—before I look out for my own. And while I can't say I'm familiar with the inner workings of the bratva, I imagine it's not very different for you.'

'Then we're at complete odds,' Oleksiy said, violently jabbing a finger on the tabletop for emphasis, 'because my life's one purpose is to step out of my father's shadow.'

Payal steeled herself against recoiling at the spite in his words. 'I've said all I have to say. I don't have a problem with you being with someone else.' She fished out a fifty from her purse and slapped it onto the table before rising to her feet. 'If you have an objection, I suggest you take it up with the men who brokered the deal. Otherwise, I'll see you at City Hall.'

Two

OLEKSIY WAS AT THE DOOR TO HIS PARENTS' condo at a quarter to eight the next morning, showered, beard trimmed, hair slicked back, dressed for work in a sharp suit and freshly shined shoes. Emanating power and control.

'*Pane* Oleksiy,' Liza remarked warmly as she let him in. 'Your mama had a feeling you'd be coming today.'

'Liza.' He mustered a smile for the family's long-time maid.

His parents were in the kitchen: father at the table in his pyjamas, reading the paper; mother at the stove, pouring blini batter onto a skillet. Oleksiy shrugged out of his jacket and handed it to Liza before joining them.

The gilded frame of the painting over the living room mantlepiece, he noted, had been switched out for a rustic one. Something that suited the painting's landscape subject better. Unlike its predecessor, it carried no delusions of decorating a Tsar's palace. No, this frame was much more appropriate for a modern luxury condo.

His mama had been making tiny improvements like this since his grandmother, the family's last living elder, died six years ago—around the same time he'd braved his first steps towards making his own way. Change had to be incremental in the Karmazin household. As it had to be in the world of thieves. Anything too drastic would trigger an uproar powerful enough to stamp it out and bar the way for repeat offenses.

Oleksiy had never officially pledged nor renounced the bratva. Early in his life, when Mama was tasked with educating him about the inner workings of the crime syndicate, she had cautioned him against drawing attention to himself. She'd conditioned him to be a benign non-entity to the bratva, bereft of any remarkable talent. Incompetent, even, if the situation called for it. To cultivate the right connections with the utmost care. To be wary of those seeking favour, and to never put himself in the position of needing a favour. To avoid the hotspots bratva brigadiers canvassed for new recruits. To always have a compelling excuse at hand to extricate himself from assemblies where thieves might catch on to his intelligence. And to never *ever* ask his *tato* for money.

Mama's advice had worked so far. Much as Tato bemoaned having to groom his son-in-law as his successor instead of his own son, Oleksiy's apparent ineptitude for bratva matters had managed to convince him he'd be more of a hindrance than an asset.

Or so Oleksiy thought.

A bratva-ordained marriage threatened to undo everything.

Tato looked up from the paper, his mouth sloping into an unimpressed grimace. 'Bit overdressed for the gym, no?'

'Ah, Petro!' Mama admonished, gently swatting Tato's shoulder with a kitchen towel. 'You're just jealous he looks better in a suit than you do.' Pulling Oleksiy's face down to her height, she planted a kiss on each cheek, bluntly adding, 'It's because you take after my side of the family.'

Bitten by self-consciousness, Oleksiy pulled up the chair across from Tato. The suit was meant to be his armor, yet it had failed to keep him from feeling exposed. Rolling out the stiffness in his right shoulder, stretching the sides of his neck, he sat down. 'I'm meeting prospective clients for the security firm.'

'Yeah?' Tato returned to his paper. 'And how many of my thieves is that gonna cost me?'

It was difficult for a vor zakone's son to steer clear of the bratva, but even more so for a low-ranking thief. Since he was a boy, Mama had drilled it into Oleksiy's head that systemic discrimination and poverty drove people into the bratva's clutches. That it was up to the more fortunate to create better opportunities, and pull them out of the unrelenting web of petty theft, contraband, extortion, prostitution and violence.

So, while Oleksiy didn't partake in bratva business, his chosen path was still entwined with the world of thieves. The fitness centre he co-owned with a friend from Stern hired retired thieves as trainers and others from vulnerable households around Brighton Beach as support staff. His newer solo venture relied almost entirely on sharp-eyed, able-bodied thieves who'd left the bratva in their prime. Some of them were a decade younger than his thirty-two years.

He responded to his father with a disingenuous shrug. 'You're the one always telling me there's an excess of labour in a free market.'

'Every trained thief lost,' Tato folded the paper and set it aside, 'is a loss to the bratva.'

'They're low-level crooks with a powerful right hook, Tato. A dime a dozen.'

'Loyal men are in short supply.'

Back at the stove, Mama shot Oleksiy a warning look over her shoulder. *What have I taught you about drawing attention to yourself?*

But Oleksiy wasn't in the mood to play dumb today. 'Well, they sure as hell didn't think twice before taking me up on my offer. So, maybe I'm doing you a favour, eh?'

Tato's quiet chuckle held a note of menace. The kind capable of making politicians and pickpockets alike break into a cold sweat. 'Kid, I'm gonna make something very clear before you start filling that head o' yours with fantasies of playing American saviour. Those men you think you're "reforming"? They don't come to you 'cause you showed them the light, all right? They go to you 'cause I let 'em. 'Cause my word is law.'

'Petro,' Mama interjected sweetly, setting a platter stacked high with blini on the table. 'The child's come home after so long—'

'Now, you being my son buys you a bit of elbow room,' Tato continued, 'but there's a point past which you won't have that luxury anymore.'

'Christ, Tato, I'm not blackmailing anybody to come work for me, all right? I'm putting out job circulars like any other business, and when they apply, I give 'em higher preference, is all. What's so wrong with that? Westerners hire by preference all the time, diversity statement or no. And I keep telling you they're all lower rung. Your ex-military guys, your brigadiers, your enforcers—I'm not touching any of 'em unless they're retired.'

Mama caressed his arm, willing him to calm down. 'What will you have on your blini? Sour cream or varenye?'

Not that she needed an answer. Apricot varenye was his favourite.

'Not now you're not,' Tato snorted. 'But tell me this. What happens a few years from now when you've done what you can with high-rise security? What happens when you set your sights on something more lucrative like, say VIP security? You have a network of US marines you can recruit from, or are you going to start eyeing my bulls, my brigadiers, my enforcers, my surveillance boys?'

Oleksiy's jaw clenched. VIP security *was* something he'd set his sights on. For a future so vague, so distant, he hadn't bothered discussing it with anyone. That Tato could pinpoint his ambitions without him ever uttering a word about them turned his feet to ice. And Tato was right. Oleksiy didn't have his own connections. If business expansion factored into his long-term plans, sooner or later, he was going to be at the mercy of the bratva's goodwill. That is, if he wasn't already. Was there really a way out of the bratva's shadows, or had he spent all this time kidding himself?

Forcing a bite of blini down his throat, he watched Liza clearing the kitchen's countertops, eyes lowered, quiet as mouse. She'd been trafficked into America by one of the bratva's prostitution cells, and would have endured every imaginable violation and more had Mama not rescued her.

Oleksiy's muscles relinquished their grip as he regained some perspective. Over the years, Mama had tried rehabilitating as many victims as she could without stirring the hornet's nest. One person, one change at a time. The goal wasn't outrageous. He just wanted to help as many people build a life outside the bratva as possible. If VIP security meant getting in too deep with the bratva, he wouldn't do it. A lucrative business was a means to an end. It couldn't be the end in itself.

'Petro, enough please,' Mama tutted. 'You won't need any sour cream on that blini with that mood of yours.'

Oleksiy bit back a snort at Tato's answering huff. The blini went down easier now.

Mama poured out three cups of coffee from the French press.

'Better add an extra spoon of sugar to mine,' Tato griped. His long, bracing inhale was a blaring horn in Oleksiy's ears.

Gritting his teeth, Oleksiy focused his attention on his plate, hoping against all odds he could steer through what he knew was coming next.

'So,' Tato prodded. 'The Lohani girl. How did it go?'

He'd spent the entirety of the night before trying to think of a compelling argument he hadn't used before, and came up empty-handed. 'I can't marry her.'

'That's what you keep saying,' Tato said between chews. 'The others were too young, too unsophisticated, uneducated, blah blah blah. Fine, we respected your wishes. We found you someone who's from a trustworthy family *and* closer to you in age. Went to Cornell. Is starting at Columbia in the fall. If this is about looks, well, that's too bad. Pretty was never a requirement.'

'It's not about looks,' Oleksiy snapped, not so much because his father had insinuated that he was shallow, but because Payal Lohani was a fucking knockout. He may have sworn never to marry anyone but Alice, but fact was fact. The woman would lose nothing if this arrangement was scrapped. Any man she trained those large, perennially half-lidded almond-shaped eyes of hers on would gladly go down on his knees to do her bidding. Hell, before Alice, he would have gladly vied for her attention, seduced her, pinned her up against a wall someplace secluded and dark as she muffled her cries of ecstasy against his shoulder.

Oleksiy was aware that Indian women were beautiful. Men in those parts didn't just build one of the seven wonders of the world to pay tribute to the good hearts of women. Payal looked like she'd walked out of an ad for a luxury brand, her skin so luminous and cheekbones so defined there could have been a ring light shining on her at all times. She had the same mocking, close-lipped smile, the same chastising glare, the same air of defiance and steely determination as the South Asian girls he'd attended business school with. She lacked their soft edges, though. Their extravagance, their perfectly straightened and shiny hair. Her hair had been swept over her shoulder in a messy braid, and in spite of her loose-fitted blouse and terrible posture, Oleksiy could tell she was built of lean, hard muscle.

Then there was the fact that she threw back her vodka like it was lemonade.

In a way, she was the perfect choice for a bratva bride—cunning, astute, smart-mouthed, assertive. Intimidating, but not enough to be considered an outright threat. Someone of her character could quietly strengthen a thief's influence within the brotherhood.

Which was precisely why Oleksiy could not—*would not* marry her.

'Her family is trustworthy to you,' Oleksiy said to Tato. 'Not the rest of Brighton. You really think this hood's going to be all right with the vor zakone's son marrying a Hindu?'

The table shook with Tato's incredulous laughter. 'You hear that, *myliyy*?' he asked Mama. 'Your *sonechko* cares about upsetting community sentiment now.' He turned to Oleksiy. 'And where was this conscience of yours when you were seeing that Alice girl, eh?'

The sound of her name on Tato's tongue turned Oleksiy's vision red, his breath aflame. Alice was the most precious thing in the world to him. The taste of an increasingly elusive life completely severed from the bratva. No one involved with this cursed world was allowed to speak her name. Not unless she could be a part of it, at his side.

'Well, allow me to put these new-found concerns of yours to bed,' Tato said. 'The Lohanis are Muslim, and Abrahamic religions are allowed to marry amongst themselves. It's all been verified with Rabbi Pasternak.'

'For fuck's sake!' Oleksiy's cutlery clattered onto his plate.

'Oleksiy!' Mama reprimanded.

'I'm a grown man. I should be allowed to marry whoever the hell I want!'

'You,' Tato emphasised each word with a jab of his finger, 'are a Karmazin. You will marry who your vor zakone orders you to marry. Now, I've given you your time. Your "space". More than enough of it. What, you think you're the only kid who's ever been roughed up a little?'

Oleksiy drew a sharp breath. Phantom pain shot through his right shoulder. He was back in the alley again. Strong hands bolting him to the ground by each limb, wrenching them to their limit. Boot heels driving into his flesh, shattering his bones. He flattened his hands against the tabletop to stave off the cold shivers, tried to ground himself to the present.

'It's high time you did your part,' Tato carried on. 'If you'd bothered taking any interest in the family business, you'd know things aren't as peachy as they used to be. We've had a few transactions go south.'

'And I keep telling you surveillance has gotten too sophisticated to be dealing in physical goods anymore,' Oleksiy retorted. 'If it's crime you want to commit, you're better off doing it in cyberspace.'

'Oy!' Tato slapped the table, making the others jump. 'I'm the one talking here. We owe some big people in high places a lotta money, you understand? Money the Lohani girl's dowry will cover.'

'I'm not cleaning up your messes for you.'

Tato shot Mama an exasperated look before saying, 'Did they teach you about corporate takeovers at that overpriced business school of yours?'

Oleksiy glared at him.

'Assuming that's a yes, and assuming you understand we're all fish food if we don't pay up, your refusal to marry leaves us with one other choice.'

'Getting on in years, aren't you? About time to be thinking about retirement,' Oleksiy goaded, his eyes narrowed. 'A takeover wouldn't be the worst thing that could happen.'

'Not for me, it won't. But you think the Berezivkas will be as accommodating of your rescue shelters as I've been?'

Paralysis seized Oleksiy again, harder, drilling deeper. His collar dug into his neck as all mental barriers gave out and his mind plummeted into that deserted alley. His ears filled with cruel jeers and laughter. His eyes burned with tears, of pain, yes, but mostly of the deep betrayal he'd suffered. He rolled his shoulder, then his neck, desperate for some relief. Desperate for air.

'You think they'll allow you to keep that gym of yours running if you refuse to wash their black money?' Tato taunted him. 'You think they'll turn a blind eye to you plucking their thieves and whores for your business ventures? You think you can stomach answering to those fellas for the rest of your days?'

Oleksiy flinched at something brushing his hand. It was only Mama draping her hand over his. He flipped his palm over and squeezed her slender fingers. *Thank you*, the first squeeze said. Then, *please get me out of this.*

Mama's hand was impassive. Like the rest of her. The reality of his position sank in as the silence drew out and Tato's questions hung over them like a thick fog. Mama may have encouraged him to be independent of the bratva, to create safer, more respectable opportunities for those caught in its snare. She may have been an open-minded, loving and supportive mother to him. But her role as wife to the vor zakone, as Tato's support system, his shrewdest adviser, his most inconspicuous intermediary and protector—that took precedence over everything else. Because as much as she hated the bratva, she loved Tato more and was prepared to do whatever it took to keep him alive.

Including forcing her own son's hand when it came to marriage.

Oleksiy untangled his hand from hers.

'Kid,' Tato said softly. 'I'm not asking you to put a bullet in someone's head for the money. I'm asking you to take a perfectly respectable bride to save this family—yourself included. I—we've given you everything you've ever asked for. All we're asking you is to do this one thing.'

To do as the thief king ordered. To fulfil his princely duty to the brotherhood.

If you have an objection, I suggest you take it up with the men who brokered the deal.

The echo of his future wife's words made his nose wrinkle and mouth curl in disgust. She'd passed the onus onto him so casually, so flippantly. As if it didn't matter that she was ruining his life.

As if he'd really ever had a choice.

'The boys in our family don't just have two left feet, they have hooves!'

Payal looked at her younger sister Saira's reflection in the rear-view mirror, wishing she shared in her zest for wedding preparations. Beside Saira, their mother glared at the passing cityscape through the car window, sitting arrow-straight, more so from the effort of bottling in her anger than out of habit.

'Flailing donkeys, the lot of them,' Saira continued. 'My left foot is still blue from getting trampled on at Parvin Apa's wedding. I'm not taking any of them in the dance.'

'Then do an all-girls choreography,' Payal said, resigned.

'Uff! Appi, this is wedding choreography, okay? Not some university cultural show where everyone's too distracted by white people doing bhangra to notice if it's any good or not. As sister to the bride, my social clout depends on this coming across as immaculately synchronised'—a starry look glazed over Saira's eyes—'but also as flirty and cinematic. I love you, and this is your wedding, but my showmanship better be what everyone talks about at your *sangeet*. I've been compiling the set list since high school.'

Well, it isn't exactly the wedding anyone had in mind, is it? Payal wanted to snap.

She had never given too much thought about what her wedding might be like. She'd attended enough to assume there'd be too many events, too many people, too many outdated, eye-roll-worthy rituals and too many lights and cameras pointed at her for comfort. She'd also assumed it would be a cause for her parents to celebrate. A reason for them to be happy. Looking at Mumma's stoic demeanor now, Payal couldn't have been more wrong.

Scandalised by the decision to forego any religious rituals in favour of a civil ceremony and a modest reception after, elders from the family (and the community at large) had shamed her parents into hosting a sangeet and a haldi ceremony. Their demands didn't require the groom's side to attend. Why would they need to be there? This wasn't about getting to know the family that Payal was marrying into. It was about making Mumma and Papa pay their social dues, to make them repent for associating with seedy outsiders.

There was nothing to celebrate about this wedding. Everything was for show, everyone was miserable. And Payal was terrified of what awaited her on the other side.

Saira was the only one in a festive mood, antiquated dowries and mafia involvement be damned. She wasn't oblivious to the wedding's circumstances—she and Mumma had been Payal's primary caregivers during her prolonged recovery. Saira had held Payal through all the late-night panic attacks that followed; patiently listened to every one of Payal's frustrated rants about her wasted potential, how she was losing precious time being held prisoner in the house, how she absolutely refused to move to India. Saira understood how dangerous the bratva was.

Yet, she still celebrated. Because she only had the one big sister.

And she had every right to recreate her favourite Bollywood number at that sister's sangeet.

'Why don't you reach out to your school friends?' Payal softened her tone. 'I'm sure some of them are in the area for the summer. Or what about the boys you volunteered with at the soup kitchen? Or the ones you met at Model UN. Or the ones you know from the rec centre.' God, her baby sister's networking skills were unreal. 'You literally know half the state of New York. How hard is it to find a handful of boys open to being bribed with free food?'

'I guess I might know a couple. But I was wondering …' Saira shuffled to the edge of the back seat to rest her chin on the passenger seat, behind Payal's shoulder. 'What if Oleksiy Bhai had some tall, dark and handsome cousins?'

Payal didn't have to look at Mumma to know how she bristled, or how her lips pursed into a thin, angry line.

'Saira,' Payal hissed through gritted teeth. She had, regrettably, let it slip to her sister that her intended was a gorgeous specimen of a man.

'Friends and uh … associates would be fine too,' Saira said in a lowered voice, as if that would prevent their mother from hearing. 'Come on, he owns a gym. Mafia gyms have boxing rings. Boxers are supposed to have great footwork. And just think how good they'll look in kurtas.'

'Saira!' Mumma slammed a curled fist onto the car window.

Poor Nasir broke into a sweat behind the steering wheel, his Adam's apple bobbing up and down.

'Enough,' Mumma ordered, her voice as coarse as sandpaper. Angry, on the verge of tears. It shattered Payal's heart. 'You'll arrange a dance with your cousins or not dance at all. This family has to endure enough embarrassment as it is without you shamelessly grinding up against some tattooed gang member off the street.'

'We're here, madam,' Nasir squeaked, pulling up into the parking lot.

The Lohani women rode the elevator up to the bridalwear showroom in hostile silence. Upon exchanging terse pleasantries with their consultant, they were whisked off to a private room where Mumma busied herself with selecting sarees to distribute among relatives while Payal and Saira tried on their designer outfits for the reception.

Payal had ordered a blush pink lehenga embroidered with flowers inlaid with mirrors and pearls. A shop assistant loaned her a pair of five-inch heels to accommodate the skirt's generous fall. The transformation was instantaneous: Feeling regal, Payal stood taller as the shop assistant cinched the ties at the waist and draped the dupatta of delicate cutwork interwoven with pearls over her shoulders. Her hands forgot their usual itch to shield her abdomen, resting at her sides instead.

To give her a sense of the outfit's full effect, the assistant gathered her hair in a quick updo and decked her in some costume jewelry. The woman in the mirror staring back at Payal seemed untouched by trauma and the insecurities it spawned. She looked lovely and carefree. Giddy, even. A bride like any other.

For the briefest moment, Payal felt like the confident girl who spent Tuesday mornings modelling for a roomful of strangers. The overachiever who graduated top of her class, and made a name for herself at Brigham & Barr in a matter of weeks. The willful girl who once put everything on the line to do the right thing.

Mumma gave her a sharp once-over when she emerged from the changing room. 'Good,' she said with a curt nod before returning to her pile of sarees.

Payal exchanged a deadpan look with Saira. That was the most enthusiasm Mumma had shown towards anything to do with the wedding.

'I think the blouse could use a little tightening,' Payal said to the consultant, fanning out the excess fabric down the curve of her waist.

'Yes, an inch off each side should do it,' the consultant nodded. She tugged at the hem which touched the top of Payal's thighs. 'How about the length? I usually suggest this length to avoid any excessive puffing around the waistline, but with your figure, you can go shorter.'

Behind Payal, Saira's eyes rounded with excitement. 'What about over the midriff?'

Payal froze. She didn't dare look her mother's way.

'That would look splendid. See the border here?' The consultant indicated two or so inch below Payal's breasts. 'We can make the cut and reinforce the fabric here.'

Bouncing on her toes, Saira squeezed Payal's shoulders. 'Appi, you'd look like a proper Bollywood heroine. Do it, na? Please, please, please!'

'Saira—'

'Have you all gone mad?' Mumma reprimanded, eyes aflame with liquid anger.

Payal's palms flew up to her abdomen.

'But Mumma—'

'Just think of the questions that's going to invite! Think!' Mumma cut Saira off. 'Can the two of you, just for once, think about the consequences of your actions before doing the first stupid thing that comes into your head?'

'It's nothing some colour corrector and full-coverage concealer can't fix,' Saira retorted. 'Besides, the dupatta's going to be pinned over the front anyway.' She gave Payal's shoulder an imploring squeeze. 'Come on, Appi. Your silhouette will look amazing in the photos.'

'Photos,' Mumma scoffed. 'As if anyone would want to revisit this travesty.' Tearing her cold glare from Payal's reflection, she said to the now disquieted consultant, 'The blouse is fine as it is. Now if you'll be so kind to see to Saira's lehenga. I don't have all day.'

Payal walked back to the changing room on unsteady legs, a lump in her throat and her heart lost somewhere in the pit of her stomach. She had always cringed when families hung giant, tackily-edited wedding portraits in their living rooms. Little did she imagine she'd have reason to envy them some day. Mumma didn't want any physical reminders of her big day in the house, not as a frame on the mantle, not even as a photo album in the cabinet they seldom opened, housing their other neglected albums.

A travesty. An embarrassment. Hell, why not add abomination to the list as well? That was what Payal was to Mumma. Not just for what she was marrying into but also for what she had done to wind up in such a compromising position in the first place: refusing to turn a blind eye and keep her head down like the good Indian girl she'd raised her to be.

Tears eluded Payal's attempts at composure, streaking her face as the shop assistant removed the costume jewelry and undid the pins and ties securing the lehenga to her person.

'Don't worry, ma'am,' the assistant flashed her a sympathetic smile. 'We'll fit the blouse so it sits on you like a second skin. Your silhouette will still look lovely in the photos.'

Three

ON THE DAY OF THE WEDDING, THE CONEY Island Channel shone a vibrant blue a few shades darker than the clear summer sky above it. Incensed by the universe's mockery of his fate, Oleksiy shoved his shirt buttons into their holes and unceremoniously tucked the garment into his pants. The incessant baritone chatter and the sound of unfamiliar footsteps outside his childhood bedroom set his teeth on edge.

His sister Marisha had evicted him from his apartment on the grounds it was unfit to house a new bride, thereby in urgent need of redecorating. He'd been staying at his parents' since. In the thick of wedding preparations, without a moment's reprieve from the grim reality, his chances of getting back together with Alice were growing slimmer. He couldn't even get to a bottle of vodka to drown his sorrows in! Security associates—ordinary citizens under the bratva's employ and protection—had been trooping in and out of the condo the last three days, bearing generous tributes in honour of his wedding along with intel from the streets. Leaving his bedroom risked getting reeled into conversation with them. Drawing attention to himself. Getting involved in bratva matters.

He lanced his arms through his waistcoat and slung his tie around his neck, scouring it from side to side until his collar relented and took it under its fold. His airways burned as if he could breathe fire. How was it only 8.00 a.m.? This day already felt like it'd been going on for an eternity.

'*Sonechko*?' A knock at the door. Mama came in, looking dignified as always in a shin-length, full-sleeved teal dress and a matching hat. 'All ready?'

'Hang on a sec.' Oleksiy forced a lopsided tie knot up to the top button of his shirt. Then, grabbing his jacket, he said brusquely, 'Right, let's go.'

'Oleksiy.' Mama's disapproving tone was gentle. The door clicked shut behind her. Straightening his tie and collar, she buttoned up his waistcoat. 'I didn't raise you to be so childish.'

'No,' Oleksiy sneered. 'You raised me to believe I could be free of all this.'

His venom didn't faze her.

'And after today, you'll be that much closer to your goal.'

'By being forced to marry against my will.'

'By marrying someone *outside* the bratva.' She jostled him by the waistcoat, her shrewd, narrowed eyes the same glimmering black as his. 'My beautiful, stupid boy, you're too blinded by your feelings to realise how lucky you are that we found the Lohani girl.'

'Lucky? Do I get a cut out of the five-million-dollar dowry?'

'Lucky that you won't live the rest of your life owing another thief your allegiance. *Sonechko*'—she cupped his cheek—'marriage was never something you could escape. Whether you're an active thief or not, as your tato's son, you were always expected to marry for the bratva's interests. The arrangement with Lohanis bails it out of its debts, and buys you a ticket out of any future obligation to it.'

Oleksiy tilted his chin up, scrutinising his mother over the tip of his nose. A moment's consideration forced him to admit she was right. But far from being grateful, he found himself resenting her. All this time, he'd blamed Tato for brokering the marriage deal when she was probably the one who'd instigated it, orchestrating the most favourable terms for the bratva behind the scenes. Securing Oleksiy's independence and robbing him of his free will at once. Snuffing out whatever chance there was of Alice returning to him.

'She's a lovely girl, Payal,' Mama said, drawing him out of his fury-fueled stupor. 'Doesn't seem like the type who'll give you trouble.'

'I don't love her.'

'And Alice didn't love you enough to accept where you came from.' She gave his shoulders a final brush and smoothed the front of his jacket. 'She refused to accept you for who you are.'

'I'm not … ' He stayed her hands, grasping them to his heart. His eyes burned and a lump in his throat obstructed his words. He was a fourteen-year-old boy again, delirious from pain meds, his right arm an unresponsive heap of flesh and bone, the shock of what happened too fresh to fully fathom he'd just lost his best friend. He'd dedicated his entire life to healing from that incident. To walking away. Alice was supposed to be the most tangible proof of his success. 'Mama, I'm not a thief.'

'No, you're not,' Mama smiled, though her gaze lost none of its gravity. 'It doesn't change the fact that you were born their prince. That girl *chose* to leave you, to dismiss everything you've done to make your own way. Your Tato and I have got you a good deal. Don't let *the idea* of her ruin your shot at a better life.'

Oleksiy's chest ached from the indignity of having to beg. 'If I gave her more time—'

Mama's lips straightened and pursed into a thin line. 'Enough. It's Payal now, or someone inside the bratva tomorrow. Your options are scant. As is my patience for this … sentimentality. All I know is that what Alice couldn't stomach, Payal can. She couldn't care less what you were born into, or who your parents are.'

'Her mere presence in my life is a flashing neon reminder of who I am.'

'So? Your goal is to be free, not to forget. And the life you've chosen would benefit from a reliable partner. I think we can both agree Alice was never going to fill those shoes.'

'And you're sure Payal will?'

'No, not at all. But she's intelligent and seems to come from a level-headed family.'

This earned a snort from Oleksiy. No family in its right mind married off a beloved daughter to the mafia—

not unless there was something to be gained. Payal's father was one of the biggest real estate developers on the East Coast. Though Mama or Tato had not explicitly told him, Oleksiy suspected Mr Lohani needed the bratva's muscle and influence to clear out a choice property in the city. That a man could pawn off such a beautiful and accomplished daughter for material gain sickened Oleksiy to the core—at times even more intensely than the lightheaded nausea he felt whenever he remembered he was being coerced into marriage himself.

'Who knows?' Mama continued. 'She might be to you what I am to your tato. Not that it'll come easy. That kind of loyalty is earned. You won't get it if you don't treat her with respect.'

'It's *because* I respect her that I don't think it's fair she should be stuck with a man who doesn't love her.'

Mama's unamused expression told him he'd strayed into self-parody. 'What a hopeless American you've become,' she sighed. 'Where's your pocket square? Come on, brush your hair and put your shoes on. We haven't got all day.'

She paused on her way out, looking over her shoulder and addressing him, not as his mother, but as the matriarch of the Karmazin family.

'One more thing: I better not hear talk about my son having a rocky marriage. I don't care what understanding the two of you come to, so long as you're both discreet. In public, you'll be expected to keep up appearances. I won't tolerate otherwise. And I won't be so considerate if I have to find you another bride.'

Oleksiy flinched as she shut the door behind her. Slowly turning to face his pallid reflection in the mirror, he slicked back his raven hair. If bratva-ordained marriages were all he had on the cards, he'd only subject himself to it this once. Might as well look sharp doing it.

At City Hall, the Karmazin–Lohani party was the largest in the foyer: Marisha and her husband Grigori accompanied Oleksiy and his parents, and Payal had her parents and sister with her. Yet, where the others waiting to be officiated belonged to a vibrant, technicolour world, Oleksiy's wedding party felt ensconced within a black-and-white picture from the silent era. He could count the number of words the two families exchanged on one hand. His bride offered him nothing besides slight acknowledging tilts of her head—first upon setting eyes on him, then once when they'd both signed the papers.

It'd been weeks since their first and only encounter at the bar. In his outrage over being coerced, he'd forgotten how steely and unperturbed his bride's demeanor was and how well-suited that kind of temperament was for the world of thieves. At least her brief glances his way didn't harbour any expectations of him, any silent challenges of making him come around eventually. Oleksiy didn't have a choice in who he married, but nothing and no one could make him forget what he had had to give up.

Once he and Payal were unceremoniously declared man and wife, the wedding party dispersed to get some rest before the evening reception at 501 Union, where the awkwardness of their wait at City Hall was amplified tenfold. Never in his life, not even in bratva-controlled restaurants, had Oleksiy witnessed such rigid segregation. Seating arrangements were partly to blame; the difference in garb—the muted, matte tones of his side in contrast to the flamboyant glitter and gold of Payal's family made the split down the middle of the venue even more glaring. Naturally, there was no mingling between the two sides. That is, with the exception of Payal's sister and two of their younger cousins who braved enemy territory armed with glitter pens, a guest book and a barely disguised curiosity about dangerous tattooed men.

Watching them, Oleksiy wryly wondered if Payal's marriage to him would set a precedent within the Indian community. A glimpse at the disapproval and fear slapped across most of their faces assured him that was unlikely.

With his bride . . . his legal wife, Oleksiy presented a united front, introducing her to his side, enduring the intrusive inspection of hers, making small talk, mustering a smile every now and then, posing for photos—just as Mama had ordered. Payal complied without him having to ask, always gracious, always smiling. As the evening wore on, though, her hardy veneer slipped now and then, granting him brief glimpses of the weary gloom she hid under her false lashes.

They hadn't said a word to each other all day.

She'd swapped out the white double-breasted dress she wore to City Hall for a flowing, traditional outfit. It was fit for an empress. A delicate diamond necklace draped her, its slightness exaggerating her long, slender neck that matching teardrop earrings kissed whenever she tilted her head in greeting. A red double petal hibiscus speared one side of her chignon—it didn't go with her outfit, but it added a touch of playfulness to an otherwise tense and somber occasion. A pinch of charm.

She looked lovely.

Oleksiy wanted to tell her as much several times over the course of the evening. Ever more so when he realised how draining playing the blushing bride was for her. Not that her loveliness affected him in any way. It was just a social reflex.

He made a mental note to be careful with his compliments. His messaging. The last thing he wanted was to give her the idea they could have something. This marriage was a business contract. He had no intention of taking their relationship beyond that of two business associates. The sooner they established those boundaries, the better.

There was no festive send-off with cheers, airborne bouquets or confetti at the end of the evening. Oleksiy found the morose scene by their limo more reminiscent of a funeral, where Payal was the casket being lowered into the ground. Her mother shot Oleksiy a look of wet agony as he climbed into the car himself.

You and me both, lady, he wanted to say, flashing her a dim-witted smile before ducking his head inside.

The short, deafeningly silent drive to the Hilton was excruciating. Oleksiy found Payal staring out the window whenever he looked her way, yet he felt her eyes on him whenever his head was turned. He had to say something to her eventually. But no matter how much he racked his mind for the right thing to say, all he could come up with was, *you look lovely*.

Payal's skirt and stole bunched up around her in a pink cloud, grazing his fingers despite the limo's wide breadth. In his struggle for words, Oleksiy couldn't help but fixate on the minute rise and fall of her chest. A stray strand of wavy hair grazed the slope of her neck and her partially bare back. The sudden urge to replace it with his fingers struck him like a hammer to an anvil. He tore his gaze off of her and didn't dare look back.

They arrived at the hotel before the tension in his muscles could ebb. Hands shoved into his pockets, jaw clenched to the point of grinding his molars to a fine powder, he stalked after the concierge assigned to guide them to the executive suite, trying his best to ignore the click of heels and rustle of skirts beside him.

'Relax,' Payal broke the day-long impasse, her voice hushed so the concierge couldn't hear. 'We're not expected to consummate or anything.'

She was taunting him, rubbing it in that she'd got her way after all. That she'd won and he'd lost. He glowered at her in reply, the stern set of his mouth drawing even tighter.

Detecting the hostility emanating from Oleksiy, the concierge skipped the detailed tour of the suite, promptly leaving once he'd deposited their luggage and collected his tip.

'Thank you,' Payal called after him as Oleksiy shut the door.

'Right,' Oleksiy sniffed, setting his hands on his hips with an air of authority. 'I'll take the couch, you take the bed. You need the bathroom? I can be in and out in five, and stay out of your way.'

'I could actually use the bathroom now,' Payal said sheepishly, the bottom of her skirt bunching as she stepped out of her heels. 'Kinda been holding it in all evening. And err ... thank you for the chivalry, but I think we can share the bed.'

Oleksiy's nostrils flared with a sharp intake of breath but she cut him off before he could launch into his diatribe about contracts and business associates and boundaries.

'If you think you've got it bad now, it's going to get a whole lot worse if you turn your whole world upside down trying to tip-toe around me.'

Oleksiy's mouth pulled up in an incredulous sneer. 'I'm not *tip-toeing* around anyone.'

'Okay, great. And I don't want to inconvenience you any more than I already have, so we're going to share the bed.'

'Look, we need to straighten some things out here.'

'I promise I won't come onto you, if that's what you're worried about.' Payal's mouth quivered with a suppressed chuckle, as if coming onto him was the most ludicrous thing she could think of. *Ouch.* She gestured at the contentious piece of furniture 'And just look at this bed. It's huge! We can play volleyball on it.'

Oleksiy got the feeling he wasn't going to get a wink of sleep if she didn't get her way. Clicking his jaw side to side, he relinquished with a roll of his eyes. 'Left or right?'

'Right, if you don't mind.' She paused a beat on her way to the luggage rack, nudging her chin at the complementary champagne on the centre table. 'You want to pop that open while I get changed?'

'I'm not really in the mood.'

'Oh?' Throwing her suitcase open, she pulled out a bag of toiletries and what looked like grey sweats. 'Well, how do you propose we celebrate this milestone in our lives?'

'Thought that's what we just came from.'

'That was a soulless ritual for outside eyes.' Payal leaned back against the luggage, hugging her belongings to her stomach. 'How do you want to remember us tonight?'

'I already told you I love someone else,' Oleksiy said peremptorily. 'This doesn't change that. So, whatever hopes you have of making me come around, I suggest you drop 'em. There's nothing but disappointment waiting for you if you don't.'

Smiling nonchalantly, Payal started pulling the red hibiscus and pins out of her hair. 'And I told you I have no objections to any of that. But we're still in this together. As housemates. Maybe even friends. So, as unfortunate as all of this is, maybe we can try finding a silver lining—pop open a bottle of champagne, commiserate about how unfair life is, get to know each other. Oh, I know!' Eyes rounding with excitement, she rummaged through her luggage. 'Okay, pour out the champagne while I get changed.'

Oleksiy watched, speechless, as she hurried into the bathroom, then scuttled back towards him jabbing at her shoulder. 'Undo me, please.'

'Wha—'

'Safety pin,' she clarified, indicating the spot where her stole was pinned to her top. Right by her bare back.

Glad she couldn't see how hard he swallowed, Oleksiy brushed her hair over the other shoulder, careful not to come into direct contact with her skin. She smelled of mangoes and peaches and honey . . . of summer. He fumbled with the pin, crumpling it and ripping a tiny tear in the expensive stole as he yanked it free.

'Thank you,' Payal chimed before disappearing into the bathroom again.

Oleksiy didn't know how long he stood there, dazed, mulling over the rapid string of words that had tumbled out of Payal's mouth, listening to the sound of running water behind the closed door. At some point, he realised he should at least remove his shoes and jacket. And maybe even his waistcoat and belt. The water continued running in the bathroom. He rolled his sleeves up to his elbows and poured out two flutes of champagne.

As he stood there, staring at the bubbles in the flutes, he wondered if Payal had left the tap running to make a run for it.

No such luck. A plume of blueberry-scented steam followed her as she emerged wearing a baggy grey T-shirt and black shorts that showed off perfectly toned legs. Carefully draping her wedding finery over a chair, she took the flute Oleksiy held out at arm's length.

'Thanks.' She arched a thick brow at the great pains he took to keep his distance. Heading back towards the bathroom, she said, 'You're going to need to change into a pair of shorts or something.'

When she didn't shut the door behind her, Oleksiy followed and braved a look inside: the water in the palatial bathtub looked like the inside of a busted soda machine with currents of pink and purple and every shade in between fizzing out from a bobbing epicentre. Wading through the colourful foam, Payal settled down on the wide ledge.

'Oh, yeah,' she moaned in satisfaction, resting her head against the tiled wall, displaying the long column of her neck for him to stare at. 'Exactly what my feet need right now. You coming?'

Oleksiy felt an unwelcome stirring at his core. For all her talk of not having any expectations, she sure enjoyed toying with him. Well, two could play that game.

'I didn't bring any shorts.'

Four

OLEKSIY'S FOREARM FLEXED AS HE UNDID his trousers.

Time slowed to compensate for the abrupt uptick in Payal's heart rate. The heat prickling her neck and face, paired with the dull hiss of the bath bomb, made her feel like a kettle on the boil.

The trousers dropped down long, corded legs, each knee bearing a tattoo of an eight-pointed star. He wore black boxer briefs underneath. Mercifully, his dress shirt hid his manhood from Payal's view—with her toes curling underwater and back pressing harder into the tiled wall, the sight of this much of him was flustering enough. His pitch-black eyes watched her, waited for her to flinch and look away as he prowled towards the tub. Payal didn't trust herself to breathe.

Through the bath bomb's strong bubblegum-like scent, she caught a dull whiff of him: cocoa, orange zest . . . and clean, warm-blooded man. His shoulder and thigh bumped hers as he got comfortable beside her on the ledge. She gawked at his tattoos—a stark reminder of what she had married into.

'Do they scare you?' he asked, his voice deep and silken.

Burning under his searing gaze, Payal gulped. She couldn't afford to be afraid now. She'd made it through the wedding. Now was the time to sort out terms and conditions. 'You said you're not involved with the family business anymore.'

'That's right.' He circled his free palm over his knee. 'These mean I don't kneel to anyone but my own authority.'

'And the bratva—your father, he's okay with that?'

'Oh, no,' Oleksiy chuckled wryly. 'No, he was pissed, all right. But he's got Grigori and Marisha to take care of things after him.'

Payal nodded, fighting the urge to splay her palm over her abdomen, remembering the reason for her incongruous levity moments earlier. Dirty as it felt to be so manipulative, she had to find a crack in his animosity towards her. 'I always wanted to get a tattoo. A whole constellation of stars'—she raised her left foot into the air and traced its outer edge with her finger—'right here.'

'Yeah? Why didn't you?'

'My mom,' Payal snorted, not at all keen to revisit the resentment she harboured for Mumma, but unable to escape it. 'Said I have wait to get my husband's permission. Apparently, women don't amount to anything but their husband's property.'

'Well … ' Oleksiy rolled his shoulder. 'You're free to prove her wrong now.'

'Yeah, I am,' Payal said, sitting taller. She raised her champagne flute. 'To freedom.'

Oleksiy clinked it with his. 'No price too high.'

Payal watched his Adam's apple bob with his shallow sip. Gaze unfocused and somber, his large frame slumped against the wall, with purplish-pink foam swirling around his legs.

'You know,' Payal said slowly, 'I really do mean it when I say I don't care about you seeing someone else. Think of me as a housemate who occasionally tags along to family events. And once classes start, I'll be uptown most of the time, so we'll barely see each other anyway.'

'She's none of your concern,' he said coolly, but with a deep frown over his downcast eyes. 'Our little arrangement's ruined whatever hope there was of salvaging that life, so ...'

'Oh.' Payal tucked her chin into her neck, confused by the rush of something fluttering inside her. Not hope. She wasn't that stupid. 'I'm sorry.'

'Why? Duty first, right?' His chest heaved with a long intake of breath, straining his shirt at the buttons. 'What about you? You smooth out all the logistics with your Romeo, or can we expect news of some preppy hipster raiding an organic pharmacy sometime soon?'

Payal took offense at being slotted a dater of preppy hipsters. 'I'm in between careers right now,' she responded curtly, 'so I haven't really had much time for all of that.'

Oleksiy leaned back, locking eyes with her as they spoke. There was a discerning smugness, a roguish glint in those molten black eyes. One he'd, no doubt, used on women abound before he met the supreme woman Payal ought not concern herself with.

Not that it mattered, of course. He was nothing but a glorified housemate to Payal.

Or so she kept telling herself.

'You know, when Tato first told me what you did, I thought he was bringing you in to take over the books. A reliable accountant is worth their weight in gold.'

Payal answered with close-mouthed laughter, raking her free hand over the gooseflesh erupting up her arm. *He's just making conversation,* she told herself. *There's no way he knows what kind of an accountant you are.*

'Nope,' she sputtered. 'Not about that life anymore.'

'No?' His relish at the tremor in her voice was evident, the corner of his mouth primed to smirk like he was on the brink of accosting a cat burglar. 'And why's that?'

He's just making conversation. He's just making conversation. He's just making conversation.

'I just ... wanted to do something more meaningful with my life.'

'Like?'

'St-statistics.'

The boom of Oleksiy's laughter bounced off the bathroom tiles, stunning Payal, at first, then infecting her into doing the same, albeit more from nervousness than genuine amusement.

It was a glorious sight—this tall, stoic, menacing man bent over, shaking with laughter. The act formed fine creases at the corners of his eyes. Payal wondered if he was jovial by nature, and who in his life made him laugh the most. She wondered if it was the Supreme—which is how she was referring to the unknown woman now—and she wondered why that made her feel the way it did.

'What?' she asked when her own laughter subsided. 'The proper collection, processing and dissemination of data is the cornerstone of all tangible change.'

'You mean data that's twisted by policymakers and giant corporations and—and lobbyists and all sorts of conspiracy theorists?'

Payal refused to be patronised. 'It's about as realistic an ambition as trying to run a business in this city without mafia interference.'

'Touché.'

The buzz of their laughter charged the ensuing silence. Payal watched Oleksiy lazily swirl figure eights in the water with his feet. This was her chance. Her crack through his armor.

'I—uh—I actually have a favour to ask.'

A lock of raven hair strayed from his back-slicked do and kissed his forehead as he fixed her with a pointed look.

'Just this one thing, and I promise I won't ask for anything else from you.'

'That's what they always say, but go on. What d'you want?'

'I—' Payal drew a rasping breath. 'I'd like a bodyguard.'

His brow arched in mild amusement. 'A bodyguard?'

'Yes. To watch my back. I'm going to be commuting to 116th street from Brighton Beach every day, and there are going to be evening classes, late nights at the lab, group projects, that kind of stuff. I'll be too easy a target for your father's enemies.'

'Hate to disappoint,' he said, resting his head against the wall, mouth upturned in a sly smirk, 'but I haven't been much of a big deal to my father or his enemies since I got these.' He patted his tattooed knees.

'Maybe so.' Payal's armpits dampened with sweat. It took every ounce of willpower she had to keep her voice steady. 'But say somebody does nab me at the station. Who's going to want to do business with your security firm when it gets out you couldn't protect your own wife? What's one bodyguard to you, hmm? You've already got them on your payroll.'

The idea tickled Oleksiy to no end, deepening the creases at the corners of his eyes.

'You want to try making friends at your new school with a surly-looking Ukrainian gangster tailing you?'

'Oh, you don't need to concern yourself with that. I'm very personable.'

'So you keep telling me.' Without breaking eye contact, he tossed the remainder of his champagne back with an elegant flick of his wrist. 'Now, if you'll pass me the showerhead, I'd like to get out of this unicorn diarrhoea before my toenails go pink.'

They went about their bedtime routines, skirting around each other in a not altogether uncomfortable silence. Oleksiy was asleep—or at least appeared to be—by the time Payal finished removing her make-up, cleansing, moisturising, brushing and shaking out the bobby pins and hairspray from her arm-length mane.

She climbed into bed, determined to spend the night facing her edge of the bed. She had told Oleksiy she wasn't interested in coming onto him and she planned on honouring that commitment. But as uncertainty over the next chapter of her life warded off sleep, his citrus scent rolled her onto her back, and pinned her gaze onto his tranquil face. There was something incredibly ordinary about him like this. He looked softer, wiser, wholesome. She could picture him being a father, sneaking in a good book and a nap in between indulging his kids. Who knew? Maybe that was the life he'd planned to build with the Supreme. The life Payal had stolen from him.

She rolled back onto her side.

Oleksiy was wrong about duty coming first. There was one thing that came even before that: survival. Payal felt terrible about foiling his happily-ever-after, she really did, but she was done hiding to survive. She needed to reclaim her agency, her life. She'd endured too much, come too far to get sidetracked by sentiment.

The newly-weds were greeted by bright, late-summer sunlight and the prominent scent of fresh paint and new furniture when Oleksiy unlocked the door to his apartment the next morning. Wriggling past her luggage, which Grigori's underlings had deposited in the short entryway, Payal peered over Oleksiy's back, taking a good look at the rest of her new home.

It was a spacious and functional space—no toilets in the kitchen, or bedrooms only accessible by ladder like some places she'd seen. Separated by a large granite-topped breakfast counter, the kitchen and living room had an open-floor plan. A corridor installed with linen and storage closets led to a bathroom and the two bedrooms. The common area was furnished with a commitment to warm hues and minimalist (but comfortable) design. The living room opened out to a small balcony which overlooked the street two storeys below: the conversations of passers-by were completely audible and the whirring of speeding cars was jarringly loud. Payal had never lived this close to the street, vertically or horizontally. She suspected that would be the biggest adjustment she'd have to make.

Definitely not what she had anticipated when she signed up to marry a mafia boss's son. There were no curtains reeking of cigarette smoke, no dark and depressing wallpaper, no antique leather furniture, no moth-eaten carpets, no liquor cabinets with a hissing cat perched on them. This place was downright homey.

Oleksiy appeared equally stunned by the state of his apartment. His shoes scuffed the parquet floor as he pivoted in indecisive half-turns, hands on his hips, eyes raking over his surroundings. Payal first assumed his mute, brisk, half-stunted gesticulations were an attempt at a tour of the place. Grumbling Marisha's name under his breath, he tore off a painting of the Manhattan skyline as seen through subway windows from a wall, tossed it into the storage closet and slammed the door shut with a force that sent a tremor through the rest of the apartment. Then, seemingly having forgotten she was there, he stomped to the bedroom at the far end of the corridor.

Payal waited, shifting her weight from foot to foot, listening to his heavy footfalls, his muffled curses and the screech of doors and drawers being jostled. He emerged moments later, flicking a stray lock of hair off his forehead.

'Marisha's changed out the mattress along with everything else,' he huffed, nostrils aflare. 'You can take this room.'

Payal snuck a peek at the other bedroom on the way to the one he'd just stormed out of.

'But this is the master bedroom.' She opened the closet. 'Your stuff's still here.'

'They're just clothes,' he retorted. 'I'll move them out. It comes with an en-suite bathroom.'

'Does the one in the hallway not have a bath?'

'It does.'

'Then I'll take the guest bedroom.' Squeezing past his unyielding form, she began wheeling her luggage into the guest bedroom. 'Really, dude, I'm not here to ruin your life. You don't have to give up your room.'

Payal felt his eyes on her as she pulled up the blinds and opened the lone window in the room. It had a clear view of the car service across the street. Through the establishment's glass façade, she could see the chauffeur who'd driven them to the apartment from the Hilton. He was in conversation with the male receptionist, no doubt speculating whether the Indian girl put out for the boss's son the night before.

The laundromat next door was probably a bratva front too, along with every other business she'd seen on the way over.

Her new apartment may have possessed all the essential comforts, but it was deep, deep, deep in bratva territory.

'I, uh—' Oleksiy cleared his throat. 'East is this way.'

He was pointing towards the head of the bed. Payal didn't immediately register what he was getting at: east was where the Kaaba lay. The direction Muslims faced during prayer.

'Oh! I'm not much of a prayer. But thanks, that's, um, that's really considerate of you.' Posture caving, Payal rubbed at her arm like a teenager at her first co-ed dance. 'D-do you observe anything, like Sabbath, or ... ?'

'Nah,' he said, unable to help the tiny grin lifting the side of his mouth and creasing the corners of his eyes. 'I was done with that stuff after I collected my bar mitzvah cash. But, uh—Mama and Marisha get together for lunch every Tuesday, so maybe ... only if you want to, of course ...'

Payal wanted to kick herself for not reading up on Judaism beforehand.

'What's on Tuesdays?'

'Nothing,' Oleksiy shrugged. 'Just girls' lunch.'

'Oh. Good to know. Thanks.'

Silence brewed between them. Neither moved. Neither looked the other in the eye.

'Okay, well,' Oleksiy finally huffed. 'I have to get going. I'm meeting a prospective client in a bit.'

That explained the sharp grey suit. He'd paired it with a skinny maroon tie.

'Oh. Good luck.'

Tongue darting out to wet his lips, he clapped something onto the nearest suitcase. 'Here are your keys. Small one's for both the doors downstairs and large one's for the apartment.'

'Got it.'

'You gonna be all right here on your own?'

Payal wanted to remind him she was twenty-nine years old. But he was just being nice, which was more than she would have thought to ask from a man who didn't want to be married to her.

'Yeah, I'll get unpacked.'

'Okay, well, good luck with that.'

She watched him head out. He was in the process of pulling the main door shut behind him when she realised she didn't have his phone number.

As though hearing her thoughts, he spun around before she could call after him. 'Yeah?'

It was a simple enough question: *What's your number?* Payal didn't know why it caught in her throat. They were housemates. She would inevitably have to get in touch with him for a grocery run, or a fleecing handyman, or if she got locked out of the apartment. Yet, asking for his number felt like a breach of their agreement, like giving him a sign that she was interested in him romantically.

The last thing she wanted was to live with someone who was hostile towards her.

'Nothing,' was her only response.

She'd ask Marisha or his mother for his number later.

Unpacking didn't take long. Small as it was, the guest room had a surprising amount of closet space, and Payal believed in sustainable fashion choices over volume, anyway.

A closer look around the apartment let on that, inviting as it was aesthetically, it wasn't quite equipped to support a running household yet. Payal took quick inventory of the kitchen, hallway closets and bathrooms to make a list of groceries and cleaning supplies. She paused in her search of the storage closet to admire the painting Oleksiy had taken down—it was a thoughtful piece with a very distinct style and mood. Dated two years ago. Unsigned. Going by Oleksiy's reaction to it and the two storage containers of art supplies shoved to the back of the closet, it must have been the work of the Supreme.

And supreme she was, for Payal certainly had no artistic talent. The only thing remotely close to art she'd ever done was model. And even that door was closed to her now.

It was mid-afternoon by the time she finished compiling her list. Well past a decent time for lunch. Her stomach was growling, and the fridge only had an unopened loaf of bread in it.

Ordering in was the logical option. But that left the matter of the household supplies. She could have ordered those too, only then she'd have to wait a whole day for her bag of rice *and* feel bad about not shopping local. She could have waited for Oleksiy to return—whenever that was—and have him accompany her. It was his apartment too. But much like asking him for his number, asking him to come shopping with her felt wrong. Like crossing a line. Too couple-y. A point of no return.

She had to do what she hadn't been allowed to do in over a year and a half: she had to leave the house. On her own. Unprotected.

You gonna be all right here on your own?

All her faculties of reason said yes. Oleksiy lived in the heart of Kotovsk turf, not one block from the luxury apartments on Brighton Beach Avenue where his father, the Kotovsk's godfather lived. Everyone in the neighbourhood probably knew the boss's son had an Indian wife by now. No one would allow a hair on her head to get hurt.

She headed out, one hand fidgeting with her T-shirt, the other cupping the can of pepper spray she carried in her purse.

From the patrons of the laundromat and veterinarian clinic, to the women waiting to collect their charges from the day care at the end of the block, everyone Payal passed seemed to have guessed who she was. Well, that or she'd become super paranoid during her prolonged isolation. She picked up her pace, regardless.

Her initial assessment, as it turned out, was spot on. By the time she made the return trip back to the apartment, four bags balanced on each arm and another in each hand, the day care had let out, crowding the sidewalk with a gaggle of bouncing children. Their mothers and nannies wrangled them into clearing a path for her, flashing her polite, deferential smiles as they did. Many of them were headed the same way as her, and would have probably continued on their merry way if Payal didn't struggle to get her groceries through the building's electric strike-locked entrance.

'Here,' said one of the women, holding the door ajar for her. 'Let me get that for you.'

Thanking her, Payal lumbered inside and straightened her arms to let gravity do its work on the bags.

'Oh!' The woman's eyes rounded at the swollen red imprints down Payal's arms. She was roughly Payal's age, modestly dressed in a full-sleeved top and a shin-length skirt. She had the clearest porcelain skin, brown eyes and an enviable fringe. Patting her daughter's shoulder, she said, 'I usually use this one's stroller to carry my groceries. You're free to borrow it next time, if you like. And if you need anything else, I live two streets over.'

'Don't be ridiculous,' said a tall, athletically-built woman who was part of the small congregation of women and children now gathered outside the door. 'Look at those arms on her. She obviously lifts.'

'Do you need a referral for a maid?' another woman asked, her brows tight with concern. 'I know a few who might be available.'

The first woman half-laughed, half-sighed. 'Nat's the pilates instructor at Brat Oleksiy's gym, Becca's husband works in facilities maintenance. And I'm Mary. I handle the laundry there.'

There was no processing the attention focused on her. All Payal could do was blink stupidly.

'You're very pretty,' yet another woman blurted excitedly. 'Much prettier than that redhead he'd been seeing.'

'Ellie!' the group hissed in tandem.

'Hi,' Payal finally managed. 'It's nice meeting you all.' Her tongue felt too swollen to speak and her eyes stung. What was it Oleksiy had said the first time they met? That she'd have a hard time fitting in. That the people of Brighton Beach weren't very welcoming of outsiders. She'd grown so accustomed to the fear-mongering of others, to barricading her last vestige of hope against them that this unprecedented show of warmth from a group of complete strangers left her overwhelmed. 'I'm Payal.'

'Yes, Brat Oleksiy's wife, we know,' Mary said, smiling kindly. 'We're by every day on weekdays because of the kids, so don't hesitate to give any of us a holler. You'll get a lay of the neighbourhood soon enough. And he's a good man, your husband. Most of us would still be working the gentlemen's clubs, or fishing our men out of the Channel if not for him.'

Mary's casual tone made it impossible for Payal to decide whether to look horrified or smile along with her.

Later, as she put the shopping away, Payal pondered what a shame it was that a man who brought happiness and peace to so many people should have to live out his life without the woman he loved. What a shame it was that Payal was apparently supreme in the looks department, but still not good enough for him to give their marriage a shot.

But that was his problem, not hers.

If her first day at Brighton Beach had proved anything, it was that all the naysayers were lying. She had made the right decision in marrying Oleksiy. This was her best chance at reclaiming her life, at being the woman she once was and growing into so much more. Her housemate, her husband—he was a scribble in the margins. From now on, all her energy, all her focus was to stay trained on personal and professional fulfilment. On her own contentment.

Five

THREE DAYS INTO THEIR MARRIAGE, OLEKSIY invited Payal over to Channel Fitness to introduce her to Mykola. The shaggy-haired, baby-faced kid was built like a Graeco-Roman wrestler, and he'd been making full use of that physique by getting into street fights, breaking and entering and all other kinds of petty crimes. He'd even dropped out of high school to make a full-time job of it. Small wonder he hadn't caught the bratva's eye before his mama dragged him to Oleksiy by the ear.

Oleksiy took him on out of a sense of duty—this *was* why he'd started his businesses after all, to create cleaner, safer job opportunities—but the kid's not being formal bratva meant he had neither training nor experience to be a fitness instructor or a security guard, and neither discipline nor diligence to be part of the support staff. Riding the subway with Payal for a few weeks was pretty much all he was good for.

Payal doubted he was up for even that.

'It's the perfect match,' Oleksiy insisted, baffled he had to pitch the pros of the kid's services as if she was one of his clients. 'Mykola here has his GED test coming up soon. So, while he's "guarding" you on your commute, you can help him study.'

Glowering at him for his use of air quotes, Payal intensified her scrutiny of Mykola. 'Can you hold your own in a fight?'

'Never lost one in my life,' the kid grinned, his voice grating, almost pterodactyl-like. He clenched his fist to show her the word 'OMYT' inscribed on his knuckles. 'See this? It means I'm a black whirlpool. Once you fall in, there's no getting out.'

'Hmph. And how're you with sneak attacks? Would you say you've got quick reflexes?' Turning to Oleksiy, she asked, 'Does he have a gun?'

'No, he—' Oleksiy shook his head at the absurdity of letting the kid handle a gun. 'What exactly do you think is going to happen here?'

'Hey! You don't know what it's like for beautiful Indian women out there, okay?'

Was it a stalker she was worried about? Because if that was the case, he could get a hold of Tato's security associate at the 60th Precinct and—

No, no, no! No favors from the bratva.

Three days into a bratva-ordained marriage and he was already losing sight of the principles he'd lived the better part of his life by. This. This was precisely what he'd wanted to avoid—sliding back into the black whirlpool. Oleksiy couldn't say if this bodyguard business was just a spoiled rich girl crying out for attention, or if it was part of some elaborate scheme to reel him back into the fold. All he knew was that he needed to stay vigilant. Of her, yes. And even more so of the dangerous impulses she awakened in him.

Like the one he had when Mykola said, 'Hey boss, why don't we give her a demonstration, you and me? Promise to go easy on you.' He was buzzing with an eagerness to impress, stealing glimpses at Payal. *My wife,* Oleksiy caught himself thinking. The bastard was infatuated with her.

Oleksiy wanted to smash his larynx so he could never utter another word with that godawful pterodactyl voice again.

'Hang onto that enthusiasm, kid,' Oleksiy said with an agitated roll of his right shoulder. 'You're gonna need it to make your reporting time at seven in the morning. It'll be a three percent dock in pay every time you show up late, so I'd better not hear Sestra Payal couldn't make her classes on time 'cause o' you.'

Mykola sobered instantly. His father was doing time for a botched bratva job. Mom was barely making ends meet. He needed the money.

As for his attraction to Payal . . . Oleksiy expected his icy reminder of her position as Big Brat's wife should suffice. No man under his employ would be stupid enough to make a move on her. And if Payal wanted to initiate something—

Preposterous! Payal would never be interested in someone as unrefined and incompetent as Mykola.

She will be interested in someone, eventually, a voice in his head nagged, *someone who isn't you.*

It didn't matter. Why should it? Business associates didn't care who the other fucked. They'd just have to exercise discretion, that's all . . .

'Maybe help him brush up on compound interest rates,' he told Payal, trying to deflect the discomfort of his own thoughts. 'It'll help him grasp what happens when a percentage gets docked from a principle over and over again.'

Oleksiy's threat proved unnecessary. Mykola was ringing the buzzer at 6:50 a.m. the following Wednesday with a GED review book tucked under his arm. Apparently, a pretty face was all you needed to straighten a wayward kid out.

Maybe Payal offered Mykola a glimpse of all the bright possibilities life had to offer. The way Alice had done for Oleksiy.

How fleeting and unrealistic those visions turned out to be.

As for real life, Payal stayed true to her word. Once the academic year started, she went about her day and he on his. When she was home in the evenings, she sat fixed to her desk with her headphones on, doing problem sets. She'd set the desk up to face the farthest wall in the living room so her back stayed turned to most of the apartment and Oleksiy the whole time. Sometimes, though, as he lay on the neighbouring couch watching TV, he sensed her watching along with him. He didn't know why he didn't turn his head to check. He didn't know why he chickened out of asking her to come watch from a more comfortable seat.

Probably the same reason why he never got around to getting her number.

He'd flaked the first day, and it just seemed more and more ridiculous to ask the longer he put it off.

It became infinitely more ridiculous when they began having actual conversations beyond 'good morning,' 'see ya,' and 'goodnight.' It started the day the Lohani family's chauffeur showed up, unannounced, bearing two large, three-tiered hot boxes of food.

'I guess Mumma's under the impression you don't feed me properly.'

She'd said it in jest, but Oleksiy didn't find it funny.

'To her credit, though,' she sighed, undoing the latches on the contraptions and lining the individual boxes on the kitchen counter, 'her shaaks *are* a whole lot better than the steamed vegetables I've been making.'

'Shaak' was the word she used for any kind of vegetable dish. The food deliveries from Mrs Lohani's kitchen in the following weeks taught Oleksiy there were countless vegetables to cook, and even more ways to cook them. The hot boxes also carried some kind of protein, either chicken or mutton, sometimes fish, and one box always held a stack of rolled-out discs of raw dough. Payal showed him how to roast them on a tawa, and taught him how to differentiate between bhakri, which was a bread made from pearl millet, and chapatis, which were wholemeal flatbreads.

It was nice not having to live off deli sandwiches and Papa John's pizza. But the notion of Payal's mother thinking her big bad gangster son-in-law wasn't feeding her daughter didn't sit right with him, so he started cooking dinner a few times a week.

Curiosity drew Payal away from her desk as he fumbled his way through the process. Her company made the entire ordeal less tedious, but no less nerve-wracking.

'You know what you should really use to thicken that sauce?' she said one evening, just as he was about to pour breadcrumbs into the tomato sauce he was preparing for his skampi na buzara. 'Parmesan.'

'That would be a lot of parmesan,' Oleksiy said with a straight face.

'No such thing as too much parmesan.'

Oleksiy tutted. 'Spoken like a true American.'

Her mischievous giggle resonated in his ears till he fell asleep that night.

He also began to entertain the idea of taking her out to that small place on Brighton Beach Avenue for his favourite lamb ribs.

No. Out of the question. Too easily mistakable for a date.

But he could always get takeaway.

Of course, plans to get takeaway or cook hinged on knowing which evenings Payal would be in for dinner. While Oleksiy had roughly pieced together what her weekly schedule looked like, he still had no way to be sure. Mostly because he still didn't have her phone number.

He resorted to calling Mykola under the pretense of checking how test prep was going. Several times a day. Before long, he knew what classes she had and when, what days she had lab, where she got lunch, which library carrel she liked to study at and when she used the university gym.

He also learnt that on days she didn't go into the city, she would meet for coffee with women from around the neighbourhood, many of them previously associated with the bratva, a few of them his employees. She'd made it to a few of Mama and Marisha's Tuesday lunches, and she did laundry at the laundromat next door instead of using the machines in their building's basement. When he mentioned the latter in passing, she matter-of-factly said the dryers at the laundromat were better.

He didn't believe her. He didn't want to. How could he? There had to be a catch. Outsiders didn't just take to this world—*his* world—that easily. Alice certainly didn't. Payal had to have a bratva agenda in some way, shape or form. He just couldn't put a finger on what it was.

He had to be careful. He had to keep her at arm's length.

And yet . . . he didn't want to. Not when they sat watching TV together in the same room, the space between them feeling like a veritable chasm. Not when he buzzed with anticipation at the prospect of seeing her after a long day. Not when their easy banter in the kitchen relieved the tightness in his bad shoulder. Not when her eyes rolled back and contented moans spilled from her lips at the taste of his food. Not when he caught himself fantasising about taking her out to local restaurants.

Then one Sunday morning, he couldn't help himself anymore.

He'd slept in, enjoying the crisp warmth of the mid-September sun bathing his bed. The familiar smell of coffee and a distant clatter of dishes cut through the sleep-induced haze weighing down his eyelids. They intermingled with the most unpleasant sound. High-pitched. Slurred. Punctuated with breathy snorts.

Oleksiy's eyes flew open. He pawed for his phone to check what day it was.

Sunday! It was Sunday!

Yet, there sat Mykola, on a high stool behind the breakfast bar, eating Honey Grahams with his wife.

'The hell is this?' Oleksiy demanded.

'Hey, boss,' Mykola said through a mouthful of cereal.

'Coffee?' Payal asked sunnily.

Oleksiy's eyes glazed over, his tongue momentarily forgetting how to form words.

She was dressed to go out, her glowing, smooth, brown arms bare in a loose, strappy white top that hugged her breasts just right, and her long, shapely legs, looking even smoother to the touch, in a pair of hot shorts.

Tearing his eyes off of her, Oleksiy scowled at Mykola. 'It's Sunday.'

'Yes. And we're going to Coney Island,' Payal beamed.

Her and Mykola. Together. Strolling the boardwalk. Getting hot dogs. Splashing water at each other. Building sandcastles.

What if Mykola *was* stupid and did try to work his charms on her. What if she fell for them?

Oleksiy's heart pounded his ribcage with a loud and angry *thud*.

'Season's over, isn't it?' he said, unable to contain the undercurrent of spite in his words.

'I wasn't planning on going in the water,' Payal replied, tipping the last of her cereal's milk into her mouth. 'The amusement park's open on weekends, and I mostly just wanted to see the place in nice weather.'

'And where are your books?' Oleksiy asked Mykola pointedly.

Mykola's nostrils trembled with his responding snort. 'It's Sunday.'

'A little break will do him good,' Payal appealed. 'He's been working really hard.'

'His dedication's been noted.' He directed a withering glower at the boy, his every word packing a bite. 'But seeing that it *is* Sunday and his day off, I'm sure he's got better things to do than chaperoning a trip to the beach.'

'It's no problem, boss. I got nothing better to do. 'Sides, Coney Island Beach is neutral turf. It's the one place Payal actually needs a bodyguard.'

'*Sestra* Payal's gonna be just fine,' Oleksiy nearly growled. 'I'll take her. Now get outta here. See if your mama needs any help around the house.'

'Arright, arright,' Mykola moaned petulantly, pushing away from the breakfast bar.

Oleksiy's ears rang with the sound of the kid's heavy, graceless footfalls even after the apartment had fallen into a death-like silence. Payal sat rigidly hunched over the table, a hand clenched around her mug's handle, her steely gaze shooting daggers at him.

'I—' Oleksiy looked away. 'I'll take you. Just—just lemme get dressed, all right?'

What had he done?

His fingers were a trembling mess as he tried to rush through his morning routine.

Why did he do it?

Because it was Coney Island, he reasoned with himself, clumsily slapping on sunscreen before pulling a T-shirt over his head and shoving his legs through a pair of cargo shorts. Because there'd be eyes and ears everywhere. Because the optics of Payal hanging out at the beach with her bodyguard on a Sunday while her husband was at home looked bad. Because Mama had warned him against giving people cause to start rumours about his marriage.

Yeah, that was it! He was doing it to make good on what Mama told him. Because if things didn't work out with Payal, he'd have to marry someone else from the bratva. And as far as bratva-ordained marriages went, Payal wasn't so bad.

He definitely was not doing it because the thought of Payal going out on a long, romantic walk on the beach with another man—a man like Mykola, no less—made his blood boil.

Payal was no less irked by his impulsive, borderline imbecilic decision when he returned to the kitchen. Her chest positively heaved with fury with her every breath.

'Ready?' he asked sheepishly.

She answered with a clipped grunt, aggressively planting a wide-brimmed sun hat on her head and grabbing her sunglasses and hand bag off the countertop. Oleksiy trailed a few paces behind her as she stomped down the stairs and made for Brighton Beach Avenue.

She was remarkably fast. He had to lengthen his strides just to keep sight of her. His legs itched to pick up speed. But then what? She clearly didn't want him near her. He smiled, nodding at familiar faces he passed, and slid his sunglasses on to appear like he was out on a Sunday stroll like any other. Like his wife wasn't running away from him. He'd signed up to take over bodyguard duties, after all. Not be her date to the beach.

But damn it if the ground didn't feel like it'd been yanked from under his feet when she whipped around and fixed those disdainful black eyes on him.

'Go get a bagel,' she ordered, swinging an arm at the shop they'd halted in front of. Oleksiy was transfixed by the way she sucked her bottom lip into her mouth as she waited for him to comply. They were naturally purplish and brown, her lips. Plump and juicy. He wanted to run a thumb over them. Taste them. Know what they felt like against his skin.

What was that about bagels?

'I don't—' He cleared his throat, rolled his shoulder. 'I don't want a bagel.'

'You haven't had breakfast.' Those lips flattened into a stern line. 'Go get a bagel. You need cash?'

'No.' Mildly affronted, he made a discrete gesture for her to put her wallet away. 'You want anything?'

'No,' she said, turning her back to him, arms crossed over her chest.

They carried on in awkward silence all the way down Coney Island Avenue, him eating, her walking a few paces ahead. By the time they got to the Riegelmann Boardwalk, the bagel was gone and Oleksiy had had enough.

'Didn't realise you'd get so crabby 'bout losing Mykola's company for a day.' He snidely added, 'Kid must be a real charmer.'

'I can pay him overtime if you don't want to,' Payal snapped, picking up her pace. Oleksiy fell in step with her, his brows pulled together in a frown. 'Same goes for the rent and all other household expenses. I may not have a job now, but I made a pretty penny when I did, and I invest my savings. I'm financially independent, and I don't need you to babysit me.'

'Hey, hey, hey!' He set a hand on her bare shoulder to get her to stop. Then promptly retracted it as if he'd been burned. 'I'm just horsin' around, all right? The overtime's not why I—'

Fuck. Why'd he do it? Why was he here?

'It's just I—I've never been.'

Payal looked at him a long stretch, then arched a brow. 'To Coney Island?'

His bottom lip jutted out as he shrugged.

'It's literally a stone's throw from where you grew up.'

'Yeah, well … ' He resumed walking. 'Coney Island's not the safest place for a young boy. It's swarming with bratva informants, and I knew I'd have to steer clear of their radar if I was ever going to make a clean break.'

Payal froze, concern etched across her face. 'Then why go now?'

'Well,' he leaned in closer to her, a teasing grin tugging at his lips. 'I don't know if you've noticed, but I'm a big boy now. Much harder to lure over to the dark side. And a local business owner, besides. Everyone who's anyone can put a name to the face.'

'But what Mykola said about it being neutral turf—it's not just your father's informants there, is it? It's *all* the bratvas' informants.'

'Yep. Exactly why it's dangerous for a vor zakone's kid to be hanging around the place.'

'Or his daughter-in-law,' Payal added.

'Or his daughter-in-law,' Oleksiy chuckled. 'Though they tend to be tougher targets.'

Payal's chest rose and fell with an anxious sigh. Oleksiy watched her from the corner of his eye as they continued up the boardwalk. She didn't come from this world like other daughters-in-law. There was no telling which of the unspoken rules he took for granted wouldn't apply to her. Unlike the others, she *could* easily be a target.

Shameful as it was, Oleksiy hadn't grasped how frightening all of this must have been for her until now. Of course she'd want a bodyguard. She had no idea what could befall her in his world.

Yet she wasn't frightened enough to go running from it. From him. She made every effort to blend in, to live her life on her terms. And here she was today, walking shoulder to shoulder with him, straight into the lion's den.

'How many bratvas are there in all?' she asked, distracting Oleksiy from the strange fullness radiating through him.

He pumped his cheeks full of air and exhaled heavily. 'A bunch. It's not just the Ukrainians, right? You've got bratvas coming up from all over Russia and the ex-Soviet states. There used to be way more, though. Smaller cells with roots in different administrative divisions. Tato heads the Kotovsk bratva, which originated in Kotovsk Raion, which is actually the Podilsk Raion now. Obviously, not all of 'em could sustain operations, what with leadership and manpower being a precarious bitch, and surveillance and security getting so sophisticated. So, the sharks moved in on the minnows, and the number of bratvas shrank.'

'Is the Kotovsk bratva a shark or a minnow?'

'Sharkier than most, minnow to a few.' His voice dropped and the bad shoulder tightened. He tried to focus on the cool, prickly wind beating his face, the way it whipped loose strands of Payal's braided hair across her face, the honey-peach scent of her it flooded his nostrils with. Anything to keep him from the imminent slide into the black whirlpool. Onto the damp asphalt of that deserted alley all those years ago. 'The Berezivkas being the sharpest thorn in our side.' As though hearing the echoes of his trauma, Payal shuddered at the name.

'The Kotovsk was in real trouble before you and your dad came to the rescue,' Oleksiy continued, his descent into the shadow pool slowing. Oddly, he felt lighter the more he spoke. Like he was sharing the burden of an invisible weight. 'But now that Tato's out of sons to trade for money, there's no telling what'll happen next time a job goes south.'

Oleksiy took Payal's contemplative silence to mean that they were done discussing the matter. But then she asked, 'Do you ever worry they'll come after you? Your businesses?'

'Every fucking day,' he said with a sardonic chuckle. 'But don't worry, all right? I don't see you being sworn into the bratva as a sestra any time soon.'

He stopped in his tracks when he spotted a Ferris wheel peering over the New York Aquarium and the beachside kiosks. 'So, this is it, huh? Coney Island Beach.'

Payal spread her arms out wide. 'Tada!'

She did a little—kind of adorable—pirouette as she took it all in. It was a beautiful day, not too hot, not too cold. No swimmers or surfers since it was off-season and the beach was technically closed. Just the odd family picnicking on the beach, schoolkids harassing seagulls, athleisure Instagrammers and their minions, couples brushing up against each other, sharing ice cream.

Ice cream. His inner voice wouldn't stop repeating the damn word.

He rather begrudged people who ate ice cream.

'It's a lot different than I remember it.' Payal's words cut through his brain's absurd tirade on everything wrong with couples who ate ice cream together.

'You been here before?'

'Ages ago, during undergrad.' Her face lit up with a wistful smile. 'It was so stupid. My friend Ramisa decided to spend the money she got for her twenty-first on a girls' trip to the city. She booked one hotel room for the five of us, but we didn't even use it. You see, we were on a mission to have the greatest night on the town ever known to man.'

'Oh boy.'

'Uh huh. But as it turned out, nightclubs really weren't our scene and we were in too chatty a mood to sit through a Broadway show, so after a fancy dinner and some drinks, we hopped from one subway line to the next, paying absolutely no attention to where we were headed.

Next thing we knew, we were being kicked off the D and following the sound of waves to Coney Island Beach. In sub-zero temperatures, in the dead of night. Ended up huddling together for warmth on one of these benches and passed out. Sun was up high and bright when we came to. Had to pay half a day's extra for that hotel room.' The shock on Oleksiy's face drew an embarrassed chuckle from her. 'It's a miracle none of us got frostbite.'

'You're lucky you escaped the bratvas' notice,' Oleksiy said brusquely. A bunch of drunk, defenseless girls on a deserted beach in the dead of night would have been too easy a haul for a prostitution racket.

It was a long time ago, though, and nobody got hurt. It definitely didn't warrant the irrational anger and protectiveness surging through him now.

'Yeah.' Face fallen, voice faded, Payal stared out at the sparkling water. 'Don't I know it.'

'So, what now?' Oleksiy asked, adjusting his shoulder to shake his agitation. 'We're here. Whaddya gotta do for an authentic Coney Island experience?'

Her face livened up again. 'I'm guessing hot dogs and amusement park.'

'All right,' Oleksiy sighed. 'But hot dogs after rides. I'm not dealing with any puke projectiles.'

'That'd be funny, though,' Payal said, sauntering towards Deno's Wonder Wheel, drawing his attention to her full hips. 'If that was the only thing the bratvas' whisper network got on us today.'

Oleksiy suspected their little beach outing would set many a tongue wagging, be it for strategic insight, or to speculate about the nature of his relationship with

Payal. The bratva presence was more conspicuous than he'd expected. Parking spaces along the streets leading out to the beach were packed with Harleys, and their heavy-set, leather-clad, chain-slinging, bandana-wearing owners hung about the vicinity in small groups. Watching. Always watching. Perhaps even more keenly now that the prince of Kotovsk graced them with his presence.

Payal was much calmer than Oleksiy felt. Shooting him an inquiring look to confirm the intimidating bikers were bratva, she proceeded to buy tickets and wait in line for the rides without sparing them a second glance. She did it effortlessly, like she was used to dealing with all kinds of unwanted attention.

Again, the bodyguard thing made sense.

And the thought of someone harassing, maybe even stalking her, shot a fiery jolt of anger through Oleksiy. He wanted a name. A physical form he could inflict pain upon. Something tangible he could do to keep her safe. To rid her of the fears she'd grown so accustomed to living with.

But stalker or no, she would *always* be in danger by association to his family. To him.

Not for the first time, Oleksiy was baffled by how someone like Payal agreed to an arrangement like theirs. Even more perplexing was her composure, the way she savoured the present. The way it all rubbed off on him the longer he stayed around her.

Why, he might have even had some fun.

Later, as they worked their way through an entire tray of Nathan's hot dogs, their bodies warm and slick with sweat, Payal asked, 'You ever been to the top of the Empire State Building?'

Oleksiy swallowed his bite. His answer startled him. 'No.'

'Me neither. Have you ever noticed that most New Yorkers don't actually ever visit the landmarks New York's famous for?'

'Yeah? Why's that?'

'Dunno. Just an observation.'

'Maybe we could go some time.' The muscles in Oleksiy's jaw twitched from the effort of masking his nerves. 'To the top of the Empire State Building.' A millisecond later: 'That is, if you wouldn't rather have Mykola for company.'

'No, no.' Payal looked up at him through her lashes. 'I'd love to have someone to do dumb touristy stuff with.'

She smiled then, a low contented thrum emanating from her, almost like a purr. It warmed Oleksiy's hollow heart, soothed its turbulent tides. Made him wonder what it'd feel like flush against his body.

'I mean—' He cleared his throat and angled himself towards the water, away from her. 'I'll be complaining the entire time so … '

He stopped himself from suggesting they go next Saturday out of fear he'd come across too eager. She didn't make a move to commit to any plans either. A part of him hoped she'd forget he'd even suggested it. Maybe if he didn't mention it again, she would.

He wished he could forget about it himself.

But it was all he could think about the next week: the two of them taking the long subway ride into the city, going up to the top of the Empire State Building, then maybe walking over to Madison Square Park and getting Shake Shack for lunch. No ice cream, of course—that would overstep into romantic territory—but surely there was nothing wrong with getting milkshakes.

Right?

The uncertainty over their weekend plans—whether there would even be any weekend plans—became near intolerable by Thursday. Oleksiy had to pop the question. Hastily dismissing Channel Fitness's weekly staff meeting, he headed home early, even though Mykola had told him Payal would be late getting home. He had to get his thoughts in order, word his proposition so as not to give her the wrong idea. This was about going to the Empire State Building, experiencing things he'd never done before. It had nothing to do with her, or that electric thrum he felt whenever he got close to her. She was an agreeable travelling companion, and that was all there was to it.

A large, slender package addressed to Payal waited with the rest of the building's packages behind the entrance. Against his better judgement, Oleksiy plucked the floral envelope taped to the brown paper packaging. The neat, slanted cursive on the card inside read:

You got married and didn't invite me??? For shame! Congratulations though! This one's one of your (and, obviously, my) best, if I say so myself. Take good care of it and let's catch up soon. :)

Cheers,
Tyler

Oleksiy resisted the urge to crumple the card. He shouldn't have opened it in the first place, let alone gotten worked up about this . . . this Tyler.

Who was he? How did he know her? What kind of a relationship did they have?

He begrudgingly carried the package up to their apartment. It felt like a frame.

This one's one of your (and, obviously, my) best.

What did that mean? Was Payal an artist of some sort? Like him?

Like Alice?

His chest constricted painfully at the thought.

No. He would never taint the sanctity of what he had with Alice by making that comparison.

No, this was about another man—some schlub named Tyler—knowing more about his wife than he did. Who was to say this Tyler character wasn't the reason Payal knew how to navigate unwanted attention so well, the reason she'd asked for a bodyguard? Who was to say this note wasn't some sort of cryptic, perverted threat? Who was to say this Tyler wasn't a total psychopath?

Oleksiy had wanted a name, didn't he? A living, breathing person he could punch into the ground so she'd feel safe.

The reasonable part of him told him not to tear the wrapping off the package. It wasn't his to open. But whether he cared to acknowledge it or not, it was becoming irrefutably apparent neither reason, pragmatism, propriety or his ironclad principles had much sway on him when it came to Payal. There was only an unerring duty to protect. A subversive desire to possess. And when he saw what lay underneath the packing paper and bubble wrap, there was blinding, crimson jealousy.

Six

'HEY.' APPREHENSION COLOURED PAYAL'S voice as she shrugged out of her light jacket and stowed her shoes away. 'Did you just get in?'

Oleksiy was sitting at her desk—a spot that implicitly belonged to her and her alone. Suit jacket discarded on the couch, his tie hung loose around his neck and the two top buttons of his shirt were undone. His usually immaculately brushed hair was in disarray and he looked somewhat winded. He occupied her chair—ankle crossed over knee, bare forearms perched on armrests—commanding her undivided attention.

'You got a package,' he all but growled, propping a frame on the couch separating them.

She was too fixated on his biting tone to immediately register what she was looking at. There were various shades of brown and a flourish of emerald. When she managed to shut out Oleksiy's molten black gaze, she made out the figure of a woman. A naked woman. Tactfully sitting sideways on a chair, looking over her shoulder at the observer, thick, glossy currents of black hair cascading down her back. A length of green fabric draped her lap, falling to a floor littered with random objects.

Payal knew that length of fabric. Remembered those props on the floor.

She recognised the soft crests peeking out from behind the woman's arm, those calves, those feet. She saw that face every time she looked in the mirror.

And behind the provocative portrait sat Oleksiy, thoroughly provoked, the muscles in his arms and jaw clenched, his eyes reprimanding. Maybe even disgusted.

Heat flooded her ears and cheeks, and tears sprang from her eyes as she choked on a sound that fell somewhere between a sob and a horrified shriek. 'Wh—who—'

Oleksiy sprang to his feet, his footfalls loud as a gong as he crossed the room and handed her a card.

'Tyler,' she read aloud. *Damn it, Tyler!*

'You know him?'

Payal recoiled at his harshness.

He ducked his head to be at eye level with her. 'He giving you trouble?'

'W-what? No!' She crossed her arms over her chest tightly. 'Tyler's an old friend.'

He whipped his gaze off of her, a bitter chuckle squeezing past gritted teeth. His hands found purchase on his hips. 'You let all your friends paint you like that?'

Something flared inside Payal. Made her brows pull together. She was mortified, yes. Traumatised, even, at the reminder of the unblemished body she no longer had. But she wasn't answerable to Oleksiy. Not for this.

'I used to model for studio art classes during undergrad,' she found her voice again, tilting her chin up, squaring her shoulders. 'An aunt of mine suggested it'd help build confidence.'

Oleksiy's eyes narrowed in judgement. 'If you modelled for the whole class, why's Tyler the only one sending you his handiwork?'

'Because we were friends,' she said, exasperated. She brushed past him to get closer to the painting. 'We had a bunch of political science classes together. We'd get lunch, hang out, that kind of stuff. Sometimes he'd pass me snacks while I was modelling so I didn't fall asleep.'

Oleksiy released a long, audible sigh. Payal couldn't tell if it was out of resignation or relief. 'Yeah,' he said, his voice softening. 'Yeah, I guess your limbs must've got pretty numb, huh? Posing for such long stretches.'

'Yeah.' Her own drawn-out sigh was accompanied by an exhausted shudder. 'Those studios were freezing in the winters.'

She looked at the painting. At herself. At how regal and sensual and self-assured Tyler had made her appear. A surge of melancholy overpowered any embarrassment she felt. How perfectly normal and alluringly smooth her skin was. How oblivious the girl in the portrait had been to the misfortunes headed her way.

Payal picked at the rough, wrinkled fissures criss-crossing her abdomen through her top. Her breath faltered as she remembered the impact of those three blows that irreversibly changed her life. They had felt like punches at first. Sharp, agonising pain had followed soon after, sending warm blood gushing down her legs.

Clenching her eyes shut, she drew several calming breaths. *You're safe now. At home. Painting. Tyler. Oleksiy.* Word by word, she pawed her way back to the present.

'Oh, Tyler,' she finally said with an air of levity, shaking her head. She took the painting to the storage closet in the corridor.

'What're you doing?' she heard Oleksiy ask as she tried to clear some space.

'The painting's too obviously of me, so we can't throw it out. And we're most definitely not hanging it up in the apartment, so—'

She let out a frustrated groan. There was only one way to make enough room for it in the closet. She wriggled the painting of the Manhattan skyline out from behind the storage containers. Sliding Tyler's painting in its place, she shut the door and fell back against it as if it might try kicking its way out.

'Here'—Oleksiy strode over to her, an agitated spring to his step—'give it here. I'll take care of it.'

Payal snatched the frame out of his reach. 'Take care of it how?'

'When I take out the garbage.'

'Absolutely not!' Ignoring the daggers his eyes shot at her, Payal lifted the painting up to admire it. 'It's charming.'

'It's mine.'

'Then you shouldn't be so quick to throw it out,' Payal retorted, her tone flat. 'It's not healthy being so unsentimental about your own belongings. Someone might make the mistake of thinking you're emotionally detached.'

'As its maker, I'm free to sell it or shred it as I please.'

'Wait.' Payal retreated a few steps as he tried swiping the frame from her again. 'You're saying *you* made this?'

His shoulders slumped with irritation. Combing his fingers through his raven hair, he asked, 'That so hard to believe?'

Payal stared at his long, slender fingers as they mercilessly tugged at his hair. They were an artist's fingers. She imagined them being smudged with charcoal as he dragged them over paper. She imagined the concentration on his face as he worked in a studio similar to the one she used to model at. She imagined his stray lock of hair kissing his forehead as he looked up from his work at her, naked on the dais.

'No, but ... ' She swallowed hard, trying to grease her parched throat. 'That's even more reason not to throw it away.'

'It's not—' He scraped his teeth over his bottom lip. Then his tongue darted out to lick it. 'It's a reminder of a time I'd rather not be reminded of, all right?'

'Then we won't hang it up where you can see it.'

'This isn't up for negotiation.' He was quivering with mounting anger. 'Hand it over. Now.'

Payal's knees threatened to buckle from being under fire like this. 'How much do you want for it?'

'What?' he snarled.

'How much do you want for it?' Payal repeated, the tremor in her voice clear as day. 'I think it's beautiful, and I won't let you destroy it.'

'I'm not selling.'

'I'll give you a hundred bucks.'

Oleksiy's head jerked back in narrow-eyed astonishment. Looking away, he uttered a quiet, spiteful chuckle. 'All right, then. One sitting.'

'A sitting?'

'One sitting.' He stalked closer and closer, flooding her nostrils with his cocoa-orange zest scent. Voice low and velvety, he said, 'As a model. Like you did for Tyler.'

Payal's eyelids fluttered. Tiny flashes of warmth detonated all over her body. She pressed the dusty painting to her torso to shield herself, yet there was no shielding her uptilted face from his warm breath and his piercing black gaze. 'E-exactly like I did for Tyler?'

He rolled his shoulder and flashed her a nonchalant grin. 'I never got the hang of drawing fabrics right. The human form, though—a woman's—that's much easier. Especially, when they're … '

Payal clung to his every word with bated breath, and simultaneously hated how he relished the hold he had on her.

' … unencumbered by clothes,' he finished.

Her answering gasp echoed the resounding *thud* her heart made. Then, as though to compensate for the momentary glitch, it sped up, muddling every coherent thought she ever had.

She wanted to. Oh, she wanted to so much. She wanted to bare herself to him, wanted to know how he'd capture her on paper. How he saw her. If he admired her in any way.

But he would never admire her. Not the way she wanted him to in that moment. That privilege would always belong to the Supreme.

Besides, he wanted to draw the woman she'd stashed away in the storage closet. He didn't want her as she was now.

'No,' came her curt reply.

Incensed, Oleksiy leaned closer, shrouding her in his shadow. 'No because I'm not Tyler?'

'Because I got what I needed from that exercise.'

'So it's always gotta be a rational choice, that it?' he scoffed. 'You don't do anything that doesn't serve your best interests?'

Like our marriage.

Payal fumed at the unspoken words. As if his own family didn't get a whole five million dollars out of the arrangement.

They had a deal. To keep up appearances. To not interfere in each other's lives. To treat each other cordially. To expect nothing remotely spousal from the other.

Stripping naked for him wasn't part of it, no matter how strong her urge to comply was.

'I actually think I'm making quite the irrational choice taking your painting,' she retorted levelly, her eyes bright with fury. 'It's going to clutter my room. And now that I'm rescinding my offer of payment, it won't get you anything either. Now, excuse me,' she levered him out of the way using the frame, 'and no outside shoes in the house!'

She shut herself in her room, slamming the door in his face. But not before catching a glimpse of utterly confounded hurt in those glistening black eyes.

Oleksiy was distant after that night. Payal never saw him before she left for class in the mornings, and he stopped coming home for dinner. He was rarely in on weekends and barely acknowledged her presence when he was. On the few occasions he deigned to speak to her, he was irritable and curt.

It was infuriating.

Yes, the painting made things awkward, but rather than laughing it off and forgetting about it like a normal housemate, he'd gone and made it infinitely more awkward by asking her to model for him. And he had the audacity to get angry at her for refusing, and guilt her for modelling for someone else?

Who was he to feel entitled to her? He couldn't have it both ways. He couldn't have her while pining for another woman. He couldn't claim her while denying her a real marriage founded on love and affection.

When her anger mellowed, Payal was left lamenting over the friendship Oleksiy had stolen from her. Their trip to Coney Island Beach had been one of the loveliest things to happen to her in recent memory and she'd been looking forward to visiting the Empire State Building with him. Mykola was a decent enough bodyguard, but he wasn't the sharpest tool in the shed, which made him a very bland, at times grating travelling companion.

Oleksiy was Oleksiy. Intelligent, enterprising, altruistic, charismatic. Stupidly handsome. Hey, Payal was only human. Being around a tall, dark-haired man with chiseled features and a sense of purpose affected her as much as the next straight woman. She liked how womanly he made her feel. She liked the anticipation of sharing something with him, be it space, a conversation, or a meal. She liked the foreboding thrill and pure gratification of getting the chance to be close to him.

She liked being the reason he smiled that smile that touched his eyes.

Being around Oleksiy, spending time with him—it didn't erase the past, but it did make living with it easier. His friendship—it was more than returning to normalcy. Normalcy was being able to leave the house, riding the subway, going back to school, not having doctors', physiotherapists' and psychiatrists' appointments five times a week. His friendship made the ordinary less so. It made getting out of bed less of a chore, and more of something . . . something special. It was something to bask in, to savour with her whole heart.

And now, thanks to his petulance, she didn't have that anymore.

The Empire State Building remained a pipe dream as October rolled around and he continued pretending she didn't exist. In the first week, she received a chilly reminder from Mumma about the garba block party the Indian community in their neighbourhood organised every year. The next day, Nasir brought over a blue, floral-printed Torani lehenga along with Mumma's weekly food delivery. He also brought four sets of kurta-pyjamas in four different sizes. One of them was bound to fit Oleksiy.

That is, if Oleksiy went to the party.

Payal's first impulse was not to invite him. Dick that he was being of late, he'd probably try making another deal out of it. *A modelling session in exchange for my gracious presence at your quaint block party.* Payal would much rather go alone.

But when she tried on the lehenga's beaded, midriff-covering choli, she remembered Mumma's anger at her decision to marry Oleksiy. How Mumma had practically disowned her for it.

Just think of the kind of questions that's going to invite! Mumma's hoarse voice hissed in her ears. *Think!*

Questions. Judgement. Ominous and pitying looks. All seared in Payal's memory. She'd fended them off at her wedding reception with a blank smile and small talk, but she'd also had another weapon in her arsenal that night: her strikingly intimidating husband. Without him at her side, those unspoken questions, judgements, consolations, and prophecies of imminent doom wouldn't stay unspoken for long.

His attendance fell well within the terms of their agreement. He would come. Payal needed him to come.

She laid the four outfits on his bed. When he got in at half-past eleven that night, she was at her desk with her back turned to him. Neither acknowledged the other. Payal listened to his movements intently as he locked the main door, put his shoes away on the rack, poured himself some water from the Brita in the fridge, strode down the hall to his bedroom. She resisted the urge to swivel her chair around when she heard him retrace his steps, waiting, instead, till he cleared his throat to get her attention.

'Hey.' She looked over her shoulder. 'What's up?'

Oleksiy nudged a thumb behind him. 'There's, uh, what—'

'Oh, right. Mumma sent those over for a party back home this weekend.' The words surged out of her at full speed. 'It's this garba block party we have every year to celebrate Navaratri, though it's more about the photo ops and networking than anything religious, seeing that we're Muslim and half the guests are white. Food's good, though, and Saira's flying in from D.C. for the weekend. You don't have to come, if you don't want to.'

'No, I'll come.' He gave her a one-shouldered shrug. 'If that's what you want.'

'I—' Payal's throat dried. 'I think I'm fine either way.'

'Well, we gotta let people know we're good, right? Won't help your dad's circle much if folks think he's made a bad investment in his son-in-law.'

Exactly. Payal released a grateful sigh, even though the stern set of his jaw and the scrutiny in his pitch-black eyes unsettled her.

'Right.' Why was she out of breath? 'So ... Friday, then.'

'Friday. When should I tell the car to pick us up?'

Seven

BOISTEROUS DRUMBEATS, PLAYFUL SHEHNAI music and a DJ's appeals to get on the dance floor blared through Cohawney Road. Multicoloured lights, streamers and lanterns canopied the entire street. The lawns on either side were carpeted over and fitted with awnings and patio heaters; mouthwatering aromas of fresh puris, samosas and yam cutlets wafted through the crisp autumn air. Payal and Oleksiy left the driver to park the car in a driveway at the edge of the street and walked the rest of the way to the Lohani house.

'You came!' Saira's eyes rounded with excitement when she opened the front door, darting from Payal to Oleksiy and back. 'They're here!' she called over her shoulder before reeling Payal into a tight hug. She then turned her attention to Oleksiy. 'And you chose the green kurta! That one was my favourite of the lot.'

Payal chanced a peek at him. Something she'd been struggling to avoid the entire drive over. The olive kurta, dark and metallic, accentuated his broad shoulders and lean frame. His muscular forearms were on display thanks to its three-quarter sleeves, and the strip of black-and-copper embroidery around his neck and down his chest lent his chiselled profile the air of a prince.

He *was* a prince. Her prince. Yet he wasn't hers at all, and never would be.

Biting back a grin, Oleksiy arched a brow at her baby sister. 'Guess that explains why the others were a hair shy of being the right fit.'

Responding with an impish chuckle, Saira ushered them inside. Papa joined them in the foyer before Saira could take Oleksiy on a tour of the house. He pulled Payal into a hug and greeted Oleksiy with a deferential handshake, enquired about their drive over and how their studies and businesses were going, respectively. Mumma was predictably prickly in that stoic way desi mothers were wont to be when displeased in public. She didn't shirk away from Payal's longer-than-necessary hug, nor was she rude to Oleksiy. She simply didn't bother to hide her disapproval of her daughter and her distrust of the man she'd married.

They headed out to the party as a typical family unit: with grown children tailing—in Payal's case, cowering—behind parents who were a good foot shorter than them. Mumma and Papa discreetly matched names to familiar faces for the girls' benefit and asked after children with vaguely recognisable names studying or working at highly reputed institutions. They offered up brief updates about Payal and Saira's lives in return and, of course, introduced everyone to Oleksiy.

It was a lot easier than Payal expected. Unlike her wedding reception, the garba party wasn't about her. So, as blatant as people were in judging her marriage, their judgement was fleeting. She was mildly amused, even, by the curious, almost wistful stir her tall, handsome and unerringly gracious husband caused among the hawk-eyed aunties in attendance.

Eventually, Papa and Oleksiy joined the huddle of uncles at the coffee tent, Mumma was waved over to a seat with a good vantage of the dancing and Saira hopped into the garba circle, falling in step with the other dancers without missing a beat. Payal caught up with a few familiar faces whose names she did remember.

'I didn't think you'd be here,' said Aditi, an old friend Payal had known since middle school. They'd drifted apart during college, and fallen out of touch altogether after Payal's attack. 'Aunty said you were at some accountants' conference in Switzerland last year, and in Belgium the year before that. I thought it was going to be an annual thing or something.'

Payal drew a deep, calming breath and identified three things in her surroundings to remind herself of where she was and when. No one besides Mumma, Papa, Saira and the household help knew what had happened to her. No one knew that she'd been in the ICU, on the brink of a coma the Navaratri before last, and no one knew she was still suffering from violent panic attacks the same time last year.

She wished she'd been attending some stuffy accountants' conference in Belgium and Switzerland.

'Yeah, well,' Payal persevered through her palpitations, 'I realised the accountant thing really wasn't my scene, so no more conferences for me.'

'Good for you,' Aditi nodded in approval. 'You're too hot to be an accountant, anyway. Speaking of which, you and I need to have a chat about your Insta game. No European travel pics, I can forgive, but when you have a snack of a husband like that'—she tilted her head towards the coffee tent—'girl, you need to give the rest of us a heads up. I was almost going to go make a move before my mom told me who he was.' Scooting closer to Payal, she lowered her voice. 'She also said he was dangerous. How dangerous are we talking? Like extreme sports or on parole?'

'He's not dangerous.' The words came out more defensively than Payal intended. She looked his way to check if he'd heard, which was silly because he was halfway across the lawn. Still, he'd come here tonight for her and she wasn't going to let anyone offend him. 'He's a business owner. He owns a gym in Brighton Beach, and he's trying to get a security firm off the ground. He mostly hires out of the local community so they don't, you know, turn to crime. Or sex work.'

'So he's not a doctor or an engineer, *and* he helps poor people? No wonder mother doesn't approve.' Brazen in her appraisal of him, Aditi let out a moan. 'But God, Payal, he's gorgeous.'

As if hearing the compliment, Oleksiy turned his head their way, his black eyes locking onto Payal's, setting her heart aflutter. The corner of his mouth quirked up in a smile of solidarity as he lifted one hand in a muted wave.

'And judging by the way he looks like he could practically eat you right now,' Aditi teased, nudging Payal's shoulder with her elbow. 'He must have it *real* bad for you.'

Aditi's words faded to a barely audible muffle as heat flooded Payal's cheeks and her heart pounded in her ears. He was still looking at her from across the lawn, reading her, waiting for her to beckon him to her. Payal wondered what he'd do if she did. If he'd take her someplace dark and secluded so he could have his way with her.

No. Of course he wouldn't. Because they had an agreement. Because he was in love with the Supreme.

Her head knew, but her heart wouldn't let her break the connection and it didn't help that he kept feeding the fire.

'Oh!' Aditi tugged at Payal's arm. 'This is our song! Come on, stop ogling your husband.'

Payal snapped out of her trance to find herself being dragged to the dancefloor. *Dholi Taro Dhol Baje* was playing on the sound system.

'Aditi,' Payal protested, trying to wriggle her wrist free from her friend's grip, 'it's been ages.'

Aditi halted at the edge of the revolving circle of dancers. 'And we're still better than most of these kids. Come on!'

Another sharp tug on Payal's wrist, and they were both in the circle, doing half pirouettes, squatting, skipping, clapping and giving each other high tens in time to the music—moves that were second nature to Payal. The physical exertion was a welcome distraction from her imprudent urges. Turn by turn, as her lehenga flared out and swirled around her, she returned to a time when she didn't have a care in the world.

'Hungama, hungama, ho gaya hai hungama,' the DJ sang into the microphone. 'Hungama, hungama—naw, naw, naw, dawgs, there are too many of you just sitting there. I wanna see some more of you dancing. Hey, baaje re, baaje re!'

Saira thrust a pair of dandiya sticks into Payal's hands as more people trickled onto the dance floor. Two concentric circles revolving in opposite directions gradually formed. Every count of eight brought everyone face-to-face with a different partner. They crossed sticks, flourished their arms as if they were swimming freestyle, then spun on over to their next partner. Her worries forgotten, Payal beamed with encouragement as embarrassed teenaged boys and uncles and aunties with no rhythm awkwardly tapped her sticks before moving to their next partner.

A whiff of cocoa and orange zest was all the warning she got before she found Oleksiy in front of her, smiling, holding his sticks out for her to tap. Payal stared at him, a lump forming in her throat, her heart growing so much her ribs felt like they might crack. It was a warm and uncomfortable sensation and it made her want to cry.

His brows pulled together in a questioning frown as their eight counts passed them by. Payal shuffled over to her next partner. She had no idea who it was, or whether she was dancing in time to the music. Everything became a muted blur. Everything except for Oleksiy's obsidian eyes that were burning with an intensity she didn't have a name for. It didn't matter who he danced with. That look stayed trained on her and her alone. And it was making her sick with want.

She extracted herself from the garba circle before he could loop back to her, and practically bolted over to the meal tent. Hastily filling a thali from the buffet, she sat down, uninvited, at Mumma and her friends' table just as Oleksiy strode into the tent looking for her.

She pretended to be too engrossed in her food to see him. Something she would've been in earnest, had it not been for him.

Why was he intent on making this so difficult? He had no business endearing himself to her. He had no business flustering her the way he did.

Even more maddening was that he technically hadn't done anything wrong. The modelling request was out of line, but this? He'd dressed in an outfit *her* family had sent him. He'd accompanied her to a party *she'd* invited him to, and he was being a sport by dancing at a garba party.

Payal didn't know what was happening to her. Maybe it was the adrenaline of attending a proper social gathering after so long. Maybe it was the stress of having to manage her anxiety. All she knew was she didn't trust her wits around him.

After finishing her mains, Payal moved from Mumma's table to the one Saira and her friends occupied, and stayed there, picking at an assortment of halwas, barfis and kheers as the night wore on. Oleksiy came looking for her again when things started winding down. The girls' unfiltered banter quieted as he approached their table.

'Ready to head home?' he asked, voice low and inappropriately sultry.

One of Saira's friends couldn't hold back a giggle but Oleksiy didn't seem to notice. His attention was fixed solely on Payal.

'Um.' Payal ducked her head and hunched her back in the far-fetched hope she could retreat into a shell like a turtle. 'I think I'll stay here a few days.'

His eyes darkened, and the muscles in his jaw strained with the effort of keeping his voice level. 'A few days?'

'Yeah, until Saira flies back out.' Payal bit down on her bottom lip as Saira broke into cheerful applause. 'You go head on home without me.'

'You have class the day after tomorrow,' Oleksiy said coolly, his nostrils flaring ever so slightly.

'Oh! Well, Nasir can take me. I'll call Mykola to meet me on campus.'

He glanced up at the awning overhead. 'If that's what you want,' he said sourly. He acknowledged the others with a slight nod. 'Ladies.'

He'd barely turned his back to them when the table burst into a flurry of girlish *aww*s and giggles. Payal didn't see what was so funny.

Payal moaned in sweet relief as her aching back touched the mattress. Using her last reserves of energy to draw a quilt over herself, she was just about to surrender to a heavy sleep when a familiar weight jostled her mattress.

Grumbling in annoyance, Payal hugged the arm snaking around her to her chest and burrowed back into its owner's warmth.

'You asleep?' Saira asked.

'Not anymore.'

'Hey, you wanted to stay back on my account, so here I am.'

Oleksiy's stony face flashed before Payal's shut eyes, sending a faint shudder down her body. 'Yeah, I guess I did.'

Saira tightened her arm around her. 'Is everything okay?'

'Yeah.' Payal snuggled deeper into her sister's embrace, tried to draw strength from it. 'Why wouldn't it be?'

'Well, you weren't planning on staying over.'

'No.' *I wasn't expecting the sight of Oleksiy dancing to blindside me the way it did,* Payal wanted to say. 'It's funny, I didn't realise how much I was missing this place until I was back again,' she said a moment later. 'I mean, I'm glad I finally get to reclaim my life again, but so much has happened so fast that a change of pace—and a return to what's static and familiar—feels nice.'

'So ... your mafioso husband isn't treating you badly?'

'He's not mafioso.' There it was, that defensiveness rearing its head again. 'And no, he's not treating me badly.'

Even though he did seem to find some sort of masochistic pleasure in toying with her.

'It was nice of him to come tonight and put up a show,' Saira said. 'Almost passed for a real husband. Nakti, Kanika and Crystal are beyond jealous of you, by the way. They wouldn't shut up about how hot he was.

Even Parveen Aunty. She just got divorced. Though she did ask if he was Kashmiri, so she might not be as interested now that she knows he's not Indian.'

'They're all welcome to shoot their shot.'

'What, is the Supreme not in the picture anymore?'

'The Supreme is *always* in the picture,' Payal said drily.

'We have got to stop calling her that. What's her name?'

'I don't know.' And that was a good thing. She knew she wouldn't be immune to looking her up on social media and obsessing over her if she did.

'But how supreme is supreme, exactly?' Saira pondered. 'Like are we talking Rihanna supreme? She's gotta be, right? If he'd rather be with her than with you?'

'I don't know,' Payal repeated testily. 'She's got red hair. That's all the intel I've got.'

'Huh, didn't take him for the type. No wonder he's not into you.'

Payal thought she might snap if Saira said that one more time.

Saira clicked her tongue. 'But forget these goras and their vanilla love lives. What about you? Have you met anyone yet?'

Releasing a piqued breath, Payal burrowed her head deeper into her pillow. She thought of the hallway at the Brighton Beach apartment. Of when she was trapped between Oleksiy and the storage closet's door. Of how he looked down at her, his breath scorching and uneven against her face.

'Columbia's gotta be teeming with cute, nerdy boys,' Saira pressed. 'And what about Tinder? I hope you've changed your location. Otherwise, it's just gonna give you a catalogue of other mafia types.'

'Uff, Sheru, I need time. The wedding, the move, school—this may come as a shock to you, but it hasn't been an easy adjustment.'

Silence. Then, salaciously, 'What about your bodyguard?'

'Who, Mykola?' Payal gagged. 'God, no.'

'I don't get it. Dating was part of the plan to get back to normal. You know, if I didn't know you any better, I'd think you went and caught feelings for Oleksiy Bhai.'

Payal's eyes flew wide open. A kaleidoscope of butterflies seized her, chasing away the day's exhaustion along with all her confusion.

No. It couldn't be.

Shit, I have feelings for him.

'Oh, Appi,' Saira said with unbearable pity. 'You have, haven't you?'

'Have not,' Payal snapped.

Saira let out a long sigh. 'Maybe he's not exclusively attracted to redheads.'

'Stop it, Sheru. I don't like him. And you know me well enough to know I'd never be okay playing second fiddle to another woman.' She removed Saira's arm from around her and wound the quilt around herself tightly. 'Now go to sleep, or go back to your own room.'

Saira rolled onto her other side with a defeated huff. 'It's not that big a deal, you know.' Impending sleep slurred her words. 'You've had a long dry spell, and you live with a gorgeous guy who doesn't smell like a toilet and doesn't make you want to strangle him when he speaks. A lesser woman would've YOLO'ed and tried jumping him already.'

Payal lay wide awake mulling over that. Sex. Saira was right. That's what Payal needed. Relief swept over her. Lust! The feelings she had for him were just lust!

She couldn't risk acting on it, of course. A deal was a deal. And even if Oleksiy's behaviour of late suggested he could be open to renegotiating, she couldn't risk revealing herself—all of herself—to him like that.

A forceful tremor rocked her body as visceral flashes from that subway station nearly two years ago suddenly threatened to overwhelm her mental shields. Eyes burning with tears, gasping hoarsely, she grabbed hold of Saira and squeezed her close before pain and dread came flooding back in full force.

My Bed. Safe. Saira. Home. Oleksiy. Yes, Oleksiy! You were thinking about Oleksiy!

Her breaths steadied. The pressure in her chest eased.

She wanted him. And maybe he wanted her back. But she couldn't let him see all of her. And he was still stuck on his ex.

And they were supposed to carry on living together like this? Outrageous.

Good thing, then, that she'd decided to stay back. A few days apart might be just what she needed to get her libido in check.

Eight

OLEKSIY SAT SLUMPED OVER THE BREAKFAST bar, pondering how much Papa John's was too much Papa John's while reaching for another slice. He decided he didn't want to know. The combination of excessive cheese, tangy tomato sauce and grease-soaked crust was the only thing that seemed to make coming home to an empty apartment bearable the past few days.

It was Tuesday night. Payal had come into the city two days, but not returned to Brighton Beach. Mykola didn't know when she planned on coming home. Oleksiy had been tempted several times to ask her himself, but that meant getting her number from someone first—either Mykola or Mama or Marisha—and he wasn't in the mood to deal with their ridicule.

Besides, what was he supposed to say if she didn't give him a definitive answer? They'd never explicitly agreed to live together at all times. She technically didn't have to see him again unless they needed to make an appearance at something like the block party over at Cohawney Road, and Oleksiy didn't have anything to invite her to. His newly discovered dislike for his own company wasn't grounds enough to get her to come back.

He groaned in frustration. Saira was a student at George Washington University. She had classes to attend. She must have flown back to D.C. by now. So why hadn't Payal come home yet?

You know why, you asinine pervert.

The treacherous image of Payal's supple, luminous, nude form flashed before his eyes. He hadn't laid eyes on the cursed painting since she'd stashed it in the storage closet. He didn't need to. It was seared into his memory, tormenting him day and night. Humiliating him. He'd lost all common sense the night it had shown up on their doorstep. All self-control. He didn't recognise the man who had cornered Payal in the hallway. He didn't want to admit what the painting had awakened in him, nor did he want to acknowledge how eager he had been to abandon his ideals in that moment.

It was bad enough he'd made a complete ass of himself, but he'd also been plagued with lurid fantasies of her ever since. Fantasies no amount of sprinting, weightlifting, boxing or working long hours could quash. Unable to bring himself to look her in the eye, he'd started acting like an intruder in his own apartment, hiding in his bedroom till she left for class, sneaking out before the sun came up on weekends, dodging her at every turn. His one slip had cost him a perfectly functional living arrangement.

He thought he'd done a decent job redeeming himself at the party. He'd worn what she gave him without argument and spent the night pretending to be interested in Mr Lohani and his cohorts' discussions, even though he didn't understand half of what they said because they'd switched between English, Hindi and Gujarati so rapidly. He'd suppressed the urge to tell Mrs Lohani off for her standoffishness. It was one thing to keep him at arm's length, but Payal? This was the first time she'd returned home after marrying a spawn of the criminal underworld. Her mother should have been overjoyed to see her healthy and unharmed.

Everything seemed to be going well. Payal was radiant as she danced, her movements so fluid and feet so light on the ground, she could have been a butterfly. When he relented to Saira's repeated appeals to join them on the dance floor, he did it to be the obliging brother-in-law, yes, but mostly to share in Payal's delight. The way he'd shared hot dogs with her at Coney Island Beach. He did it to be a part of her world.

He didn't realise the sight of him dancing would bring her world crumbling to the ground.

The hell was she expecting from a white man from Brooklyn, though?

He stuffed more pizza into his mouth. Maybe he was overthinking this. Her extended stay at her parents' probably had nothing to do with him.

But she should be here, damn it!

He missed the ordinariness of having her around, the unpredictability of what every day with her brought. He missed watching her eat the food he cooked. He missed the frustrated huffs and elated squeaks she made as she did her problem sets at her desk. He missed believing he had someone to do dumb tourist stuff with. He missed her saccharine summer scent.

He missed her. His wife.

He stilled mid-chew.

Feeling dirty all of a sudden, he tossed the half-eaten pizza slice back into the box and shoved himself away from the counter.

The black whirlpool. He was sliding deeper and deeper into it, losing sight of who he was. Who *she* was. Payal was a bratva-ordained bride. An added tether to a way of life he'd worked years to distance himself from. The last nail in the coffin keeping him and Alice apart. Payal was a contractual obligation, not someone to agonise over. Most definitely not someone to miss.

And yet, the faintest whiff of her honeyed peach scent stopped him in his tracks. Nudging her bathroom door open, he switched the lights on and stared at the sparklingly clean surfaces, the crisp, colour-co-ordinated towels, the two-ply toilet paper, the baby pink watering pot by the toilet—*wait, a watering pot?*—and a vast array of cosmetics, implements, and toiletries occupying the counters and shelves. He opened a jar of peach body butter with trepidation. Took a cursory sniff. Then drew a long, lungful of its scent. Her scent. Holding the jar to his nose, he looked through the rest of her things like a kid at a candy store. The woman really liked her body butter. Aside from peach, she also had the stuff in shea, cocoa, vanilla, mango and gingerbread, of all things. Like her greatest purpose in life was to be edible.

Or be eaten out.

Adjusting his pants, he squeezed his eyes shut to exorcise the thought from his mind.

Payal kept an assortment of oils on hand too: coconut, argan, almond and castor. Her shower gel was honey-scented and her shampoo and conditioner were regular supermarket brands. The ledge at the end of her bathtub was decorated with a tray of soaps that resembled lemon bars, a half-used scented candle and a jar of familiar colourful balls.

Returning the peach body butter to its rightful place, he pulled a bath bomb from the jar and rolled it in his palm. A fond smile tugged at his mouth as it took him back to their wedding night. To the electric jitters he had felt as they sat side by side, soaking their feet in the colours of the rainbow, ironing out the details of their arrangement.

She's not gonna miss this, he told himself, surreptitiously closing his fist around the powdery orb. A few minutes later, he was naked in his own bathroom, lowering himself into steaming, bubble-gum coloured water. The dull nips of the bath salts made him tingle all over, soothed the soreness in his muscles, got them to unclench. Letting out an uninhibited groan, he lay back and followed the bath bomb's colourful and bumpy path across the water's surface.

He felt like a perfect fool—a fool submerged in unicorn vomit. But the memories the streams of colour invoked cut through the noise and reminded him what he'd lost sight of. His arrangement with Payal was meant to be convenient. It was meant to manage expectations and keep the peace. And up until their encounter in the hallway, it had done just that. Payal may not have been the woman he loved, but as far as bratva-ordained brides went, she was as good as they'd come.

Payal was his peace.

He needed to fix this . . . somehow. He didn't want another bratva bride. He didn't want to risk getting saddled with someone out of sync with him.

His body jerked back, then. As though a gun had gone off.

He didn't want to be with another Alice.

Oleksiy checked his watch and flicked his jacket sleeve back in place. Twenty minutes past the appointed time. He tried focusing on the view from the reception area's floor-to-ceiling window. No luck. His shoulder was beginning to bother him.

He didn't have a reason to be nervous. Silver Properties Development had been effusive about hiring him for Sarsfield Tower and he'd gone over the service contract his lawyer had drawn up with a fine-tooth comb. The five-year contract, his security firm's first large-scale gig, should have been a done deal, but the unexpected summons to Silver Properties' office set him on edge.

He strode over to the receptionist's desk after another ten minutes. 'Hi.' Flashing her a genial smile, he nodded at Ken Danesh's closed door. 'Everything all right in there?'

The receptionist didn't bother looking up from her computer monitor. 'He'll call when he's ready for you.'

The call came another fifteen minutes later, at which point Oleksiy was convinced he'd missed something in the contract, and his right arm felt primed to snap off.

'Oleksiy, hey.' Danesh was a small, bald, bespectacled man agitatedly shuffling papers around on an inversely large desk. 'Come on in, have a seat. Sorry for calling you in last minute, but I thought it'd be best to talk face to face.'

'No problem.' Oleksiy eyed the fidgety man. Masking his own nerves with a lopsided grin, he unbuttoned the front of his jacket and settled into the visitor's chair. 'Everything in the contract all right? You never got back to me with any comments or questions.'

'What? Oh, yeah, no, the contract's fine. No changes or addendums from my end. But'—Danesh arranged his pens in a neat line before steepling his fingers—'here's the thing: we've run into a bit of a situation ... in that we—as in, Silver Properties Development—can't give you the Sarsfield Tower contract at this point in time.'

Oleksiy cocked his head sideways. A growl threatened to escape him. 'And why's that?'

'The owners of a few of the Tower's commercial spaces have objected to you because of your affiliation with the Kotovsks.'

'But I'm not affiliated with them,' Oleksiy said sternly, his voice gravel. 'I'll admit to a family connection, but I don't—I've *never* worked for them. And just so we're clear, neither of my businesses are involved in anything illegal.'

'Hey, I'm on your side,' Danesh said, his fear of Oleksiy animating his gestures. 'And frankly, I don't care if you *are* bratva. Your logistics for the Tower had some of the most meticulous, cost-effective, borderline paranoid security measures I've seen in all my years in the business. And these guys technically shouldn't have a say in who the real estate developer hires for building-wide security. They don't have majority ownership!' He leaned forward, his voice dropping. 'But they're Berezivkas.'

Oleksiy stiffened.

'They've got serious pull with the folks who *do* have majority ownership and they're never gonna be okay with Kotovsks setting up cameras and patrolling the premises.'

Oleksiy glowered at Danesh a long moment, his thoughts spiralling back to that deserted alley. To that afternoon when he was pinned to the asphalt and had his arm wrenched out of its socket.

'Shit,' he hissed, rolling his neck in a circle, then his shoulder, desperately willing the phantom pain to go away.

'My hands are tied on this one, bud,' Danesh said quietly. 'But look, it's just the one project, all right? Silver Properties has plenty of other high-profile buildings in development. You'll be hearing from us again sooner than you think.'

Relaxing his jaw, Oleksiy reeled himself back to the present. He and his ex-bratva recruits had spent weeks drawing up the plans for Sarsfield Tower. He'd already put in orders for customised equipment so they could get to work as soon as the papers were signed. A different building requiring a whole new set of plans and differently configured equipment in the unforeseeable future was small consolation.

'Right.' He got up and held his hand out to Danesh. Signed contract or not, a good relationship with the right contacts meant everything for business. 'Thanks for taking the time to tell me in person. I'd have been tearing my hair out if you'd just shot me an e-mail telling me I'm fired.'

'Oh,' Danesh chuckled, running a hand over his shiny head. 'I wouldn't wish that on anyone.'

Outside the office building, Oleksiy drew a lungful of chilly autumn air. Getting himself a coffee and a chocolate chip muffin, he took a roundabout route to the station to put off the muggy train ride from Manhattan to Brighton Beach. He had a long day's work ahead of him, and he knew he wasn't going to get any of it done if his foul mood persisted. He wished he could speak to someone. Someone who'd listen without telling him to toughen up, that this was what he'd signed up for.

His phone rang at that moment, as if in answer to his silent yearning. It was an unknown number.

Payal.

'Hello?'

But the voice on the other side wasn't hers. 'How's it going, Lucky C?'

Oleksiy's heart skidded to a dead halt. Nobody had called him that in sixteen years.

'What do you want?' Oleksiy spat, spinning on his heels, searching his surroundings for a face that matched the voice. 'Where'd you get this number?'

'Oh, come on, C. You know a personal number's no biggie with a spy network like ours. But I guess you wouldn't know much about that, would you? Last I heard, you'd got yourself a fancy business degree and gone straight.' The deep, bear-like voice boomed. 'Even gotten hitched!'

Oleksiy winced. His phone threatened to crack in his grip.

'Mazel tov, brother. Though I'm kinda hurt I didn't get an invite. Always hoped we could put the past behind us by the time one of us tied the knot—you know, became real men.'

Oleksiy scoffed. The man on the other end of the line had been initiated into manhood sixteen years ago. At Oleksiy's expense.

'But, hey, I get it. Word on the street is the missus is a real stunner. Of course you didn't want me around. The ladies always did like me better than you.'

'My wife,' Oleksiy seethed, 'is none of your concern. Now, what do you want?'

The son of a bitch had the nerve to chuckle. 'Just wanted to say it wasn't personal—Sarsfield Tower.'

Oleksiy blinked in outrage. It was bad enough that he'd lost the contract because of the Berezivkas. But now, knowing who had given the order . . .

He didn't think this day could get any worse.

'It never is with you, though, is it?' he sneered.

'I do what I have to, C. Not everyone's got it as easy as you.'

Oleksiy wanted to throw up. 'Don't ever call this number again.'

He hung up. His thumb hovered over the screen a moment, intent on calling a number he didn't have saved. Shaking his head, he shoved the phone back into his pocket.

Everything inside the shower stall was obscured by a thick fog of steam. Oleksiy braced his hands against the wall, tired and bruised from hours of boxing, but no less angry than he was in the morning. Hearing the night janitor's trolley wheels approach, he reluctantly turned the faucet from hot to cold, rinsed off and got out. He put his work clothes back on and headed back to his office. A wall-to-wall window behind his desk overlooked the main fitness centre of his gym down below. He watched the janitorial staff wipe down the equipment, then the floors and remained watching as the overhead lights went out. When the night guard came barging in, thinking someone had broken into his office, Oleksiy finally forced himself to head home.

He called Mykola when he turned onto his street to see the apartment's windows dark. Again.

''Sup, boss?' came Mykola's pterodactyl voice. Oleksiy seemed to have caught him mid-chew.

'Is she coming home tonight?'

'Mm, don't think so. She called Nasir after her communist meeting to pick her up at the Beer Parlor.'

'Her what?' He rubbed his eyes, letting out an exasperated breath. 'No, never mind that. Just text me the address.'

He didn't believe what he was doing, yet he also couldn't fathom how else he was supposed to hold onto his sanity. Borrowing a car from the service across the street, he made his way up to Manhattan for the second time that day.

The Beer Parlor was a cozy, dimly lit basement establishment, where tables were decorated with candles and expensive wood-panelled walls that showcased paintings and photography from up-and-coming artists. Not the aesthetic Oleksiy usually associated with hard-line communism. Then again, it was probably best to take anything Mykola said with a grain of salt.

He spotted Payal as soon as he entered. She was huddled at a long table at the back of the dim room, running her fingertips over her wine glass, deep in conversation with her friends.

'That was quick,' Mykola said, a snort accompanying his grin when Oleksiy joined him at the bar. 'You bring a car?'

Payal looked their way, then. Straightening on seeing Oleksiy, she looked around at her friends before raising her hand in a meek wave.

'Yeah,' Oleksiy answered Mykola, returning Payal's gesture with a half-nod. He ordered himself a beer on tap and slid Mykola a few dollar bills. 'Here, go and call yourself a ride back home.'

'That's okay. I'll just head back with you.'

'Kid, I said go home,' Oleksiy ordered in a low, threatening growl.

'Okay, okay!' Mykola slapped an open palm onto the counter to retrieve the money. 'Just trying to save you some cash.'

Payal's brows pulled together on seeing Mykola leave. Extracting herself from her posse, she threaded her way through the other patrons to the bar. She was in a sheer, burgundy button-down blouse and a grey plaid skirt that ended just above the knees. Those gorgeous, bare, body-buttered-up legs had Oleksiy taking a long swig of beer. Her black, high-heeled ankle boots made them look like they might go on forever.

'Hey.' She flashed him an anxious smile and nudged her head at the exit Mykola had taken. 'Everything all right?'

'Yeah.' Her summery scent undid the knotted muscles down his neck and right shoulder. 'He had to go deal with something. I'll keep an eye on you till you're done.'

'He didn't have to—' Those dark, plump lips puckered in distress. 'I wouldn't have kept him if he had to be somewhere. Why didn't he—'

'Hey, don't sweat it, all right? I was in the neighbourhood.' He took another sip. 'You go back to your comrades. I'll wait here.'

'Easy there, Senator McCarthy. They're democratic socialists.' Payal looked over her shoulder at her friends. Only a few of the large group seemed intrigued by who she was talking to. Sliding onto the bar stool next to him, she added, 'And they seem to be doing just fine without me.'

Oleksiy wondered if they knew he was her husband. He wanted them to know. 'What's a nice rich girl like you doing hanging out with those types?'

'Same thing a pretty bratva boy like you does every day.' Resting her elbow on the counter, she propped a cheek on her knuckles. 'Helping the working class. Seeing what you do, speaking to Mykola and the women whose lives you've touched around the neighbourhood—it got me thinking about the larger systemic issues depriving vulnerable people of basic dignity. Employers who genuinely care about their employees are few and far between. We can't just sit around waiting for giant corporations to grow a heart. The working class needs to organise and force their hand. And I want to be a part of that.'

'As a newly minted statistician,' Oleksiy said, suppressing a sceptical grin.

'Absolutely!' She angled her torso to face him. 'There are so many discrepancies in how lower-income and marginalised communities are represented in data, in what data gets cherry-picked for widescale dissemination, how much of a role corporate lobbyists have in the entire process. With enough training and field experience, I could do something about it. I mean, somebody should.'

Oleksiy stared at the foam in his glass, tongue-tied by her mind and passion. And to think it was his own actions that spurred this . . . his chest felt tight. Full. Yet he couldn't bring himself to trust it. The day's bitterness and anger still held him in a vice.

'Well,' he said solemnly, 'here's hoping your endeavours are more successful than mine.'

He felt her eyes on him as he took another long swig.

'Hey,' she said softly, leaning closer. 'Is everything okay? Did something happen?'

He shook his head petulantly. 'Just a shitty day, that's all.'

'You want to talk about it?'

'Not really, no.'

'Well, what're we going to do then?'

'About what?' he asked, tired.

The brush of her thumb against the furrow between his brows startled him out of his skin.

She leaned even closer, her voice husky. 'About this.'

Tempted to turn into her touch, he twisted his head away instead and fixed her with a hard look. 'I'm open to suggestions.'

'Are you?' Her large almond eyes searched his for a sign he was bluffing.

Oleksiy's gaze was steadfast.

'We could play a game. One where we pretend that we met at a bar.'

A throaty chuckle escaped him. 'We did meet at a bar.'

'True.' She tilted her head, contemplatively brushing her knuckles up his forearm. 'But we could pretend you picked me up at a bar.'

Catching her hand mid-caress, Oleksiy rasped, 'You'll come home?'

'If that's what you want,' Payal replied, eyes fluttering at the intensity of his grip.

Oleksiy dropped her hand as if it burned him. 'Tell Nasir to go home.'

'Wait here.' She slid off the stool. 'I'll go get my stuff.'

Tearing his eyes off her delectable backside, he glanced at her friends. Her friends who may or may not have known she was married, that he was her husband. Her friends who may assume she was going home with a stranger. 'Wait.'

She looked over her shoulder, eyes half-lidded.

'Your friends ... you don't want to introduce me to them?'

'Why would I?' she smirked, sauntering away. 'You're just some guy I met at a bar.'

Nine

PAYAL PULLED THE PASSENGER SEAT'S BELT across her chest, and folded her hands on her lap. The heat rolling off of Oleksiy as he started the engine was excruciating. It took every ounce of self-control she possessed to sit still and keep her eyes glued on the road ahead.

For what it was worth, she *had* managed to make some headway in getting her desire in check. The extended stay at her parents' had allowed Saira's words to sink in and percolate. Payal's lust was the culmination of an overlong dry spell. It didn't matter if it was Oleksiy or someone else—someone available—who took care of it. Oleksiy just happened to be the only one around for her to latch onto.

Of course, all this was easier said than done when they were miles apart. In his presence, under his pitch-black scrutiny, she was pitifully powerless. He had resembled a starved panther on the prowl when she'd spotted him across the bar. And he wasn't there for any old prey. He'd come there for her. To take her home.

Her seat belt strained against her chest painfully. The majority of streets in the area required cars to drive in one direction. Oleksiy would have to drive around Columbia Business School, then half the island before they could make for Brighton Beach. By the time he turned onto Riverside Drive, Payal was certain she was going to combust well before that.

Fingers playing with the buckle of her seat belt, she eyed the walkway that bordered Riverside Park. It was empty. As was the street they were driving down.

'Slow down.' Her breath caught at her own words. 'Park in that empty spot over there.'

Oleksiy did a double take, then pulled over by the wide road verge separating the street from the walkway. A nearby tree's branches obstructed the light from the street lamps. Once he switched the car lights off, they were blanketed in darkness.

Payal undid the buckle and demurely watched the belt's strap slide through her fingers. Oleksiy's fist stayed curled around the gearshift, his knuckles tensed.

'This can't change anything,' he said, his voice a delicious, gravelly baritone.

'I know,' she nodded at the empty street ahead, willing herself to be strong. Of course it couldn't. He was in love with someone else. But she wasn't after love. She wanted things to return to normal. She needed for their arrangement to work. And after tonight, she knew, without a shadow of a doubt, he needed the same. 'Consider this something we both need to get out of our systems.'

'There you go with the rational choices again. You know … ' he relaxed, leaning back against the headrest, licking his bottom lip as he took her in. 'If I'd been a genuine thief, you'da made a very useful sestra.'

I'd have been your ideal match. Letting out a rueful chuckle, she angled herself towards him. 'If I didn't know any better, I'd think you were starting to like it.'

His seat belt coiled back with a *snap*. Letting go of the gearshift, he pushed a strand of hair off her cheek.

'Not me,' he rasped, shoving his fingers in her hair, cupping the back of her head proprietarily. He pulled her closer. Met her halfway. 'The guy you picked up at the bar.'

The words were barely out before his mouth was on hers, consuming her like she was water and he'd been stranded in the desert without any. Taking her stunned gasp as invitation, he slid his tongue into her mouth, tasting, exploring, learning. A primal moan escaped the base of Payal's throat. She tilted her head to grant him more access. The feverish urgency in his kiss, his practiced tongue and delicious cocoa-citrus scent intoxicated Payal to the brink of senselessness. Oleksiy firmed his grasp on her head to keep it from lolling back. She set a steadying hand on his neck.

'Who is he?' she purred against his mouth, revelling in the dull scratch of his beard. His neck and jaw were granite, the shifts in their muscles distinct to the touch. 'This poor schmuck putting his neck on the line, seducing a bratva thief's wife.'

His answering chuckle shot a flush of warmth to her core. He scraped his beard up her cheek to whisper her in ear. 'I'm not the one giving the orders to park, sweetheart.' Nuzzling into the crook of her neck, breathing her in, his fingers glided along the length of her skirt, then her bare thigh. 'If anyone's doing the seducing here'—he played with the skirt's hem—'it's you.'

Emboldened, Payal spread her legs and guided his fingers under the skirt.

'Fuck, you're soft,' he hissed.

Lavishing her neck with bites and open-mouthed kisses, he traced hot trails up and down her inner thigh, inching closer and closer to the sweet spot between her legs with each stroke and retreating just short of it every time.

'Oleksiy,' Payal whined, breathless.

She lifted his head from her neck with a sharp tug to his thick, silken hair. His irises seemed larger and darker than normal. Combined with his dishevelled hair, he looked like a man possessed. A feral beast contained by the flimsiest restraints. Payal's heart thundered. As his seductress, she'd be the one to bring him to heel.

'I don't have time for skittish men.' Giving his hair another sharp tug, she bucked her hips against his hand. 'If you're going to do something, do it with conviction.'

Jaw tightening, gaze piqued, Oleksiy brushed his thumb over her clit through her panties. 'That what you want?' he snarled.

Tendrils of tingling pleasure reverberated through her limbs and pooled at her core. Biting back a moan, Payal clutched his hair tighter. 'Yes,' she rasped, eyes rolling back, lips seeking his again. 'Yes, just like that. Don't stop.'

He came at her with ferocious zeal, prying her mouth open with his tongue, denying her respite for air and leeway to suppress her moans. A tormented growl poured from him when his fingers wandered lower to find her underwear seeping with arousal. Thighs clamping around his hand, Payal grabbed his shoulders and curled into the sound, into him, like a metal object to a magnet. Only—

—the storage compartment wedged into her hip.

Payal withdrew with a tiny yelp. Cursing under his breath, Oleksiy wriggled his hand free from her thighs. Then, pushing his seat back a few notches and reclining it, he set a guiding palm on the small of her back. 'Come 'ere, pussycat.'

'You really know what you're doing, huh?' she asked, levering herself up and over the cup holder.

'Well.' He flashed her a smug grin. 'I *was* a hormonal teenager once.'

There was no elegant way to do this. By the time Payal managed to straddle his lap, she had knocked her head, knee and elbow against various surfaces, and they'd both dissolved into belly-aching laughter. It was all worth it, though. Because Oleksiy's laughter touched his eyes.

Payal combed a stray lock of hair from his forehead as their giggles died down. She traced the creases at the corner of his eye, his cheekbone and jawline, then the shape of his lips. Watching him watch her with baited breath all the while.

Bowing her head, her lips hovering over his, she rocked her hips against his straining erection. A quiet shudder seized them both. She rocked her hips again, and again, and again.

Oleksiy pushed her jacket off her shoulders, his hands lingering, sliding down to her breasts and cupping them. Payal's head tipped back as he found her pert nipples through all the layers she had on and rubbed circles over them. Purring in contentment, she closed the hair's breadth remaining between their lips, kissing him, silently begging him to never stop.

His hands slid lower. To her abdomen. Over wrinkled, hyper-sensitive scar tissue. She sprang upright, fists clenching his shirt, a frightened whimper tearing through her chest.

'Whoa, hey.' Oleksiy's hands flew off of her immediately, his brows pulled together in a concerned frown. 'What's wrong? You okay? Did I—'

'No.' Payal caught hold of his hands, resolutely planted them on her thighs and led them up her skirt to her ass. She leaned over him again and bit his bottom lip, resumed rocking her hips over his crotch. 'I'm fine.'

I am *fine,* she told herself over and over again as Oleksiy palmed her butt cheeks. *I'm with Oleksiy.*

The past would always be a part of her, but it didn't have to have power over her in this moment. Here, in this car, she was a sestra of the bratva. A woman powerful enough to have a man like Oleksiy under her spell. Tonight, she was boss.

She reached between them to tug his dress shirt from his pants and undo his belt and zipper. Oleksiy buried his face in her breasts. His growl reverberated through her body as she stroked him through his underwear. Cradling his head to her, she slid her free hand under his waistband to pull his cock out.

'Wait,' he rasped, fingers digging into her flesh. 'We can't. I don't have any protection on me.'

Neither did Payal. *Shit.*

Well, she wasn't going to let that rain on her parade.

She gave him a little peck and eased him onto his back. 'I thought you said you had a lot of practice being a hormonal teenager.'

Bracing her hands on the edge of his seat, she rocked against his crotch, moulding her slickened cleft against his shaft through their underwear, rolling her hips at the top of each stroke so the head of his cock rubbed her clit.

'I did, but I'—Oleksiy writhed underneath her, mouth agape with ecstasy, palms roughly roving over her ass and thighs—'kinda hoped my one-night stands'd get a little further than second base in a borrowed car by now.'

'You're cute,' Payal said with a throaty giggle. She rewarded him with another kiss. 'We can stop if you like.' She rocked her hips deliberately. 'At a CVS.' Another languid rock. 'Get some condoms.' Another rock. 'So you can fuck me like a big boy.'

His hips bucked into her. He gave her waist a jerk, urging her to move faster. 'I oughta fuck you senseless,' he panted. 'But I'm not driving anywhere till this'—he thrust his pulsing cock at her clothed slit—'gets taken care of.'

Whining petulantly, Payal nibbled on his earlobe. 'Not even back home?'

'No,' came his stern reply. He yanked her by the hair to get her to look at him. 'That going to be problem?'

The slight sting of her scalp mingled with the crackling friction between her legs fanned the flames coursing through her. She doubled the squelching pressure on his crotch. 'Does it *feel* like it's going to be problem?'

Muscles in his jaw twitching, he clamped her flush against him and sealed her lips with his. They moved in harmony with each other, greedily, vehemently. Forcefully, yet tenderly. Payal's impending release—those explosions of heat stemming out and taking over every inch of her like an untended vine—gave rise to hoarse cries. Cries Oleksiy hungrily lapped up and returned with shallow, low-pitched grunts that pierced through Payal's core and nudged her over the edge.

Oleksiy followed soon after, squeezing her to him as the tremors took their course.

Payal's lids grew heavy as she listened to his breaths even, felt the erratic but robust thrum of his heart under her breasts.

'You okay?' he asked softly. He tucked her hair behind her ear, the feather-light graze of his fingers triggering a slew of aftershocks.

'Mhm.'

They both looked between them as she lifted herself off of him.

'Here, hold on a sec.' Payal clumsily manoeuvered back into the passenger seat and reached for her backpack. She fished out a pack of wipes from the front pocket and handed it to him.

'Thanks,' he said awkwardly.

Righting her own clothing, Payal looked out the window to give him some privacy as he cleaned up—as if they hadn't just dirty-talked and dry-humped their way to an orgasm that teenaged Payal couldn't have conceived of in her wildest dreams.

Payal felt a sharp thrill just thinking about it. But more potent was the thrill she felt knowing she'd be returning to Brighton Beach. That was her dry spell solved. Sure, the solution was far from ideal, but it was serviceable. At least for the time being. It was the rational choice, as Oleksiy loved to put it. She could only hope it was enough for things to go back to the way they had been.

They returned the car to the service and strolled across the street to their apartment, shoulder to shoulder, like they'd just come back from a date. Only they didn't have to kiss each other goodnight at the door. They weren't going to kiss at all. They were going to go up to their apartment and carry on with their lives, business as usual.

Their footsteps sounded louder than usual as they climbed up the two flights of stairs. The irrational side of Payal feared Mumma might crane her neck over the banister and tell her off for staying out so late with a boy.

The apartment smelled of stale air. They slid out of their footwear and jackets at arm's length, and made for the hallway in unison. On second thought, maybe the hall was too narrow for the both of them. Payal changed course to the living room and busied herself with opening the balcony door for some fresh air.

'I, uh—' Oleksiy shoved his hands into his pockets. The corners of his mouth quivered with a bashful smile. 'It's good to have you back.'

Echoes of his grunts and scorching breath against her person set Payal's cheeks aflame. She bit her bottom lip. 'Goodnight.'

'Goodnight,' he nodded before disappearing into the hallway.

Payal took a look around her. *Well . . . home sweet home.*

It was late. She'd had a long day, had a glass of wine, engaged in some . . . vigorous physical activity. She should have been exhausted, yet she felt like she'd just downed a tall Americano.

Washing the outside world's grime off her hands, she poured herself a glass of water and sipped on it, dazed. How did her bedtime routine go, again? When she heard Oleksiy's door swing open and his feet pad back down the hall, she sputtered what she had in her mouth back into the glass.

'So, here's the thing.' His cuffs were unbuttoned and folded up to his elbows, hands dripping water. His harried expression reflected the buzz pulsing through Payal. 'What if I haven't got it out of my system?'

'Hmm.' Wiping her mouth, Payal set her glass down. She leaned back against the countertop, gripping its edge for support. 'I'd say that'd be a real problem. But ... I wouldn't be opposed to helping you out.'

'No?' He studied her through narrowed eyes, one side of his mouth pulling up in a devious smirk. 'I mean'—prowling towards her, he reached for her hips—'I wouldn't want you feeling pressured into it on my account.'

She yanked on his tie, bringing his nose an inch from hers. 'Let's get one thing straight, hun. No one pressures me into anything. Ever.'

The corners of Oleksiy's glimmering eyes creased. 'I believe you,' he murmured against her lips.

Payal collapsed into his warm embrace. Her hands roamed the expanse of his muscular chest and lean arms, while his skated past the small of her back to fondle her ass again.

'I don't have any protection,' she said, breathless, her nimble fingers making quick work of removing his tie. An active sex life *had* been a part of her plan to reclaim her life, but only hypothetically. She hadn't thought she'd actually make the leap so soon.

'I've got condoms.' Oleksiy raked his teeth down the column of her throat. 'Or I should—unless Marisha tossed 'em when she redecorated. In which case'—he plucked Payal off the floor by her thighs, eliciting a surprised squeal from her—'I'm cutting off all familial ties with her.'

Payal wound her legs around him as he bumped and stumbled over to his bedroom. The master bedroom. The room that, under normal circumstances, would have been hers too. It was something she'd neither expected nor wanted from their arrangement, but there was something about Oleksiy bringing her into his personal space himself. Not out of obligation or resignation, but from a place of desire, of primal need. It made Payal feel invincible. Like nothing in the world frightened her.

She shoved him up against his bookshelf when he set her down, rattling the books, startling him with her strength. Muffling his incredulous chuckle with a feral kiss, she tore his shirt open, sending buttons clattering all over the parquet floor.

His face was indignant. His erection, on the other hand, betrayed his enthusiasm with a twitch.

Payal ran her palms over his damp skin as she pushed the starched fabric off his shoulders. She stilled at the feel of a long, slender strip of wrinkled, satin-soft skin on his right shoulder—something she was all too familiar with.

He'd masked it with a tattoo, his scar. With the image of a spider descending from its web.

Payal brushed it tenderly, afraid it might still hurt.

Oleksiy stroked up her forearms and circled his hands around her wrists. 'My tattoo scare you?'

She looked him in the eye, undaunted. She knew scars. Better than anyone else. It would take a hell of a lot more than this—than her own scars, even—to get her to back down tonight. Without breaking eye contact, she leaned down and kissed the string—a purplish-brown gash in a composition of greys—by which the spider left its web.

Spurred by his throaty moans and shivers, Payal licked a trail down to his pecs and took his nipple in her mouth. Below, she undid his belt and zipper and shoved his trousers down. Oleksiy kicked the garment aside while undoing the buttons of her blouse. Letting it fall to the floor, he cupped her breasts through her spaghetti top and bra, hooked his fingers under their straps to lower them—

Payal spun around and pressed her ass into his erection. Oleksiy groaned into the nape of her neck as she ground into him slowly, sensuously. It didn't diminish his desire to strip her, though. Her abdomen clenched under his eager exploration. He cupped the underside of her breasts, squeezed them together and rubbed circles around her straining nipples. It felt incredible. So incredible she wanted to give in and get naked for him. Which was precisely why she *had* to make him stop. Forcing his hands lower, she hooked his thumbs under the waistbands of her skirt and panties.

Once those dropped to the floor, he spun her back around to face him, kissed her, then sank to his knees. Knees marked with an eight-pointed star each, declaring he bowed to no one.

Well . . . no one but her.

He pressed her legs apart, bit into his bottom lip and made a depraved sucking noise as he traced up her thighs. Hiking a leg over his shoulder, he buried his nose in her bush and inhaled long and deep. On her toes, quivering all over, Payal grabbed fistfuls of his hair to steady herself and braced her foot on one of the shelves behind him.

Oleksiy nuzzled against her clit, traced her dripping slit with his finger. 'Any STIs, pussycat?'

'No.' Payal licked her lips and squeezed her eyes shut in anticipation.

He tongued her clit and pressed a finger inside her in one swoop. Crying out, Payal keeled over. Round and round he circled her clit. A second finger joined the first, curling and pressing into her squelching G-spot. Payal rocked into his palm, her body covered in a layer of sweat, emitting steam. She undid her bra and untangled it from her body to breathe easier. But only just. Oleksiy's tongue was relentless, flattening over her clit, writhing from side to side till she forgot how to breathe altogether. The heat coiling at her core receded for a blink, then exploded like a new star bursting into existence.

He continued sucking on her, pumping in and out of her as she rode it out. When it verged on painful, Payal stumbled back on unsteady legs. Oleksiy slurped her cum from his fingers and slowly, predatorily drew himself up to his full height. Coming up against the edge of his bed, Payal's gaze dropped to his bobbing cock. She held out a palm for it to slide into her trembling grip, ghosted the pads of her fingers over its veins and throbbing, clean-cut head. Nuzzling into the fine dusting of hair on his chest, she breathed him in—his usual cocoa and orange zest fragrance now imbued with the musky notes of fresh sweat and her arousal.

She scraped her nails up his torso. Muscle memory from months of self-defense classes had her winding her arms around his chest and arm and tackling him onto the bed.

Oleksiy threw his head back, letting out a bewildered chuckle. 'You could give the boys in the ring a run for their money with those moves.'

Straddling him, Payal reached between them to stroke him. 'Yeah?'

'I mean'—Oleksiy thrust into her hand, eyes rolling back—'you'd need a bit o' help. But lucky for you, you've got me to practice on.'

Payal rubbed the head of his cock on her clit. 'You do make a decent wrestling partner.'

Oleksiy hissed. He shuffled higher up the bed with her in tow and reached over to the bedside table's drawer. Amused by his distress as he rummaged, Payal tormented him further by pressing distracting, open-mouthed kisses behind his ear and down his neck.

'Thank fuck and hallelujah!' he finally exhaled, holding up a foil packet.

He tore it open with his teeth and slid the latex over his shaft. Payal, sitting upright, grasped him in hand and primed his tip at her entrance. She took him in slowly. Excruciatingly slowly. Savouring the way he stretched her wide and filled her to the brim. When he was buried to the hilt, she threw her head back and cried out without the slightest hint of inhibition. Circled and rocked her hips, used this man underneath her—her husband in the eyes of the law—to get to what made her feel good. Better than good. Untouchable. Powerful.

His nails dug into her fleshy thighs as they got a steady rhythm going, snaking up her hips, under the hem of her spaghetti top.

No. Hard limit.

Payal caught his wrists and pinned them up over his head. She wanted to be seen, she did. But not at the expense of the high she was on. Never at the expense of being vulnerable.

She relished at being responsible for Oleksiy's unravelling. Denied him the tenderness and kisses he craned his neck off his pillow for. He snapped his teeth at her for it, thrashed his legs with every violent thrust of his hips. Yet he remained hers to play with all the same. Hers to ride and squeeze inside her. Hers to watch as he fought his impending climax. Payal fucked him hard and fast, filling the room with a lurid song of wanton moans and sweat-slickened skin slapping, drawing immense satisfaction from robbing Oleksiy of his control. The man could say he loved another woman all he wanted, but when it came to this—to good old-fashioned fucking—he was just like the rest of them. An animal. One who needed it given to him straight and rough.

'Payal—' he gasped, hands trying to wrench free of her grasp. 'Fuck, ah ... '

'Yes, yes, yes.' Breasts spilling out of her top, Payal rode his throbbing cock to her edge. Her walls fluttered, then clamped around him.

A guttural roar ripped through Oleksiy's chest as his back arched off the mattress and his cock seized and pulsed erratically inside her. Payal held him captive between her legs while he rode out wave upon wave of turbulent pleasure.

They stared at each other, motionless, their eyes thick with the haze of being thoroughly sated, their breaths shallow from surviving such heights.

Then Payal released him, leaning back on her palms and making a show of withdrawing his cock from her. Oleksiy massaged his reddened wrists, a smarmy grin plastered across his face. It disappeared the instant she slid off the bed and pulled her panties back on.

'Whoa, whoa, whoa, wait.' He sat up, disoriented. 'What're you doing?'

His softened expression—those puppy eyes—sent a dull ache piercing through her chest. Was this a cue for her to stay? She kind of wanted it to be.

She looked at him as if the answer was obvious. 'I'm going to my room.'

He chuckled bitterly. 'What is this, a fuck n' dash?'

That made her bristle. He'd made it abundantly clear this couldn't change anything. That they were only in this for convenience. That he'd go on mooning over someone else. But what? He wanted to cuddle? The gross male entitlement! The hypocrisy!

'Dashing,' Payal said curtly, collecting her skirt and blouse off the floor, 'implies I didn't hold up my end of the bargain, and I think we can agree that I—that we have both been very … honourable.' Masking her anger with a breezy tone, she sauntered out of his room without sparing him another look. 'Let's just call this what you always do—a rational choice.'

Ten

OLEKSIY CURLED INTO A BALL UNDER HIS comforter, reluctant to wake up from the best night's sleep he'd had in days. The smell of coffee gradually dissolved the heaviness from his eyes. He rolled onto his back and stared at the ceiling, uncertain if he'd just had a really visceral wet dream or if last night had actually happened. Stretching out his legs, yawning off any remnants of sleep, he pawed at his bedside table for his phone.

Then leapt to his feet.

8.07 a.m. Whatever the hell happened last night, he was late for work.

And buck naked.

Cursing under his breath, he shook out his comforter on the off chance his clothes were tangled in it somewhere. Nada. He stepped on a button. *The fuck?* His clothes from yesterday lay scattered by the bookshelf in a tattered heap, and his foot got snared in a bra strap. The smell of coffee wafting in, along with sounds of activity outside his room became more potent as he hooked a toe through the laced undergarment and lifted it to his fingers.

Work could wait. Payal was home. Last night really did happen. She really did ride him raw. Twice! He had felt a sharp pang of something when she got up and left. He really had wanted to feel her close, feel those purrs of hers permeate through him just a while longer. And what had he done in response? Call what they did a fuck n' dash like some asshole gamer who spent his waking hours harassing women and spewing homophobic slurs online to stroke his fragile ego.

The impulse to retreat into himself again was strong, but his need for things to return to normal was stronger. He had to take stock of how badly he'd fucked up. He had to know if she was okay. Pulling on a T-shirt and boxer briefs, he neatly folded Payal's bra in half and padded over to the kitchen.

'Hey, you're still in.' Payal sniffed the milk she got out of the fridge and added a splash to her coffee. She was in a baggy T-shirt and sweats, her dishevelled hair in a loose braid. She looked adorable. Straight up wholesome. The antithesis of the filthy pussycat who'd had her way with him the night before. 'You usually head out earlier. Coffee?'

'Sure. And, uh,'—he showed her the bra before daintily setting it to the side of the breakfast bar—'you left this.'

'Oh, thanks,' she said without a hint of embarrassment, pouring him a mug of coffee and passing him the milk. 'You want some breakfast?'

Oleksiy's stomach answered her with a prolonged grumble. Dinner had slipped his mind last night.

Making a doting cooing noise, Payal passed him a bowl and the box of Honey Grahams. 'What have you been eating? There's nothing in the fridge.'

More Papa John's than he was proud of admitting to. 'I ate out. Easier than cooking for one.'

'Right,' Payal nodded, suddenly engrossed in the stirring of her cereal. 'Makes sense.'

Oleksiy fiddled with his own, his eyes never leaving her. 'Saira make it back to D.C. in time for class?'

'Mhm.'

He set his spoon down after a bite and leaned forward. 'So what was the hold up?'

Payal looked up, a deer caught in the headlights.

'Why didn't you come home?' he pressed.

She arched a brow at the reproach that had crept into his tone. 'I needed time. Perspective. Your ambush the night Tyler's painting showed up—'

'I didn't ambush,' Oleksiy muttered under his breath.

'—and my reaction to it,' Payal continued, her voice growing firmer. 'It wasn't doing either of us any favours, and all of that put together made for a pretty hostile environment.'

'Hostile?' he balked. 'I never—'

'By my standards,' Payal clarified, raising a hand for him to stay calm. 'I'm not saying you harmed me, but I also don't like being treated like I have a contagious disease.'

Oleksiy pouted, repentant but too proud to admit he'd been wrong. 'I tried to make it up to you.'

'I know. But I was really overwhelmed, and I figured a few days away could be a good thing. For both of us. And after a day or two it, it just seemed easier to stay away.'

'Why come back at all, then?' His mind flashed to their conversation at the bar. What if she'd only fucked him out of pity? 'You didn't have to.'

'I wanted to,' Payal said simply, oblivious to the relief those three words sent crashing over him. 'Seeing you there at the bar, it became obvious what I—what we both needed. Sex is a basic human need and we haven't—or at least I haven't—had any in a while, and that can really mess with you.'

'We needed to get it out of our systems,' Oleksiy repeated her words from the night before.

'Exactly.' Payal spooned cereal into her mouth. 'Saira was right, I do need to get back out there. Set up a Bumble account or something.'

Oleksiy stopped mid-chew. 'Excuse me?'

'It's a dating app. Let's women make the first move. Definitely doesn't eliminate all the weirdos, but at least my DMs won't be overflowing with messages about where they'd like to put my juicy lips.'

He'd show them where he'd shove his fist before they so much as tried. 'I know what Bumble is.' His voice was dry as sandpaper. 'I wanna know what it's gotta do with you.'

'Oleksiy!' Payal laughed. 'What have we been talking about? Sex!'

'But we—last night—'

'Last night was a spur-of-the-moment thing,' she said matter-of-factly, her words a crushing blow. 'An emergency, if you will. But we've got a deal to uphold, and it wouldn't be right to keep using you like that.'

Using you.

It was a mutual using, of course, but something about hearing her say it, about her making sex with him sound like a Papa John's pizza you guiltily ate in the dark after a rough day made him feel hollow inside. Not to mention fucking furious.

'I'm telling you—perspective!' Payal continued. 'Like, I hadn't even realised my sexual needs were something I had to actively factor in. It was always sort of just available in some way, shape or form when I wanted it, you know? But after getting married … well, now I know. So now you'll go to your lady friend, and once I find someone, we're set and everything will be right as day. Problem solved!'

Oleksiy resented how proud of herself she was. She hadn't solved squat. 'You can't get on a dating app.'

Payal's smile disappeared as she fixed him with an affronted glare. 'I *can't*?'

'You're a married woman.' He softened his tone the moment the words left his mouth. Being harsh with her—shutting her down point-blank—wasn't going to get their domestic harmony back on track. He had to be smart about this. 'Opening a public dating profile is a bad idea. Someone from either of our family's circles might be on it. Tato's enemies might catch wind, plant someone there to match with you.'

'Huh, good point.'

Crisis averted. He let out a long breath.

'Guess that just leaves good old-fashioned bar-hopping with the gals,' Payal chirped. With a wink and a little shimmy, she added, 'Worked out quite well last night.'

Oleksiy froze. The thought of some beer-bellied, ballcap-wearing asshole's hands on her made his blood boil. 'Again, you're a married woman. We've got appearances to keep up,' he said through gritted teeth. 'A reputation. You can't be seen around and about with someone else.'

Someone who's not me.

'Relax.' That she didn't even register how riled up he was added insult to injury. 'It's not like I'll be parading him around Brighton Beach.'

'What about Mykola? You'll still have him with you every step of the way. What if he lets slip that you're having an affair? Rumour like that'll tear through this neighbourhood quicker than a hurricane.'

'You think so?' She shook her head after some consideration. 'No, I had my doubts about him at first, but whatever he lacks in scholarly aptitude and finesse, he makes up for in street smarts. Give him a little more credit. He doesn't seem like the type to let something like that slip. Not even by accident.'

'People switch allegiances on a dime.' Something Oleksiy had learnt the hard way sixteen years ago.

'Yes, I am aware, but Mykola adores you. You know, if he does somehow manage to get his GED—and that's a big if—he'll have done it for his mama, yes, but he'll also have done it for you. You're like an older brother to him. It's in his voice whenever he speaks about you.'

'You guys talk about me?' Voice pitched a notch higher, his heart skipped a beat. Hopefully, Payal was right and Mykola was loyal enough not to have told her Oleksiy kept close tabs on her whereabouts.

'Sometimes, yeah.' She tucked a strand of hair behind her ear. 'Speaking of which, did he actually have something to do last night, or did you just chase him off to have me to yourself?'

Warmth flooded Oleksiy's cheeks. He shrugged. 'Eh.'

'And was your day actually shitty or did you make that up to play the sympathy card?'

'If only,' Oleksiy said wryly.

Her face turned somber. Attentive. 'You want to talk about it?'

He did. In spite of how convoluted and counter-intuitive their relationship was becoming, he really wanted to share with her. So, he told her about losing the Sarsfield Tower contract because of the Berezivkas, about getting taunted by a Berezivka thief afterwards. She didn't tell him off for wasting precious time and resources like Tato would have, didn't tell him his chosen path needed him to have thicker skin like Mama would have. She didn't suggest some hare-brained ploy to get back at the Berezivkas like Marisha or Grigori would have and she didn't tell him to drop everything he'd built to tour Europe and East Asia like . . . well, never mind. She simply lent him a compassionate ear, allowed him to unburden himself and work through the seven stages of grief. Then she took him out for brunch to cheer him up.

Oleksiy felt better. As he knew he would. But Payal's designs to hook up with other men were never far from his thoughts. Whether it would be in weeks, or in a matter of days, she *would* find someone eventually. Someone to take her out on dates. To fuck. Maybe even love. Someone who wasn't him.

It shouldn't have bothered him. Why should it when he'd devoted himself to loving Alice?

He couldn't help it, though. It just didn't feel right.

The rickety elevator opened out to the sixth floor of the Butler stacks. Mykola's directions played on a loop in Oleksiy's head as he climbed the staircase and threaded his way through the dark aisles. The place smelled of dust, stale air and old paper. Lights fit for an interrogation room lit up over him with loud *clacks*, then blinked out once he was no longer under them. Oleksiy kept his head down and steps quiet—he didn't want to attract the attention of the odd student studying at their carrel.

He felt like a burglar casing the joint. Hell, in his leather jacket and combat boots, he *looked* like a burglar.

It wasn't intentional, of course. Nothing about this trip to Columbia University's library was intentional. He'd started his day bent on enjoying a lighter workload. No incoming shipments, no fires to put out, no scheduled meetings with staff or clientele—hence, the casual getup—but his idle thoughts always circled back to Payal. More specifically, to whether or not she'd found someone to get her rocks off with yet.

Life at home had more or less gone back to the way it had been before her nude portrait shot everything to hell—warm, companiable, homey. Payal seemed content. Too content. And Oleksiy . . . he was relieved that peace had been restored, but he still harboured an insidious itch to hold her again, to feel her writhing flush against him, to be engulfed within her.

Sex is a basic human need. So why didn't he see his own frustrations reflected in her? Was he really so expendable that she could get him out of her system after the one time?

Oleksiy spotted the reading chair Mykola said he usually sat at. Payal's carrel was tucked in a secluded corner across the aisle, only visible from the moth-eaten chair through a strategic gap in the shelf behind her.

Poring over R code on her laptop while scribbling and scratching out statistical gibberish on a legal pad, she gave a start when Oleksiy appeared at her side. 'What are you doing here?' Her fingers unconsciously hit *ctrl* and *S*. 'How'd you get in?'

Oleksiy pulled out Mykola's visiting card from his jacket's pocket.

'Oh.' Payal looked around him, through the books at Mykola's empty post. 'I didn't even realise he was gone.'

'Gotta stay more alert,' he tutted, then jerked his chin at her laptop. 'Save everything?'

'Where'd he go?' she asked with a dismissive wave at her laptop. 'Is everything okay?'

Oleksiy closed the laptop. 'Everything's fine.'

'Then why're you here?' Payal tried to look him in the eye, but she couldn't tear her eyes off his hand slowly and deliberately sliding her laptop to the side of the desk with the rest of her belongings. 'You're scaring me.'

The library's dankness had frizzed her hair. Her shoulders and back were hunched from stooping over her laptop too long, and her eyes looked glassy, almost deranged from concentrating too hard. It was high time she took a break, and Oleksiy was going to make sure she did.

Tugging her chair away from the carrel, he scooped her up and onto the desk in one deft manoeuver. The muffled yelp that escaped her spurred him to situate himself between her legs. 'You don't ever have to be scared of me,' he said inches away from her stunned face, gently gripping her waist through her hoodie. He hated how many layers she had on. 'Ever. You understand?'

Releasing a shuddering breath, Payal nodded.

He drew out his next words huskily. 'And I came to see if you'd like to take part in a time-honoured Columbia tradition.'

Payal's brows pulled together in a dubious look.

Oleksiy licked his lips and rolled his bad shoulder. 'That is, if you haven't done it with someone else already.'

'You want to—?' Her eyes widened with realisation, then disbelief. '*Here*?'

Brushing her hair over her shoulder, he ghosted his lips over the side of her neck. 'Yeah.'

'We could get caught.'

He chuckled into her ear, nipped at its lobe. 'Part of the charm, pussycat.'

She arched into him at that, squeezed his thighs with hers. Arousal replaced the overworked haze in her eyes from moments ago. Oleksiy smirked as he took in the telling dip of her lashes and the part of her luscious lips.

'Up to you, though,' he said nobly. 'We can always go get lunch instead.'

Payal's hands clamped around his face. 'The hell we can,' she hissed, crashing her lips to his.

Her touch drew him in like quicksand, and he yielded to its infinite, unknowable depths without fear of running out of air or losing himself. He leaned into her wet, open-mouthed kisses hungrily, taking in as much of her into his mouth as he could. The brush of her jeans-clad crotch against the swelling in his pants had him swallowing a groan, kissing her with greater fervour. His hands dropped from her face to cup her breasts and trace their shape with his thumb.

Winding her arms around his middle, Payal yanked him closer by his ass. A throaty cry spilled from her at the added friction—one Oleksiy couldn't muffle with his mouth.

'Uh-uh-uh, pussycat.' Breaking their kiss, he pressed a finger to her lips. 'We can't do this unless we're real quiet.'

Payal nodded sheepishly, mischievously, even, then drew him back to her. Her hands encircled his wrists as he resumed fondling her, tracing every rise and dip of her torso. God, he wanted to bury his face in her summer-scented tits. Her grip on him tightened the instant he tried getting under her hoodie with the same unusual strength she tossed him around with the other night, the same blink-and-you'll-miss-it stiffness that seized her every time he'd tried to take her top off. Clearly, it was something she wasn't comfortable with—he could chalk his brief glimpse of her glorious breasts off to

Divine Providence—and this wasn't the time or place to hash it out.

So, he got to work on the button and zipper of her jeans. Her sneakers had to come off—their fall to the floor echoed through the stacks, making his heart pound harder in his ears—before he could free her ankles of the annoyingly clingy garment and her underwear, and reinstate himself between her legs.

She chuckled into his kiss as she unfastened his jeans and pushed it down just enough to free his erection. 'This is so irresponsible.'

With a scoff, Oleksiy unearthed a foil packet from his jacket, tore it open and rolled the condom on. 'We're using protection, aren't we? Besides'—he shoved a hand into her hair and tilted her head back to fix her large, black, almond-shaped eyes squarely on him—'what's marriage to a thief without breaking the rules once in a while, huh?'

The carrel rocked as he yanked her to its edge and traced her slit with tip of his cock. She was already sopping wet.

'Hmm. It seems like living on the wrong side of the law suits you just fine,' he smirked, brushing his head over her clit, prodding her opening with it, but not entering.

Payal swatted his hand away. She rotated her wrists as she stroked him, smearing every inch of his shaft in her juices, sucking back saliva that threatened to dribble from her mouth as she watched. Something in Oleksiy's chest gave out when she angled her hips up and guided him inside her—his heartbeat jumped up an octave, the sound clearer than it'd ever been before, and his head fell back from a heady rush of adrenaline.

He thrust into her. Hard. The carrel rocked in tandem with a *clip-clop.* Mesmerised by the slack-mouthed ecstasy etched across Payal's face, by the feel of being sheathed in her wet warmth, Oleksiy pulled out to the tip and slammed back into her.

This time the carrel's hind legs scuffed the floor, its screech piercing through the stacks' silence like a fucking fog horn. Payal's eyes flew wide open, and her inner walls and thighs clamped around him in a vice. Neither of them dared move or breathe. Torturous seconds passed. Oleksiy listened for the *clacks* of overhead lights turning on. For approaching footsteps. All while being cock-deep in Payal.

Fucking mass-produced furniture and their uneven legs.

'It's okay,' he mouthed moments later. Even though he was very much not okay at the prospect of not being able to pound into her.

He tried a shallower stroke. *Clip-clop.* An even shallower one. *Clop.*

Blowing out a long exhale to contain himself, he hooked one of her legs in the crook of his arm and rolled his hips, brushing the head of his cock against her G-spot. No racket this time. Just the mute gasp caught in Payal's pretty mouth. Reaching between them, Oleksiy coated his fingers in her arousal and smeared it on her clit. Circling it. Rolling and rolling his hips. Minutely. Excruciatingly slowly. And when she began to thrust and thrash for more, he flattened his palm on her pubis to still her and muffled her whimpers with his mouth.

'I got you, pussycat. I'm here.' Alternating between plucking and rubbing her clit, he savoured seeing her eyes roll back into her head and her brows pucker with the need for more. 'At your service,' he panted, 'anytime, anywhere. I want you to use me and only me, you got that?'

'Oleksiy,' she whimpered under her breath, fingers clawing at his arms. 'Oh god, oh god, oh god.'

'Not until I hear you say it, sweetheart.' He stilled his fingers. 'Who're you gonna use from now on?'

'But that wouldn't be—it's not—we shouldn't—'

He thrust into her with delicious force without a care about being discovered. Payal's answering squirm suggested she didn't either.

'You sure about that?' he asked.

'Fine,' she all but sobbed. 'You. Only you. Just please—'

Oleksiy's thumb got to work before she could finish, flicking, stroking and rubbing her clit faster and faster. He ignored his throbbing dick's demands to thrust, focusing, instead, on the woman underneath him—on how she trembled at his touch, how erratic her breaths were becoming, how vehemently she cleaved to him. An agonised yowl escaped his chest as her walls clamped down and drenched his shaft in hot cum. His head dropped to her shoulder and his hand slammed onto the edge of the carrel to stay his hips, and keep his knees from buckling.

He let go of Payal's leg when her walls relaxed their grip on him. Purring out a serene, satiated moan, she sat up and pressed herself flush against him.

'Now show me how you're going to use me,' she breathed into his lips, winding her limbs around him tightly.

Clip-clop, clop-clip, the carrel rattled as she sprang off of it and mounted him. Oleksiy caught her by the rear, stumbling back a few steps until he regained his balance. She did the rest of the work, digging her sock-covered heels into his ass for leverage, bouncing up and down his dick. His lungs were devoid of air. All of it seemed to have pooled in the pit of his stomach, stoking a fiery coil that was thickening and tightening, scattering pulsating embers all over his body.

He stumbled some more. Knocked into a bookshelf once, maybe twice. Then pinned his wife against a small expanse of wall and rutted into her.

'That's it,' Payal said into his ear, caressing his hair. Her walls fluttered around him with the promise of another orgasm. 'Use me. Come for me. Only me.'

Drawing a sharp inhale, Oleksiy took her mouth hostage, feeding her guttural grunt after grunt as the fiery coil inside him snapped. Her walls clamped around him again, milking his cock, ensconcing it in exquisite liquid heat.

She went limp when it was over. Her limbs fell from around him, and she slid down to her feet. Foreheads touching, they held onto each other, hearing nothing but their ragged breaths in the muggy stillness of the stacks.

'You okay?' Oleksiy asked when he'd somewhat recovered.

Payal nodded.

Oleksiy brushed his knuckles against her cheek. His lazy smile vanished when he recognised the affection behind the gesture. Pulling away, he busied himself with removing the condom.

'Wouldn't have those wipes on you, would you?' he asked, cupping his penis to prevent any cum dripping onto the floor. They'd done enough damage to the stacks for one day.

Worn out in the best way possible, Payal shook out her hair and sauntered over to her backpack, her beautiful, bobbing butt and long legs on full display like she was in her living room and not in a public library.

Later, once the carrel had been wiped down and she'd pulled her jeans back on, she asked, 'So, were you actually going to get me lunch, or was that just a line?'

Oleksiy propped himself against the shelf, hands shoved into his jacket pockets. 'I could get you lunch.'

'Good.' Payal slid her sneakers on and hopped to her feet. 'Because I'm starving.'

This is good, Oleksiy decided. A housemates-with-benefits situationship. Really, what was their situation if not an amalgam of eclectic benefits, anyway? What was one more sordid clause to their agreement? This way they both got something they actually wanted, and Oleksiy didn't have to deal with rumours of his wife having an affair making the rounds in Brighton Beach. Or worse, deal with Payal bringing some asshole home with her.

This was good. It could be great. All he had to do was keep to the central premise of their arrangement—he was devoted to someone else, and they were only married on paper. Those little bursts of lightness he felt around her, of generosity and tenderness and vulnerability—they were nothing. Nothing that couldn't be expunged. He was a consummate professional. A man of unerring integrity who never went back on his word.

Why, then, did a voice in his head, however small, keep prodding him to let go and give in?

Eleven

PAYAL REREAD THE SAME THREE SENTENCES over and over again. The trajectory of her thoughts had been so crystal clear mere moments ago. Then poof! Gone, just like that. Could there be anything more grating or tedious than writing detailed methodologies on what search parameters are used to extract and streamline data from a whole assortment of databases?

Then there were results tables. And labels for said tables. And detailed discussions of the results. Conclusions. Footnotes. Endnotes. All of which Payal still had to do.

And to think this was just a mid-term paper, a small fraction of the work her final thesis would entail. That made Payal even less keen to continue.

Of course, the problem might not have had anything to do with the colossal amount of writing she had to get done, and everything to do with her being at home, within grabbing reach of her contractual husband-cum-fuck buddy.

I want you to use me and only me, you got that?

Payal felt parched, and squeezed her legs together every time her mind wandered back to their encounter at Butler Stacks. To the way Oleksiy's low, raspy voice dripped sex in her ear, the way every cell in her body reverberated under his touch, the way he made her feel like his filthy little fuck toy while making her feel safe at the same time. She'd thought dry-humping in a car on an empty street was risqué. Little did she know. She hadn't been able to look at her carrel or the librarians or any of the regulars at the stacks in the same way since.

Still, she would have probably made better progress on her paper at those stacks, with the East River separating her from Oleksiy. At home, on a beautiful Saturday morning, when he seemed to have nothing to do but parade himself around in her peripheral vision in a threadbare T-shirt and boxer shorts? The temptation of availing herself of his offer was too damn high.

Alas, Mykola had weekends off, so unless there was a real emergency, Payal would have to tough it out at home.

Her lips quirked up as she continued grappling for the right words to type. As far as problems went, being in close quarters with a handsome and willing man with a mid-term deadline looming on the horizon couldn't even be classified as an inconvenience. It was a minor predicament, at best. All in her head. One she could reframe as an incentive to hurry up if she chose to—a little reward for when she crossed the finish line.

'What's so funny?' Oleksiy's voice pulled her out of her thoughts.

He was beside her, hair dishevelled, beard untrimmed, broom in hand. Payal rolled herself away on her chair so he could sweep under the desk.

'Nothing,' she said, eyeing the way his back muscles rippled as he swept dirt into the dustpan. 'Just remembered a stupid meme. Need any help?'

'No, I'm done. Scrubbed my bathroom down. Laundry's in the dryer. And we've still got a bunch of your mom's food in the fridge, so we're good to go another few days.' He emptied the dustpan in the kitchen trash can and put the cleaning implements away. Washing his hands, he ran them through his hair. 'Hey, you know, I was thinking: why don't we go into the city? Do some touristy stuff like we talked about?'

An incredulous giggle caught in Payal's throat. She wanted so badly to say yes. Not just because it got her out of working on her paper, but also because the trepidation and sweetness in Oleksiy's words made it hard to refuse.

She gestured at her laptop remorsefully. 'I still have a ton of work to do. It's thirty per cent of my grade.'

'Yeah, no, I get it.' Rolling his right shoulder, he set about tidying the counters and breakfast bar.

'But you could go without me,' Payal suggested.

'Yeah ... yeah, maybe I will.'

His small, polite smile vanished when he looked up from the counter at her.

'What?' Payal peered over her shoulder to see what he was looking at. She'd drawn the blinds across the window behind her desk, but adjusted the slats to allow streaks of bright, golden sunlight through. The view of the street below was no different than it usually was on Saturday mornings.

Oleksiy was still looking at her, studying her, when she turned back around.

Payal's fingers flew up to self-consciously tuck a strand of hair behind her ear. 'What are you looking at?'

'The light.' He padded across the living room, head tilted sideways like he was in a trance. Squatting before her, he craned his neck this way and that to take her in from every angle.

Payal tried shielding her face with her hands. 'Oleksiy, what—'

'Let me draw you,' he said softly, catching her hands mid-air.

Panic seized her. Not this again. Things were going so well. Why, why, why did he keep doing this?

'With your clothes on,' he hastened to add. Gently setting her hands on her lap, he adjusted her hair so it framed her face, and rolled her chair a fraction of an inch so a ray of light hit her hair and warmed her cheek. 'Right here, just as you are, with the light turning your hair red.'

'But I … I have to … to … '

The pure black of his eyes and the contrasting forces of power and gentleness in them chased all coherent thought from her tongue.

'You can keep working on your paper.' He flashed her a sly grin. 'It'll be like I'm not even here.'

Easy for him to say. All Payal wanted to do at that moment was lean forward and kiss him. Grab him by his soft T-shirt, climb on top of him. Take him slowly and gently on the freshly swept floor.

Nodding sceptically, she returned her hands and attention to her laptop. 'Okay.'

'Mind if I get some paper off o' you?'

'Sure.' She fished out some printing paper from the desk drawer.

'And a pencil.'

Payal shook her head and chuckled. 'You're ridiculous.'

An understatement, as it turned out. Because the next thing he did was grab their chopping board to use as a lap desk.

Payal made considerable headway on her paper over the next few hours. Apparently, the secret to productivity lay in external scrutiny and a fear of being judged for procrastinating.

She stopped to stretch out her back and fingers once the first subsection of her results was done. 'Well?' she asked Oleksiy. 'Let's see what you got.'

Giving his work a finishing smudge with a long, graphite-smeared finger, he gave the sheet a little shake and held it up for her to see.

'Oleksiy,' Payal softly gasped. 'That's—'

It was definitely her in the picture, but filtered through an enchanted lens. The woman in the picture didn't look like an unkempt, strung up and sleep-deprived graduate student. She was the picture of comfort, peace and contentment. A whimsical working away in her secluded and picturesque cottage.

'I look like a hyper-realistic Studio Ghibli character,' Payal remarked, her voice full of wonder.

'Eh, I'm outta practice,' Oleksiy shrugged, scratching his beard.

'No, it's incredible.' Payal held her palm out. 'Can I keep it? We should get it framed.'

'Come on,' he snorted dismissively.

'No, please sign it and let me keep it. No one's ever drawn a halal portrait of me.'

Oleksiy grimaced at that, no doubt thinking of her nude portrait stashed in their storage closet. The pencil scraped against the paper as he signed his work and he handed it to her as if it was a tissue she could blow her nose on. 'What about your wedding pictures?'

The portrait now in her possession, Payal frowned. She rotated her chair away from him in case he changed his mind and tried snatching it back from her. 'What about them?'

'You oughta be framing those up instead of my sloppy sketches.'

Thin but sharp pain skewered through Payal's chest. *Photos*, Mumma had spat months ago. *As if anyone would want to revisit this travesty*. Her words had left an open wound in their wake, one which bled to this day. The wedding photographer had emailed Payal a link to a gallery of all the wedding photos, but Payal hadn't bothered clicking on it, let alone order any prints.

'I don't think your sketches are sloppy,' she said, hoping he'd drop the matter.

'Okay, so maybe they're not.' Oleksiy leaned back, arms crossed. 'But I'll bet you look a helluva lot better in the wedding portraits. You were … you looked pretty that day.'

'Yeah?' Cheeks aflame, Payal ducked her head before she broke into an unhinged fit of giggles. 'Well, you didn't look so bad yourself.'

'So, then, find a picture of the both of us for that shelf,' he said, gesturing at the television unit.

A year ago, Payal would've scoffed at the idea of putting her wedding pictures up on display around the house. But after getting written off by Mumma, after going five whole months without really acknowledging or absorbing what a momentous milestone getting married was, Oleksiy's suggestion felt seismic.

'All right,' she said, drawing a deep, grateful, nourishing breath. 'I'll see what I can find.'

Payal opened their wedding photo gallery with half a paper left to write—a rookie mistake if there ever was one. She spent the rest of the weekend sending photos back to the photographer for touch-ups, deciding on sizes for single prints and assembling her favourite into an album on the photographer's online studio before ordering physical copies. After that, it was a mad dash to finish the mid-term. She cut it close. Stupidly so. Completing and submitting it two minutes before the 11:59 p.m. deadline. It wasn't proofread and her references were out of alphabetical order.

The next morning, she played hooky. To recoup. And to be at home when the photos arrived. Besides, she reasoned with herself, she and Oleksiy had to be at the penthouse for Oleksiy's father's name-day dinner at six, so she would've missed afternoon lab anyway.

With a steaming cup of coffee close at hand, she lounged about in an oversized hoodie and surfed the internet for a nearby place that could frame Oleksiy's sketch of her. Then she went to the storage closet to get his art supplies out. There would be more drawing from here on out, Payal decided. But drawing on a chopping board even once was one time too many.

The majority of Oleksiy's sketchbooks were filled cover-to-cover with practice sketches. Everyday observations. Different iterations of the same things, people and places over and over again until he got the form and mood just right. Like his sketch of Payal and his painting of the Manhattan skyline, there was a distinct charm in his work. He saw the world through a prism of something better, something serene and magical. Something that felt a lot like hope. It was positively criminal he had kept this part of himself hidden in a storage closet the whole time Payal had known him.

A photo strip containing Oleksiy and a redhead fell out of one of the sketchbooks. The Supreme. It had to be.

Payal recognised her from her studio modelling days—she was a sculptor or something—but her recall was a bit fuzzy. A lifetime's worth of social conditioning, of being told she was less for not fitting Eurocentric beauty ideals had just punched her squarely in the solar plexus.

Of course, it wouldn't have been fair to give misogyny and racism all the credit. The Supreme was a genuinely stunning woman. Her porcelain skin looked airbrushed despite the impromptu nature of the pictures. Her emerald eyes popped against her thick, lustrous tresses, and her wide Julia Robertsesque smile was enhanced by high, razor-sharp cheekbones and a long, slender nose.

Her ethereal looks were not what affected Payal the most, though. It was how happy, carefree and downright silly Oleksiy was with her. One of the photos had him trying to fit the crown of her head in his mouth, while another had him blowing raspberries in her ear—a far cry from the miserably stoic and tortured man in the wedding photos Payal had been so excited to get her hands on.

She should've put the photo strip back in the storage container, pretended that she'd never found it. That it didn't even exist. But her impulses got the best of her. She took a photo of it and sent it to Tyler, asking if he remembered who the woman was.

> **Tyler:** *Ooo, Alice Brisset! She had that installation up at the Johnson Museum our senior year, remember? Even held a workshop. She was pretty cool.*

> **Tyler:** *Skin was to die for too. Not a pore visible to the naked eye. It's what got me into Korean skincare, but I sure as hell didn't get those results.*

> **Tyler:** *Where's the pic from? And WHO is the yummy snacc with her?*

My husband, Payal typed, then deleted.

It was the last healthy decision she made before throwing herself down the rabbit hole. Alice Brisset. A quick internet search revealed she was a bit of a wunderkind. A prolific installation artist who'd had exhibits at MoMa, and other museums and galleries across the USA, Mexico, Argentina, the Netherlands, Germany, Turkey, Japan, South Korea and New Zealand. She was a regular attendee at New York Fashion Week, and attended the Met Gala two years ago wearing Zuhair Murad. And, oh, she'd also designed the sets for a fucking Lady Gaga video.

Supreme, indeed.

All Payal had to show for her life's achievements was a derailed accountancy career and a maimed body.

Stung as she was, it made sense why Oleksiy was still hung up on her. Alice Brisset was the human embodiment of the innate ease, unassuming glamour and boundless possibility Oleksiy imbued in all his artwork. She was the antithesis of a life tied to the bratva.

And Payal . . . Payal had exploited bratva custom to insinuate herself into his life.

But was that *so* bad? Whatever Alice Brisset was to Oleksiy, she wasn't there for him now. He wouldn't have had to come looking for Payal in bars and public libraries, asking to be used if she was. Whatever happened between them was over and done with. Alice Brisset was his past, and Payal was his present.

His legal wife who he'd sworn he could never love.

Well, Payal didn't need love. She refused to drown in the cocktail of guilt, jealousy and self-pity brewing inside her, to feel small and worthless, to be second-best. She was dignified. Honourable and courageous to a fault. She once had the most dangerous crime syndicate in New York in a chokehold and had returned from the brink of death to tell the tale. So what if she wasn't best friends with Lady Gaga? No one, not even the Supreme, was going to make her feel like she wasn't the star of her own life.

Payal regretted every life choice she'd ever made.

She was loitering in the third-floor hallway outside Oleksiy's office at Channel Fitness, her gloved hands shoved deep into her beige trench coat's pockets to offset—unsuccessfully—the bone-deep chills racking her bare legs. Oleksiy had been too engrossed in his meeting to notice her poking her head into his doorway, and maybe that was for the best. The November winds had claimed whatever confidence or zeal Payal possessed as its own, leaving her with little besides feet frozen numb in her boots and an ever-growing dread she was setting herself up for ridicule.

It wasn't too late, though. If she left now, Oleksiy and the Channel Fitness employees in his office would be none the wiser.

'What are *you* doing here?'

The pterodactyl voice had Payal biting back a petrified yelp. Rearranging her features into the picture of composure, she turned on her heels to face Mykola.

'Oh, hey. I'm just waiting for your boss,' she said, smiling in spite of her chattering teeth. 'We had plans.'

'Yeah?' Brows pulled together, Mykola looked her up and down. Evidently convinced by the trench coat and high-heeled boots, he shrugged and sidestepped her to get to Oleksiy's door. 'Then why're you out here, waiting?'

'Oh, don't, I was just on my way ou—'

Too late. He knocked. 'Hey, boss, Sestra Payal's here for you.'

Payal reluctantly stepped into the doorway and waved.

'Hi, everything okay?' Oleksiy checked his wristwatch. 'We weren't supposed to head out for … ' his brow quirked up as he noted the tight bind of her coat's belt. ' … a *while*.'

The smug, conspiratorial look in his dark eyes warmed her blood. But nice as it was to feel her toes again, Payal was mortified they had a rapt audience of burly ex-bratva associates.

'I just needed to run something by you.' She offered the others an affable smile. 'In private.'

'All right.' Smoothing his tie over the plane of his chest, Oleksiy dismissed his men with a tilt of the head. 'We were finishing up here, anyway.'

They filed out, showing deference to Payal, barely suppressing their grins. Mykola didn't budge.

'You too, kid,' Oleksiy said.

Mykola waited for Payal's orders.

Oddly touched that she outranked Oleksiy in his eyes, she gave him leave with a nod. Then softly locked the door behind him.

'So … ' Oleksiy sat back in his chair, looking amused and none too pleased at the same time. 'What's the emergency?'

Payal's hand was still on the knob, her back pressed up against the door. The fear of being ridiculed—or worse, kicked to the curb—was still potent. But she'd come too far, put her legs through too much hell to back down now. She was a survivor. The greatest good he could ever hope for. And nothing was going to make her apologise for being who she was.

She pushed off the door and cut across the office in deliberately long, confident strides. 'Hope I didn't interrupt anything important.'

'No.' Oleksiy watched her undo her coat fastenings with bated breath, only to be slapped across the face with the most delicious look of frustrated disappointment. She had clothes on underneath. A black, cross-necked bodycon mini-dress. Provocative for sure, but not quite so much as skimpy lingerie.

Draping the trench coat over his desk, Payal glanced out the triple-glazed, wall-to-wall, floor-to-ceiling window behind it which overlooked the aerobics machines, free weights area and exercise stations downstairs on the first floor.

Oleksiy cleared his throat. 'Probably best not to make a habit of showing up unannounced, though. Wouldn't want anyone getting the wrong idea.'

'What kind of idea is that?'

'The kind where my staff thinks I'm being unprofessional during work hours.'

'Oh.' Payal feigned concern. 'No, we can't have that. I wasn't planning on staying long. See, the thing is, I submitted my paper.'

'Ah.' Oleksiy settled deeper into his chair, twining his fingers together. 'Mazel tov.'

'Thank you. And, well … I thought I'd treat myself to some coffee and chocolate babka at La Brioche.'

'That's a good plan.'

'Only, when I left the house—'

'Wearing that,' Oleksiy added, looking pointedly at her dress, the pitch of his voice dropping a few notches.

Payal pivoted a little to offer him a better angle of her behind in the form-fitting dress. '—I realised I wasn't really in the mood for baked goods ... or anything edible, actually.'

'Well,' he clicked his tongue. 'Signing up for a gym membership is an unusual way to reward yourself, but I'm happy to be of service.'

'Oh, so we have a comedian in the house,' Payal said dryly. She did another quick survey of the view from his window. The opposite side of the fitness centre was walled with tinted glass and fitted with automated shades to prevent glare. There were no rooms or open galleries in her eyeline, either on Oleksiy's floor or the one above it. The place was designed to give him the best vantage of his dominion without offering up an inch of himself for surveillance. A very mob boss set-up for someone who technically wasn't in the mob. 'Any of those security cameras pointed at you?'

'Just the one outside my door.' Oleksiy spun his chair towards his desk and whipped out a sign-up form. 'So, were you thinking of a one-year membership or one of our specialised training programmes? Our ladies' kick-boxing classes are quite popular.'

Swivelling him back around, Payal bent from the waist so their eyes were level. 'If I remember correctly, Mr. Karmazin, you offered me another service. Anytime, anywhere.'

The corner of his mouth pulled up in a smirk. 'Offer's still valid, pussycat.'

A low snarl escaped the base of his throat as he launched at her. Payal sprang away before he could take her lips, drawing an incensed chuckle from him. Hands gripping the armrests, chest heaving with mounting frustration, he narrowed his obsidian eyes in a silent promise he'd make her pay. Payal sank to her knees, crawled across the carpeted floor and stroked his lean, sinewy legs through his trousers.

'I thought you were the one getting the treat here,' Oleksiy said, his voice strangled.

'Mm,' Payal mused, sounding an awful lot like she was considering what to order off a menu instead of unbuckling his belt and unzipping his trousers. 'As far as chocolate babka alternatives go, this isn't so bad.' She freed him and took him in hand. 'Wouldn't you say?'

He cursed under his breath, fidgeted his hips, refusing to look away on the off chance this was all a dream. His nostrils flared with shuddering breaths as Payal hovered over the head of his cock, grazing her lips against it, but only just.

'I don't have anything,' he offered, his tone pleading. 'In the way of infections.'

Payal placed a chaste kiss on him. Teased him, branded her smile along the sensitive underside of his shaft. Then, she wrapped her lips around him. His thighs tensed around her ribs, locking her in place, and his low, long-drawn moans pierced right through to her core. She kept her sights trained on him as her lips and tongue worked his length. On the way his neck muscles strained to keep his head from lolling back, the way he ground his teeth to stop his eyes from glazing over.

She quivered at the care with which he brushed her hair off her face. All so he could look at her. Admire her. Sear this image of her in his memory. Payal could tell he was fighting the urge to thrust into her. She cupped him, stroked him, swiped and swirled her tongue around him, coaxed him in every way she could think of, and still he held on to his restraint. Allowing her to set the pace. Trusting her enough to give her control.

Power surged through Payal alongside her arousal. So what if she'd never be privy to this man's carefree silliness, his abandon or his enduring and unconditional love? She was his tormentor and saviour all in one, and she would have him at her heels, doing as she bid whenever she pleased.

'Payal,' he mumbled, brushing his knuckle against her cheek. His breaths were hoarse, his eyelids hooded. 'I can't ... I'm gonna ... let me take care of you.'

Too drunk on her own power, Payal didn't care if her needs were taken care of. She pumped and sucked harder. Raked her teeth over his engorged flesh.

'Fuck. Payal—' Wrapping an enormous hand around her neck, he made her spit him out. Lips pressed together in a thin line, he tightened his grip on her, tilted her head up so he had her full attention. 'Don't mistake me for one of your uptight Ivy Leaguers,' he said with menace. 'In this part o' town, we don't leave ladies high and dry.'

Fingers digging into her cheeks, he reeled in her lips to his, leaving her no room for escape this time. Not that Payal had any intent of escaping. She surrendered wholeheartedly, clashing lips, wrestling tongues, yanking him closer by his jacket's lapel.

His imploring caresses drifted under her dress as she rose to her feet. Concern momentarily overshadowed his signature smugness. 'You're covered in goosebumps,' he said into her stomach, vigorously rubbing up and down her thighs.

Cradling his head to her, tenderly threading her fingers through his thick hair, Payal hummed at the heat his touch stoked. Down her legs and between them. His hands stilled when they travelled higher to find she didn't have any underwear on.

'You didn't think I was going to show up in a trench coat, a dress *and* underwear, did you?' she chuckled in response to his tortured groan.

'In this weather? You're fucking insane.'

'Well, don't just sit there,' she chided, bending over his desk. 'Be a big boy and warm me up.'

'Yes, ma'am,' he said, rolling and squeezing her butt cheeks in his palm, positioning himself behind her. 'You on any kind of birth control?'

'No.' And at this point she wasn't sure why. Maybe it was because she hadn't foreseen herself having sex on the regular so soon. Maybe it was because she didn't want to believe it'd be under *these* circumstances. But whatever the reason, this was most definitely going to become a regular thing. 'Condom in the coat pocket.'

Oleksiy circled her clit as he spread her, filled her, pummeled into her. His free hand splayed over her abdomen, but fell away before she could think to bat it away, finding purchase of the desk instead. Twining her fingers with his, resting her forehead on the desk's top, Payal drew him over herself like a cocoa-and-orange zest-scented blanket, lost herself in him to the point his grunts and erratic breaths, the swirls of his fingers and the thrusts of his manhood all felt like a second heartbeat.

He was never going to look at this desk without thinking of her, nor would he ever be able to imagine his home without her in it. She was going to etch herself into his psyche, into every nook and cranny of his existence. So what if he didn't love her the way he did Alice Brisset? Payal was his partner in every other sense of the word. Relegating her to a container in his storage closet wouldn't just be difficult; from this point forward, she was going to see to it that it was impossible.

After—once her climax swept through her like hot blasts of air in a furnace, leaving her flushed and unsteady—she sat shivering on Oleksiy's lap, her last reserves of warmth spent. Oleksiy wrapped his arms around her tightly, rubbed the bare expanses of her arms. Blew hot air over her neck. Pressed his lips into her hair.

Payal should have read it as a trivial gesture, but she couldn't help it. It made her heart lurch.

What if she hadn't come here to mark her territory? What if she wanted more than to just seduce him? What if she wanted him to . . . ?

'I should go,' she said, sufficiently unnerved. Terrified of growing too accustomed to his affection. She tapped his arm to be released. 'Any longer and your staff will think we're getting nasty up here.'

'Pretty sure they've already come to that conclusion. Besides'—he pressed his bearded cheek to hers—'what're they going to do, fire me?'

'Getting a little cocky, are we?'

'Can you blame me?' His chest rumbled with a chuckle. 'Shit, you're turning cold again. Maybe wear a thermal or something next time.'

Arching a brow, Payal twisted in his arms to look at him. 'Next time? I thought you said I shouldn't make a habit of this.'

'Well, maybe not tomorrow,' he conceded, 'but definitely not never. A month from now, two months, a year. We've got time for all sorts o' mischief.'

His words sent a thousand butterflies fluttering in her stomach. Gave her permission to hope.

Alice Brisset, with all her accolades and haute couture and famous friends, may have had Oleksiy's silliness, his public displays of affection and his adulation. But Payal had the one thing Alice Brisset could never have with him.

A future.

Twelve

OLEKSIY SIPPED ON HIS MEDOVUKHA, pretending to listen to whatever it was Marisha and Grigori were talking about—the usual low-down on current bratva affairs, he assumed. Turf skirmishes. International arrivals. Local distribution. Itinerary discrepancies. Laundering and extortion operations. Who'd had their ass handed to them, got off with a few scrapes, wound up in the ICU ... the works.

As a business owner in the neighbourhood, it was imperative he kept his ear to the ground.

As a man who'd enjoyed a surprise visit at his office a few short hours ago, he only had eyes for his wife.

Payal sat wedged between Mama and Tato on the two-seater across the living room, flipping through the wedding album she'd had printed, asking them names of guests from his side and how they were related if they were family. The so-sexy-it-should-be-illegal black dress had been swapped out for a pair of skinny jeans, an oversized festive sweater and a pair of silver filigree earrings.

Mama had offered her a glass of uzvar so she didn't feel pressured to drink alcohol. She didn't know Payal could down a whole Mediterranean Mule without so much as wincing. She didn't know what the sweet, modestly dressed girl next to her had done to her son at his office earlier that afternoon.

The duality of her, of his dynamic with her—it threw him for a loop. Was this what all marriages were like? Schtupping each other senseless one minute, appearing innocent the next?

Was that what he had with Payal—a marriage like all marriages, a marriage that was *real*?

She got up to use the bathroom before Liza called everyone to the table for dinner. Not the powder room for guests, though. She went to use the bathroom in Oleksiy's old bedroom.

He'd never brought a girl up to the penthouse before, let alone hooked up with one in his room. The possibilities Payal's being there now presented . . .

It was outrageous. He couldn't. His family was right there.

But it didn't have to take long. He could have her peaking around his fingers, muffling her cries against his lips before dinner was served.

Besides, if their arrangement was indeed evolving into a real marriage, he wanted to know more about this duality, about finding the balance between carnality with civility. One might even say his interests were academic.

He threw back the rest of his medovukha and made to stand up.

'Where do you think you're going?' Marisha demanded, yanking him back onto the couch.

'I, uh—' His eyes darted between his room and his company, which included his parents.

'She's a smart cookie, your wife,' Marisha said. 'I'm sure she can find her away around the bathroom without your help.'

'Now, now, Risha,' Grigori chided, his attempt at playfulness falling flat. The man's aura was as chilling as his stature was pale and slight. Unscrupulous and tech-savvy, he was the perfect successor to Tato—a vor for the highly surveilled digital age. 'Brat Oleksiy might have an urgent domestic matter that needs discussing. Or maybe'—his smirk made Oleksiy's skin crawl—'he just wanted to show her the lay of his old mattress.'

The benign jibe sounded lecherous coming from Grigori. Marisha, her attraction to her husband still a mystery to Oleksiy, dissolved into giggles nonetheless. Oleksiy shot daggers at both of them with his eyes. Thankfully, his parents were too engrossed in the wedding pictures to notice the sniggering beside him.

This was what lusting after Payal got him.

'It's just the honeymoon phase,' Grigori said. 'Trust me, it'll pass.'

That earned him a punch from Marisha.

Good.

'She seems to be doing okay, though,' she said to Oleksiy. 'Which tells me either Indian women have a freakishly high tolerance for bullshit, or you're not being your usual pissbaby self.'

Oleksiy's mouth curled into a contemptuous smile. 'Try saying that to me when Mama and Tato aren't in the room. I dare you.'

Grigori gave Marisha's arm a light squeeze, telling her that was enough. 'She means to say you two seem ... compatible. Content.' He shrugged. 'Maybe the Prince of Kotovsk has found his "happily ever after" after all.'

The words were laced with spite and meant to provoke, and Oleksiy almost took the bait. Luckily, Liza saved him, announcing dinner before he launched into a tirade denying the charges against him.

After the mains, Marisha and Payal took on the painstaking task of lighting sixty-four candles on Tato's name-day Kyiv cake. Having helped Marisha haul it over to the dining table, Payal's eyes rounded when the family started singing *Mnohaya Lita.*

'Mananalita?' she asked Oleksiy, her brows adorably furrowed in distress.

'Mno-haya lita,' Oleksiy enunciated while his family carried on singing.

'Myo-hay-lalita.'

'No, it's mno, mno ... '

By the time she got it right, the song had been sung and Tato had begun blowing out his candles.

'Oh no,' Payal pouted, her shoulders slumping. 'Can we do that again?' She frantically gestured for Tato to leave the candles he hadn't snuffed out yet. 'You can make another wish when we're done.'

Everyone around the table did a double take, then, throwing their heads back in delighted laughter, indulged her by singing the song again. Her flawless pronunciation, more than Tato cutting into his cake, was met with rapturous applause when they finished.

Oleksiy looked at Payal, a burgeoning pressure in his chest. Here was the first and only woman he'd ever brought up to his parents' penthouse. The first and only woman not to shrink from his lineage, or turn her nose up at his family despite having nothing to gain from the family business. The first and only woman to accept who he truly was and where he came from.

Difficult as it was to admit, Grigori might have been right.

Maybe Oleksiy *was* happy.

Payal rolled over to her other side, groaning in annoyance. The incessant blares and screeching engine of the garbage truck outside refused to let her fall back asleep. Her eyes flew wide open when a thunderclap pierced through the chaos and jostled the apartment's windows. The truck's lights made the rain spattering her window glow red in the dark. She watched the droplets hit the glass and trickle down, willing the noisy vehicle outside to hurry up so she could go back to sleep.

She heard heavy pads of feet in the hallway. The kitchen faucet turning on and off.

'Oleksiy?' she called out.

His broad-shouldered frame darkened her doorway a moment later. 'Hey,' he whispered. 'Thunder wake you too?'

'Garbage truck,' Payal said, propping herself up on her elbow. 'Gotta give 'em credit for working in this weather, though.'

'Well, that's how the Guns N' Roses lyrics go, isn't it? Nothing lasts forever in the cold November rain, except the dedication of the good folks at DSNY.'

Mercifully, the sounds of the truck began to retreat and fade.

'You know,' Payal mused aloud, 'if the thunder's got you scared, you're most welcome to stay here with me.'

Flicking the comforter off the side of her bed, she gave the empty spot a pat.

Oleksiy came to her without a moment's hesitation. He made an indignant tutting noise at his Manhattan skyline painting, which Payal had mounted over her headboard.

'It won't bite,' Payal said.

By the sound of his huff, he wasn't convinced.

The bed dipped under his weight. Shuffling closer to her, he pulled the comforter up to his ears and let out a contented sigh.

The added warmth of him in bed made her blood sing and her eyes droop at the same time. 'Hi.'

'Hi,' he said, mouth tilting in a lazy, boyish grin.

She longed to scratch his dark beard so much, kiss his face and nuzzle his nose, feel the strong and steady beat of his heart against hers. But she was too afraid of shattering the illusion, so she kept her hands to herself. 'Mumma's sending over more outfits for you tomorrow.'

'Another party?'

'Diwali at Roma Aunty's,' Payal confirmed wearily. 'It's a big deal.'

'Well, I do look pretty sharp in those outfits,' Oleksiy said. 'Even though it's kinda scary your mom and Saira got my measurements down by just looking. Those pants from last time fit better than my custom trousers.'

'I should take you to an Indian lingerie store someday. They're always in the seediest basements, and the guys that work there can tell you you're a C-cup the second you set foot through the door. But they've got *the* best wire-free cotton bras, so I always end up making a trip when I visit.'

She was met with deafening silence.

Did the bra talk weird him out? Surely not? Not after he'd casually returned her bra after their first time. Not after the countless times they'd had sex after that.

Unless . . .

'Hey, mind if I ask you something?' His voice strained with an abundance of caution. 'You don't have to answer if you don't want to.'

Shit! Shit! Shit!

'Why won't you let me see all of you? Like the top of you. Is it some kind of phobia, or did something or *someone*—shit, I dunno. You know what, forget I even asked. It's a limit for you and I respect that. And if there's anything else you're not comfortable with, or if you ever feel like I'm crossing a line, just tell me and I'll stop, okay?'

'I was mugged,' Payal blurted. Evading the question altogether would leave him with a never-ending itch to find out, and the truth had repercussions she couldn't begin to fathom. This ... this lie—it was the one thing that could preserve this moment, this intimacy, this deepening and blossoming bond between them. There was no other way. 'Almost two years ago. I was on my way home from work. It was rush hour. The station was jam-packed, and I was pushing my way to the exit. I didn't even realise that … I thought my backpack got caught against something, so I pulled, and … '

She got lost in the deepening furrows lining his forehead. For a second, he looked like he'd seen through the lie.

Swallowing, she said, 'He stabbed me so I'd let go. Vanished with my stuff. I was too shocked to scream. No one realised anything was wrong until I collapsed.'

A dark shadow descended over Oleksiy's features. 'They catch the guy?'

'No.'

'Christ.' He reached out to console her, then reconsidered, resting his hand between them, instead. 'I'm sorry.'

Payal shrugged like it wasn't a big deal. 'It is what it is.'

'That's why you want Mykola around,' he said, more to himself than to her.

'Well, not Mykola specifically,' Payal said dryly.

Oleksiy scrunched his face. 'You know, if it's the scars that's got you feeling, I dunno, self-conscious or whatever, I don't care. I mean, any guy who does deserves his ass handed to him, but I'd be a piece of shit *and* a hypocrite if I did.'

'But I don't have a swanky spider tattoo covering mine up.' Payal burrowed deeper under the comforter until her eyes and nose were the only parts of her left uncovered. 'And my scars are basic. A mugging in New York: wow, groundbreaking. They're not battle scars with glorious backstories you can regale people with.'

'I was beat up in a back alley when I was fifteen, five to one.' He looked away, lips pressed together. 'The guy that ended up tearing my rotator cuff off was my best friend in the whole world.'

'Oleksiy … '

'Some glorious war story, huh?'

'But why would he do that? Why wasn't he defending you?'

'He was Berezivka.'

The name sent a chill down Payal's spine and her knees curling into her chest. 'A Berezivka?'

'I didn't have a lot of friends growing up,' he said with a distant, melancholy smile. 'Kids with strong bratva ties were more bad news than not, and the ones without any still knew I was the vor's son. They didn't differentiate between me and the rest of the bratva kids. I coulda been their ringleader for all they cared.

'I didn't have much to look forward to outside of school except a trip or two every month to Bulletproof Comics. And every so often there'd be this other kid on the bus headed there. Ruslan. Russel on the streets. I'd seen him around, knew he ran with the Berezivkas, but we were on a bus to and from Brooklyn College every month, and it seemed stupid not to compare hauls. Comparing led to borrowing and borrowing led to intense discussions about character stats and endgame theories, and before I knew it, we were hanging out on the regular, and he was teaching me how to box.

'Always hollered at me to, "Shield that pretty nose o' yours, Lucky C!"' Oleksiy chuckled bitterly. 'Probably because he'd had his own smashed in maybe six times by that point.' He drew in a breath, long and deep and sobering. 'To his credit, I did come out of that ambush with my nose intact so … '

Payal's heart wrenched on seeing the agony twisting his face. 'What happened?'

'Time. Sixteen's when you usually pledge your allegiance to the brotherhood. I'd managed to convince him to put it off till seventeen. Ruslan was a smart guy. With a bit of effort, he coulda made it to a state college, got a job someplace in the city. But there was this one asshole, a low-level enforcer moving up the ranks named Kogan—he had it out for him.'

That name.

Payal struggled to hear what Oleksiy said next over the pounding of her own heart.

No, stop. You're overreacting.

Kogan could've been a common name, for all she knew. It didn't have to be the Gavrill Kogan she knew who owned the Povnokrovnyy Gentleman's Club. It couldn't.

'Got him to pledge,' Oleksiy continued. 'Then when he found out we were friends, he and a bunch of his infantry picked me up in a van, and gave Ruslan a choice: prove his loyalty to the Berezivkas or get expelled. I told him an expulsion was good, that we'd both get the shit kicked out of us, but at least he'd be free. In the end, brotherhood trumped friendship.'

Forcibly tuning out the panic Kogan's name triggered, Payal took Oleksiy's hand in hers and squeezed. 'And he's all the poorer for it.'

Oleksiy scoffed in a bid to shake the weight of the memory.

'And you,' Payal continued. 'You didn't let what happened change how you saw the world. You kept believing it could be better, still dedicated your life to rehabilitating people and keeping the Mykolas of the world out of trouble.'

'Yeah, well, you're quite the little Batman yourself—getting mugged, helping the working class organise.'

'Instilling fear in the city's corrupt elite with colourful infographics,' Payal added dryly.

'Can't punch your way to change, even with your freakish upper-body strength.'

Payal bit back a giggle at that.

'Hey, Payal?'

'Mm?'

His voice was soft, almost child-like. 'Hold me?'

Payal untangled her limbs from the comforter and drew him in by his shoulders. Oleksiy brushed her hair off her face like she was made of fragile glass, nuzzled her nose and pressed a chaste kiss to her lips. Then, hiking her leg over his hip, he enveloped her in a firm yet achingly tender hug before burying his face in her chest and drifting off to sleep.

Trust. The sleeping man in her arms trusted her. With his past, his present and maybe even his future.

And she'd lied to him.

She'd feared the Karmazins would see her as a liability if they knew. If they didn't flat out reject the proposition of marriage, they would have restricted her whereabouts to Kotovsk territory. Columbia, the Democratic Socialists of America—all of it would've been out of the question.

If only she'd known about Oleksiy's history with Berezivkas before! She would've come clean. They had a common enemy and their traumas were not so different. He would've understood. Seen her as kindred spirit, even.

But it was too late. Telling him the truth now meant losing the privilege of idly running her fingers through his hair, of feeling the puffs of his steady breath against her breasts, of being ensconced in his possessive embrace. It meant losing the privilege of sharing a life with him.

There was no use denying it now: she didn't want to be a contractual obligation anymore. She was in love with Oleksiy, and she wanted to be loved and cherished in return. The truth wasn't going to get her that.

Maybe the past—*her past*—was best left behind. Along with Ruslan's betrayal and Alice Brisset's . . . everything. Payal hadn't heard anything to indicate the Berezivkas had connected the dots linking Oleksiy Karmazin's wife to the Povnokrovnyy raid two years ago, and it was unlikely they ever would. No bratva was a match for the affluent American Desi network's ability to bury inconvenient truths that threatened to tarnish its self-righteous image.

Leave the past in the past. Yes, that's what she would do. Forge ahead with her new life. With her husband. The man she loved.

Thirteen

'WE SHOULD GO SOMEWHERE.'

They stopped at the edge of the sidewalk, waiting to cross the street.

Payal adjusted the grocery bags in her hands. It'd barely been an hour since they had breakfast, but she supposed it was never too early to think about their next meal. 'Sure, what're you in the mood for?'

'No, not for lunch.' The cold wind had splotched Oleksiy's nose and cheeks an adorable shade of pink. 'I mean we can do that too, but I meant *go* somewhere, like on a trip.'

'Oh. Yeah, we never did make good on visiting the tourist hotspots around the city.'

The bags in Oleksiy's hand rustled as he rolled his shoulder. 'I was thinking a little bigger. You know, farther. Like on a honeymoon.'

Payal whipped her head up to stare at him, dumbstruck. She remained staring as the pedestrian signal flashed and Oleksiy took off across the street in long strides.

A honeymoon. Scurrying after him, groceries rattling and slamming into her legs, she repeated the word to herself over and over again. The man who'd once warned her against waiting for him to come around was suggesting going on a honeymoon? With her?

Sensing her amusement, Oleksiy pulled on a mask of nonchalance. 'What?'

'No, it's nothing,' Payal bluffed, her stifled laughter warming everything from the cheeks down. 'I just remembered a documentary I was watching about restoring historic landmarks. Apparently, back when India was under British rule, they used to rent out rooms at the Taj Mahal to English honeymooners.'

Oleksiy wrinkled his nose. 'But the Taj Mahal's a mausoleum.'

'Exactly.'

'Oy vey.' He flicked a stray lock of hair off his forehead. 'Taj Mahal might be a bit too much to squeeze into our schedules. How do you feel about Vermont?'

The treacly warmth inside her felt all the sweeter and more luxurious at the notion of spending a romantic weekend at a rustic bed-and-breakfast with Oleksiy. That he was even entertaining such a thought made her giddy with delight. 'Bit late for apple-picking, though, isn't it?'

He shrugged. 'There's the Ben & Jerry's factory.'

'Nuh uh, too cold to do an ice cream binge justice.'

They turned the corner into their street.

'Cape Cod?'

Payal had to chuckle now. What had gotten into him? 'Tell you what, why don't we wait till the weather's a little nicer, hmm? We can afford to be ambitious. Still have all that money we got for our wedding, remember?'

'You mean the Ben & Jerry's factory won't cut it?'

Payal handed her bags over to him as they neared their building so she could fish her keys out of her coat pocket. 'For a honeymoon? Absolutely not.'

She eyed the collection of deliveries behind the electric strike-locked door. 'Oh, you got something.'

Oleksiy gave the label on the nondescript package a quick glance before manoeuvering their groceries past the inner door she held open for him. 'That's for you.'

'For me?' Payal turned it over in her hand, gave it a little shake. 'Little light for a Ben & Jerry's sampler pack.'

'Please,' Oleksiy called over his shoulder dryly. He was already halfway up the first flight of stairs. 'Like they'd actually send an assortment of little cups of ice cream if you sign up for a monthly subscription.'

'Oleksiy, you know there are places that actually do that, right?'

'Now, now,' Oleksiy said, disguising the hope in his voice with mock reproach. 'Don't you toy with me, pussycat.'

Upstairs, Payal couldn't shed her boots and coat, wash her hands and tear into the cardboard box fast enough. Plunging her hands into the foam peanuts, she fished out a rectangular object bound in bubble wrap.

It was a photo frame. Sterling silver. Gilded in gold at the corners. With both their names and their wedding date engraved at the bottom.

Payal ghosted her fingertips over the letters, unsure whether she'd read them correctly or not, too afraid they might disappear if she made direct contact.

'Whaddya think?' came Oleksiy's rich, expectant voice. He sounded so far away, even though she knew he was right behind her, peering over her shoulder.

All coherent thought was lost in the fog blurring her vision. 'Oleksiy … '

'You've been putting off picking out that portrait like we talked about, so I thought I'd give you a little incentive.'

Payal Ayesha Lohani & Oleksiy Orenko Karmazin.

Their names permanently engraved in metal. Side by side.

He'd had it made of his own will. To put up in their living room. As a constant reminder of what they were: husband and wife, housemates, friends, lovers. So much more than mere signees of a contract.

'Oleksiy, it's beautiful,' Payal finally managed to say. She swallowed the lump rising up her throat, blinked away the sting in her eyes. 'Except we got married on the seventeenth of August, not the eighteenth.'

Oleksiy stiffened, his eyes wide with panic.

'I'm kidding,' Payal said quickly, bursting into anxious laughter.

'Fucking Christ, Payal.' Sighing in relief, Oleksiy dropped his head into the crook of her neck.

'I'm sorry.' Giggling, she pivoted on her heels to cup his face and kiss him. 'Thank you.'

The corners of his pitch-black eyes creased with his smirk. 'You're very welcome, pussycat.'

Bowing his head, he returned her kiss, deep and languorous, his hands roaming over her body. Payal wanted to feel his touch all over, and get as close to him as humanly possible. She wanted to surrender all of herself to him, mind, body and soul.

He'd trusted her enough to let her see beneath his beautiful and imposing defences. It may have been too late to tell him the whole truth, but maybe she could still let him in. Shed her guard. Muster the courage to trust him with the most vulnerable part of herself.

She nudged him away, unable to look him straight in the eye when she spoke. 'I want you to see me. All of me.'

She pulled her sweater and T-shirt off before he could talk her out of it. Trembling, breaking into goosebumps all over—from the chill or from fear, she couldn't tell—she stood up straight in her bra, angling herself so the kitchen's overhead light hit her mangled abdomen.

The silence that followed was deafening. Payal couldn't bring herself to meet Oleksiy's gaze. When she finally did, she wanted to burrow deep into the ground and never return to the surface.

His jaw was clenched, nostrils flared, eyes positively livid. As he jerked his bad shoulder, clenching and unclenching his fists, the upturned slash of his mouth looked an awful lot like disgust.

'I … ' Payal looked away, holding back tears. She tried threading her quivering arms back through her tangled clothes. 'I told you my scars aren't as cool as yours.'

Cool?

There was nothing remotely 'cool' about this.

Oleksiy's heart pumped fury into his veins. The sudden rush of adrenaline made him feel sick.

Three gashes. Three, what should have been *fatal,* stab wounds over her vital organs.

She was lucky she was even alive.

He was lucky she was alive.

'Hey.' His emotions made his voice gruffer than he meant it to be. He shook her by her arms. Again, more forcefully than he meant. 'Hey, look at me.' The sight of her big, almond eyes welling up made him feel like a piece of shit. A piece of shit choking on his own tears. 'I don't give a fuck, you understand? This doesn't change a thing.'

Payal ducked her head. A quiet sob racked her slender frame.

'Hey, hey, hey, no,' Oleksiy whispered, winding his arms around her, kissing the crown of her head. 'You made it this far—that's all that matters. I've got you. I've got you the rest of the way.'

He held her. He didn't know how long, nor did he care.

His wife was safe in his arms.

But the motherfucker who did this to her was still out there.

When Payal had first told him about the mugging, he'd assumed it was a nick to the stomach—the bare minimum to get someone to loosen their grip on their belongings. But wounds as precise as hers—three of them at that—didn't make sense for a random mugging.

More likely, the attack was premeditated. Maybe a stalker or a crazy ex like he'd assumed when she first asked for a bodyguard. Maybe even a business rival of her father's. Whoever it was, Oleksiy wanted a name so he could beat the fucker's skull in.

He tightened his hold around Payal, worried she might somehow succumb to her wounds and evaporate into thin air.

Tato's security associate at the 60th Precinct could get a hold of the incident and investigation reports. If Oleksiy called in the favour. Willingly throwing himself into the inescapable black whirlpool.

Funny thing was he didn't care. He didn't care if he owed the bratva a debt. He didn't care if his principles were compromised.

Principles were made up.

Someone had hurt his wife.

He was going to do everything in his power to keep her safe. Even if it meant killing the sick animal who'd hurt her with his bare hands.

Fourteen

'HOW DO YOU FEEL ABOUT HOSTING Thanksgiving dinner?'

They were laid up on the couch after dinner—with her nestled in his side, head on his shoulder, a leg thrown over his—watching a Christmas movie with a half-eaten bar of Swiss chocolate perched precariously beside them on the edge of the couch.

Oleksiy was too engrossed in the overlit romance unraveling on the TV screen to give her his full attention. 'I feel,' he mumbled, sweeping her hair off her neck, tracing its lovely slope with his fingers, 'you have finals coming up pretty soon, and you're wasting enough time watching Christmas movies as is.'

'Oh?' Propping her chin up on his chest, Payal fixed him with a pointed look. 'So soliciting sex in the library while I'm working isn't procrastinating, but hosting a dinner party is?'

Underneath her, his chest quaked with laughter. 'I dunno much about organising dinners, pussycat, but I'm willing to bet it takes a whole lot longer than our little escapade at the Butler Stacks. Besides, sex replenishes and rejuvenates us. Having our families over for dinner's gonna do the exact opposite.'

'It'll be chaotic,' Payal admitted, 'but your parents are doing Hannukah, Marisha and Grigori have New Year's, and Mumma and Papa will do Eid.'

'When's Eid?'

'Not until next summer.'

'Huh. It moves up a few days every year, though, right?' Drawing lazy circles on her back, Oleksiy pretended to ponder on the matter at length. He found her growing impatience with him immensely amusing. 'So, at some point,' he mused aloud, 'we'll be celebrating *everything* back-to-back.'

Payal pinched his side, eliciting something between a yelp and chuckle from him. 'Stop trying to change the subject! We're tight on time, I know, and the food probably won't be anything to write home about, but we haven't had anyone over since we got married, and maybe Thanksgiving at our place could become a nice annual family tradition.'

Oleksiy tucked his chin into his chest for a better look at this woman who'd defeated death and chosen to spend her second shot at life with a spawn of the underworld. This gorgeous, glorious woman who accepted him, chose every day to build something warm and safe and enduring with him instead of resenting him—with all his baggage—for being the one she got stuck with.

'We should do it,' he hummed. His heart swelled at her face-splitting smile. 'But only if you outsource the cooking.'

'Oleksiy, I'm not getting a dinner for nine people catered.'

His phone began vibrating somewhere underneath them, throwing the chocolate bar off balance and onto the floor. Patting down the couch, Oleksiy said, 'And I'm not gonna be held responsible for you flunking finals.'

'Please,' she scoffed, inventing a new form of acrobatics to retrieve the chocolate bar. 'I've never gotten anything below an A-minus in my life. Besides, it's the time in the oven that takes the longest. Actual prep time is relatively short.'

Oleksiy shielded his phone's screen from Payal's line of sight as soon as he saw who was calling. 'I gotta take this.'

Slipping his arm out from underneath her, he stepped out onto the balcony and shut the triple-glazed door tight before answering. 'Sergeant, hey.'

'Evening, Karmazin.' Sergeant Laing was a soft-spoken gentleman. Oleksiy imagined only the direst of circumstances could have got him tangled with the brotherhood. 'Listen, I pulled up everything we had on file. You sure Payal Lohani's the right name?'

Inside, on the other side of the glass door, Payal was asking, by way of mime, if Oleksiy wanted his coat.

Brows pinched together, Oleksiy shook his head 'no' at her. 'Yeah, I'm sure. Payal Ayesha Lohani. Critical stab wounds in a mugging two years ago.'

A laboured exhale on the other side of the line. 'Well, I dunno what to tell you, kid.'

The wintry air outside had nothing on the nefarious chill that settled deep inside Oleksiy when he heard what Sergeant Laing said next. It spread, black as night, wringing every shred of warmth from him, puncturing every pocket of hope and goodwill he'd ever known.

He remained outside after the call ended, too numb to remember how anything worked. Tendrils of the spreading chill lashed at him, scorched his insides with merciless freeze. His mind put up a fight, tried to explain away the sergeant's words. But anger obscured his vision, made it impossible to stay calm.

Then, without warning, his last vestiges of composure disintegrated, unleashing violent currents of hollowing, numbing anger through his veins, tainting everything he ever felt for the woman on the other side of the glass door.

When Oleksiy finally willed himself back inside, Payal was on a footstool in the kitchen, taking inventory of the overhead cabinets.

'Okay, so I know you're going to shoot me down,' she said, shutting the cabinet door and stepping off the stool, 'but we really should go to your parents' basement and have a look through our wedding presents. Someone might've given us fancy tableware, and I don't want to waste money on stuff we already have.'

Oleksiy's jaw muscles clenched. His voice threateningly low, he said, 'First you tell me who you are.'

Payal scrunched her nose. 'Huh?'

He held his phone up. 'That was Sergeant Laing from the 60th Precinct.'

The amusement drained from her face in an instant.

'Apparently,' he snarled, 'Payal Lohani was declared dead at Brooklyn Methodist two years ago. Right about the same time the hospital filed a bunch of disorderly conduct complaints against heavily tatted "Russian-sounding" gangsters loitering the premises, bribing and intimidating staff. The NYPD didn't think the two things were connected, but we know it's not unusual for prissy Indian girls to get tangled up with the bratva, don't we?'

'You—' Payal's voice cracked with a shuddering exhale. Her eyes darted around the room in panic. 'You had someone look me up in the system?'

'Don't you dare,' Oleksiy seethed, his entire body thrumming with soot-black rage. 'Don't you fucking stand there playing victim, acting like I'm the one who did something wrong.'

'No, that's not what I—'

'I had Sergeant Laing pull up your files for a lead on your attacker. To make sure no one ever hurt you again. Because I cared about you. Trusted you! Only to find out you've been lying to me the entire time.'

'Oleksiy, please, I can explain.' She still couldn't look him straight in the eye. Bottom lip caught under her teeth, she shut her eyes—likely deliberating which lie to tell him next. 'I'm going to explain.'

Rounding the breakfast bar with an abundance of caution, she inched towards him, arms extended, palms open. As if to say she meant no harm. Like an animal wrangler would do while approaching a wild beast.

Oleksiy resented that. Being treated like he was overreacting, like he could be manipulated into forgetting, into being complacent.

But that's exactly what she'd been doing the past few months—manipulating him, seducing him, lulling him into a false sense of newly-wed bliss. And she would have gone on doing it had he not made the phone call.

'I should've been completely honest from the start,' she said, 'but I didn't know about your history with Berezivkas then, and I didn't know how you or your parents would take it, and I was scared, and I was wrong, and if you'll only just—'

Oleksiy jerked his arm away before she could set her hands on him. His mind reeled at the mention of the Berezivkas. 'Who are you?'

'I'm Payal. Payal Lohani. Same person I've been the last twenty-nine years.'

'Then who was that at Brooklyn Methodist?'

Crossing both hands over her heart, she said, 'That was me too.'

Fuck this.

Face twisted in a grimace, Oleksiy stepped away from her.

'W-w-when I was an accountant at Brigham & Barr,' Payal said, half-panting, half-sobbing, 'we used to do the books for a tech firm called Sunela Solutions.'

Oleksiy fixed her with a searing glare. Lips quivering, she pushed on.

'It's generally accepted that every firm's going to have some irregularities, but so long as clients are paying the premium, Brigham & Barr sweeps it all under a carpet of legitimacy. Sunela Solutions was no different, but I thought it was weird it raked in millions of dollars for the most basic workplace IT solutions.

'After doing their taxes and audits for two years, I suspected they were inflating their revenue figures, but when I flagged it to the higher-ups, they told me there was nothing to flag. And they were right—all of Sunela's receipts were authentic. But the customers enlisting their services didn't make any sense. Family-run grocery stores, bars, restaurants, nightclubs, car rental agencies—none of those places had the need or means to shell out that kind of cash for computers.

'I spent the next year looking into it. Didn't breathe a word about it to anyone.' Payal drew a bracing breath. 'And one name kept popping up over and over again—Gavrill Kogan.'

That name.

It shot Oleksiy back through time, pinned him to the asphalt in that deserted back alley, showered him in phantom punches and kicks.

He'd trusted Payal with that name, with what it meant to him. And she hadn't uttered a peep about knowing it.

Because it would've blown her cover.

Seeing her in front of him now, reliving what happened that afternoon sixteen years ago—she could have been one of the boys beating the living shit out of him for all he cared.

'I knew I had to stop digging the second I found out he was bratva,' Payal continued. 'Keep my head down. Do the job I was being paid to do. Pretend that I didn't know shit. But then another audit season rolled around, and Sunela's statements listed four million in revenue from the Povnokrovnyy Gentleman's Club.

'Maybe I could've turned a blind eye if it was drugs or firearms. Out of sight, out of mind. Maybe. But the girls who worked at that club—I doubt most of them were even legal adults. They didn't speak a word of English. You know what their lives are like. You know what happens to them when they age out.

'I handed in my two weeks' notice to Brigham & Barr. Started looking for another job. But I couldn't get those girls out of my head. I felt dirty for having the life I did. Dignity, security, basic comforts, options an-and opportunity. Then when I wound up getting another job with a higher salary than the last one, I couldn't take it anymore.

'So I tipped off the FBI. Anonymously. Or at least I thought it was.'

Oleksiy knew what happened next. Every bratva in town descended into chaos—rampant distrust, tenuous allegiances falling through, cruel punishments doled out for the minutest offenses. And with the human trafficking network taking such a big hit, every bratva was scrambling to rethink one of the world's oldest business models.

That the seemingly unassuming woman in front of him set the dominoes falling only confirmed Oleksiy's suspicion she couldn't be trusted. 'You're saying the Povnokrovnyy raid was your doing?'

Tears streaming down her face, fingers picking at the fabric covering her scars, Payal nodded.

'And Kogan ordered the hit on you.'

Another somber nod. 'The seniors I'd first approached at Brigham & Barr must've ratted me out.'

Oleksiy's nostrils flared. 'Then you faked your own death to drop off Kogan's radar?'

'Papa did, yeah. Kogan's men were casing the hospital, looking for a way to finish the job.' She let out a grim chuckle. 'But lucky for me, Indians have more connections inside the healthcare system than bratvas do.'

'But he tracked you down in the end, didn't he? Kogan,' Oleksiy said, his words ash in his mouth. 'He made you a deal—immunity from the Berezivkas in exchange for Kotovsk intel.'

'Oleksiy, no,' Payal said, her tone a seemingly rehearsed mixture of hurt and reproach. It was almost convincing. 'No, I married you because they'd never lay a finger on your wife. You said as much yourself, remember? That day we went to Coney Island.'

Coney Island. *Ha!* Oh, she'd worked him well that day. Charmed him into thinking he actually admired her for being so brave despite all those thieves lurking around Deno's Wonder Wheel when really, she was probably in league with them, reporting to them about his family's dealings.

'Bullshit,' he spat. 'You coulda moved states. Hell, you coulda moved back to India. Alice,'—he began pacing back and forth—'she loved me, and she still couldn't stomach marrying into a bratva family. And I'm supposed to believe someone like *you* would?'

'First of all, I've never lived in India, so there's no "moving back" there.' Payal's voice was steadier now, though her almond-shaped eyes shone with unshed tears.

'And as for Alice—she's not here, so she must not have loved you as much as you think she did.'

'And what? You love me more, is that it? Is that what you're going to say?'

Payal pursed her trembling lips, and shot him a watery glare.

'Alice never lied to me.' Oleksiy batted away the treacherous sting in his eyes, jabbed two fingers into his chest for emphasis. His voice was hoarse. 'She didn't work for the enemy. She never tried to butter me up with talk about family traditions or sightseeing or singing *Mnohaya Lita*. She never lured me to bed to get to my family.'

Payal recoiled at that. The hurt on her face tugged at a part of him he wished was dead.

'You really had me convinced there. That you were right for me. That, somehow, you were everything Alice couldn't be.' His words were thick with venom. 'But the truth of it is, you're the walking embodiment of everything that makes me sick.'

Payal stared at him, shell-shocked.

The silence between them stretched out, and with it the mist in Payal's eyes cleared. Soon she stood straight as an arrow, chin tilted up and shoulders thrown back.

'Save some of that judgement for yourself, Oleksiy,' she finally said. 'I might've lured you to bed the first time, but you're the clown who kept coming back.'

Oleksiy's chest heaved with humiliation. There she was again, making him feel like an animal. A wounded one with an overbearing urge to lick his wounds.

'It was stupid of me to think you'd understand,' she continued. 'The thing with men like you is that you're so privileged, you can't begin to imagine being stuck in a place so bad, so suffocating, you have to resort to doing the unthinkable.'

Oleksiy let out a taunting chuckle. 'Princess, you got some nerve talking to me about privilege after *buying* yourself a husband.'

'I'm not talking about money. I'm talking about brute strength. The kind your tato exercises so you never have to get your hands dirty. Oh, you act like you're so righteous for not pledging to the Kotovsk, but the only reason you get to do what you do is because your father allows you to do it. You think anyone who doesn't make the morally correct choice is beneath you, but you never stop to think about the privileges … the dumb luck letting you make your choices. It's why you're getting all high and mighty on me now, and it's why you'll never see that your old friend Ruslan probably didn't have a choice when he broke your arm.'

Oleksiy's head reeled back, blood pounding in his ears.

How fucking dare she?

But then of course she'd defend Ruslan. Hell, given her association with the Berezivkas, the two might've even been the best of friends.

In his mind's eye, he saw a parasitic black abomination festering inside him, shooting from his fingertips, wrapping around her neck and extinguishing her from being. The worst part? His fists itched to follow suit.

'I want you gone,' Oleksiy hissed. 'Out of here. Now.'

She didn't argue.

He couldn't stand the sight of her. Pulling his boots on, he stormed out of the apartment.

Oleksiy didn't know where his legs were taking him, or how long he'd been out wandering the windy streets of Brooklyn. All he knew was he couldn't go back to the apartment.

He'd been so focused on escaping the black whirlpool out in the big bad world, he'd been blind to the one yawning open in his own home. What he had with Payal *was* too good to be true. Of course it was. Nothing could be that perfect.

Just like his friendship with Ruslan. There was always a catch.

The gall of her to throw his past in his face like that. Oleksiy had shared that part of his life with her in a sacred act of trust, and she'd weaponised it against him.

Fragments of their fight bombarded his thoughts like relentless waves of shrapnel. Her face flashed before his eyes. The imploring looks, the hiccuping breaths, the glistening eyes, the hurt, the anger and indignation—they lost their notes of insincerity the longer he dwelled on them. There were fleeting moments she didn't look anything like the conniving actress she really was.

The abomination, having taken full control of him, was quick to quash such notions. She didn't look the scheming temptress precisely because she was so good at being one. How else did he think she kept her true colours hidden so long?

Fine droplets of freezing rain drew him out of his thoughts and made him take his bearings. He'd made it all the way out to the outskirts of Brooklyn College's campus. A short walk away from Bulletproof Comics.

Walking the familiar route he'd taken countless times as a kid, he stood across the street from the comic book store, staring at the storefront with the same blue canopy topped with the same giant yellow letters as nearly two decades ago.

The abomination made kindling of the sight, used it to warm his frigid insides. It reminded him of the friendship he'd lost. The lover after it. Then the wife who was friend and lover rolled in one. The incandescence roiling through him coaxed his muscles to relax. Seeped into all the empty crevices once occupied by hope and goodwill and happiness.

It was a sensation he knew well, its familiarity oddly comforting.

That gave him pause. Made him shut out the abomination's dogged proclamations that this was good, this was how it was supposed to be.

Why was he here at this time of the night, basking in self-pity? Who did that?

Marisha was right—he *was* a pissbaby.

And Payal . . .

She'd been dishonest with him. He had every right to be upset with her. But maybe, just maybe, she was right about his privilege. Maybe he was so privileged, so keen to be righteous that he zealously courted victimhood.

Maybe he *was* incapable of understanding what drove people to make amoral decisions.

And maybe Payal was telling the truth about not being a Berezivka spy.

How could she be? Mykola kept him informed on all her whereabouts. If she was passing on information to the Berezivkas, making suspicious detours, being evasive about who she spent time with, Oleksiy would have known. As for information, what information? When she wasn't at school, she was at home studying or spending time with him. Besides, she never showed much interest in the intricacies of Kotovsk affairs. His parents, Marisha, Grigori, or any of the women she'd befriended around the neighbourhood would have told him if she seemed too inquisitive for comfort.

Blood-curdling dread crowded out the poison the abomination flooded his faculties with.

You're the walking embodiment of everything that makes me sick.

What had he done?

He bolted to the bus stop, making it onto the bus back to Brighton Beach just as its doors were sliding shut. Unable to bring himself to sit down, he bounced on the balls of his feet the entire way, twisting the straphanger around his fist tighter and tighter as if doing so would make the bus move faster.

He got off two stops early and sprinted the rest of the way. Lungs aflame, feet primed to fall off, he took the stairs to their apartment three at a time.

'Payal!'

Excepting the kitchen, the apartment was engulfed in darkness.

'Payal?'

Oleksiy crossed over to the corridor without a care for the wilted leaves and wet gravel he tracked behind him.

The door to her room was shut. He knocked.

'Payal.' Voice thick with remorse, he rested his forehead on the wood. 'Payal, I was out of line. I'm sorry.'

Nothing.

'Payal, please.'

He knew what he'd find on the other side. Still, he turned the knob and swung the door open.

Payal stood on her parents' doorstep, her luggage forgotten somewhere on their driveway, ringing the doorbell to the rhythm of her chattering teeth. The lock needed only turn halfway for her to burst in and fling her arms around her ashen-faced mother. Every question gone unanswered heightened the confused hysteria pervading the next. When it seemed Papa would gesticulate and yell and worry himself into a stroke, Mumma took charge of the situation—pried Payal off of her and gave her a thorough once-over. Once it was established Payal was physically unharmed, she sent Papa off to bed with a stern command and Payal to her old room to take a hot shower.

Then it was milk and as many chocolate digestive biscuits as Payal wanted, and straight to bed. No more questions asked.

Not that Mumma and Papa needed to ask any more. The two suitcases, a carry-on and an overflowing backpack in the driveway, told them everything they needed to know.

The next morning, Payal headed down to the dining room for breakfast. Her insides felt heavy yet hollow, and she was exhausted, but not for a want of sleep.

Her parents were an idyllic picture in the soft wintry sunlight streaming in through the sheer white curtains, contentedly cutting into perfectly round, fluffy and golden-brown pancakes. It was like the night before never happened. Payal waited for the queries to recommence, for the hand-wringing about today's youth having no respect for the institution of marriage, for the rhetorical questions about what so-and-so aunty would say.

But the two people at the table with her, companionably chatting among themselves, passing apple sauce, maple syrup, butter and muesli to one another, only radiated strength and support and, above all, love.

For the briefest moment, Payal felt like she'd gone back to a time before Oleksiy.

That such a thing was impossible, that what he'd meant to her and what he'd said last night would stay with her so long as she lived broke her heart all over again.

Papa headed to work with a habitual reminder for Payal to text him if she needed the car. Seeing him off at the front door, Payal and Mumma returned to the dining table to finish their morning drinks—a coffee for Payal, and tea with a splash of milk for Mumma—in charged silence.

Payal was the first to crack. 'You can say it. If anyone deserves to hear it, it's me.'

'Say what?'

'I told you so.' Shaking her head, Payal lifted her gaze to the ceiling to blink away tears of shame. 'I'm such an idiot. What was I thinking marrying into the Ukrainian mafia? Of all the absurd things to do. You were right. You have every right to be embarrassed of me.'

'Payal,' Mumma said gravely, reaching for her hand. 'I need you to be completely honest with me. Did he hurt you?'

Payal shook her head reflexively, but—

Alice never lied to me. She didn't work for the enemy. She never lured me into bed to get to my family.

'I have never tolerated a man speaking to me that way before, and I'm not going to start now,' she said with an air of finality.

Mumma nodded, her eyes downcast in thought, her thumb caressing Payal's hand. Payal had missed this.

'I could never be embarrassed of you,' Mumma said after another long stretch of silence. 'I was angry, but not at you. I was angry at how powerless I am. I was angry that my perfect, beautiful, brilliant daughter had to go through what she did, that I had to watch my baby fight for her life and there wasn't a bloody thing I could do about it. And then when you decided to marry Oleksiy—I'd had so many dreams about who my daughter would marry, about finding you a smart and handsome prince who'd be worthy of you. When you were left no other choice but to marry Oleksiy, I … I felt like I'd failed you.'

But Payal did marry a prince. Descended from thieves, perhaps, but no less spoiled and arrogant than the regular kind.

'Eh, princes are overrated.' Payal tried to lighten the mood. 'And they're never as handsome as they are in the movies.'

Mama cracked a smile in spite of herself. Drawing a long breath, she asked, 'What will you do now?'

'Well … I have class at one.'

'But,' Mama tightened her grip on Payal's hand. 'Your bodyguard ... '

'Contract's still in effect,' Payal assured. 'Mykola will meet me on campus.'

Or so she hoped.

In truth, she didn't know what the arrangement had become, or if there even was an arrangement anymore. If his outburst the night before was any indication, Oleksiy was fully capable of pulling Mykola off duty. For the sick satisfaction of seeing her get hurt.

So be it.

She was on borrowed time, and she wasn't going to waste what little she had left fearing death.

Fifteen

THE CROWDS AND FESTIVE CHEER AT SAKS Fifth Avenue—and the rest of the city, for that matter—were insufferable. Making matters infinitely more so, Oleksiy's head and nasal cavities itched under his blond wig and matching mustache while the lower half of his face felt naked without his beard.

He wove through the designer collections on the third floor, careful not to make a beeline for the target. Security footage had to look like it was a coincidental run-in, and said 'run-in' had to take place out of earshot from other shoppers. A near insurmountable challenge with the dense holiday crowd milling the floor.

In the weeks since Payal left him, Oleksiy had thrown himself, headfirst, down the black whirlpool, using half-forgotten Soviet-era espionage tactics Mama had imparted to him in his early teens, tapping bratva assets deep, deep, deep undercover for dirt on Kogan, and abusing his own business capital to get the ball rolling.

There was no conceivable scenario he could think of where Payal came home. She was too self-assured, too dignified, too iron-willed to ever forgive the indefensible things he said to her. Oleksiy might have lost respect for her if she did.

No, he couldn't win her back.

But he sure could take care of the biggest threat to her security.

Payal had been right about a lot of things the night she left, but wrong about one—Oleksiy wasn't above doing the unthinkable, especially when it came to her.

A window of opportunity presented itself when the target made her way to the Balenciaga section. Moving up a display rack, pretending to peruse the shapeless full-length dresses, Oleksiy faked a double take when he got close enough.

'Oh, hey, you're Majid's wife,' he said, dying a little at how obnoxiously genial he sounded. 'Majid Al Thahouri.' He snapped his fingers in quick succession in an act of trying to recall her name. 'Warda, right?'

'Yes.' Taken by surprise, Warda Al Thahouri offered him a polite smile. Oleksiy could see her appeal—the woman was a barbie doll, exuding high-end luxury from head to toe, nary a hair out of place. The brevity of her stay in the United States because of her diplomat husband's job must've been an added perk for Kogan. 'But I must apologise for not knowing who you are. My memory is coming up short.'

'Filip Steskal,' Oleksiy said. 'Czech Consulate. Majid introduced us at your National Day reception week before last.'

'Oh, yes, yes, of course!' She didn't look all that convinced. 'How nice to see you again. And here of all places. Majid would never accompany me on a shopping trip. All these nice suits for him to pick from and still, he insists on wearing the same three over and over again.'

'Ah, but he's a good man, Majid. Actually … ' Flashing her another trite smile, Oleksiy pulled out a burner phone from his coat. 'Seeing you here reminds me I've been meaning to send him a picture of the three of us from the reception.' He thumbed in the passwords, first to access the phone, then the CCTV feed. 'But I get so busy it keeps slipping my mind. Here,' he moved closer and showed her the screen. 'Why don't you have a look?'

Her brows pulled together in confusion. Pleasant politesse slowly shrivelled into dread as it dawned on her what she was looking at: a live feed of her husband, blindfolded, gagged and bound at an unidentifiable location.

'Majid,' she cried in horror, grasping for the phone as Oleksiy repocketed it.

'Uh, uh, uh.' Oleksiy was still smiling for the security camera. His eyes made a quick pass of their surroundings to make sure they hadn't attracted anyone's attention. 'I'm gonna need you to stay real calm if you want to see your husband again, Mrs Al Thahouri.'

Shielding herself with her handbag, she began backing away, scanning the floor for an escape route.

'I wouldn't do that if I were you.' Oleksiy pulled out a dress from the rack and examined its material. A glance at the price tag had his brows spring up to his wig line. He returned it to the rack. 'Majid's safe return will require your full co-operation.'

She continued backing away, one hand fumbling with the zipper of her handbag. 'Stay away from me or I'll call the police.'

'Fine by me.' Oleksiy shrugged. 'Have fun explaining your affair with Gavrill Kogan to them.'

She stilled, her feline-flicked eyes wide with a fresh wave of dread.

'You'll have diplomatic immunity so long as you're on American soil, of course, thanks to the man you're cuckolding,' Oleksiy continued, flicking through more dresses. 'But—and do correct me if I'm wrong—the Emirati government won't be too happy to hear about your adulterous escapades. Majid will be recalled, probably lose his job, and you … what *is* the punishment for adultery in the United Arab Emirates these days? Three years of imprisonment?'

Mrs Al Thahouri's teary eyes still scanned the floor. For help. A way out. A miracle.

'Come on here and have a look at these dresses with me.' His voice was soothing and friendly. When she dragged her feet to his side, he said, 'No one's gotta get hurt. If you co-operate, you can have your husband back by New Year's and we can all forget any of this ever happened.'

'How do I know you're telling the truth? How do I know Majid isn't already—'

'You don't. But it's a gamble you're gonna have to take to see him again and stay outta jail.'

She stood motionless a long beat. Then: 'What do you want?'

'The keys to your love nest, for a start.'

'I—' Mrs Al Thahouri stared at his waiting palm. 'I don't have them with me.'

Oleksiy gave her a pointed look.

Reluctantly, she detached the keys from a platinum keychain with her name spelt out in white gold studs.

Oleksiy's fist closed around the keys.

One step closer to seeing his plan through.

Anticipation turned his voice gravelly. 'Here's what you're gonna do next. You're gonna call Kogan, and you're gonna convince him to meet you there on New Year's Eve. It's gotta be New Year's Eve, understand? Not before, not after.'

Mrs Al Thahouri drew a deep breath and nodded. 'Then?'

'That's it. Just get him there on New Year's Eve, stay put at home, and you'll have Majid back the next morning, alive and unharmed.'

'And will you tell him—Majid—what I did?'

'Not unless you give me a reason to.'

The set of her face told him she was beginning to see there was only one logical way out of this mess. 'Just one call?'

'Just one call. And Mrs Al Thahouri,' he said sternly, 'the call's gotta sound genuine. You let on something's up and it's game over for Majid and prison for you, you got that?'

'Yes,' Warda Al Thahouri replied stoically. 'I get it.'

It was wrong roping innocent people into this. Wrong to blackmail. Wrong to kidnap. Wrong to have Mykola guarding the hostage. Wrong to do what he was about to do next. Yet Oleksiy didn't feel an iota of shame doing any of it. Revenge and repentance. Those were the only things that mattered.

Those were the only things making life without Payal the slightest bit tolerable.

Kogan and Al Thahouri's love nest was a southwest-facing co-op on the Upper West Side. Way out of any bratva's purview. No doorman. Negligible CCTV camera coverage. Street view through a pair of high windows in the living space. Real mood-setting fireplace separating living space from kitchenette. A ladder on the farthest wall leading up to the loft. Possibly furnished with taste, though Oleksiy wasn't going to risk switching the lights on to find out. So tiny it couldn't serve any purpose but to be a fuckpad.

If even that.

Inside the bedroom, the foot of the double bed, which spanned wall to wall without sparing an inch, obstructed the door from opening all the way. Once his eyes adjusted to the new depth of darkness within, Oleksiy realised every single wall was fitted with shelving, hanging rods or drawers. It was a walk-in closet. Which meant the loft up the ladder had been the space originally meant to be used as a bedroom.

Jesus.

Oh, Payal would've been rolling on the floor laughing if she got a load of this place.

His heart gave a painful lurch. He'd never make her throw her head back in laughter again, never hear her titter at a meme on her phone, never see the breathless, sated curl of her lips after she came.

Grinding his teeth, he stretched out the sides of his neck and loosened his bad shoulder with a sharp jerk. No point in dwelling on what was done. He needed to have his wits about him if he was really going to go through with this.

No. No ifs. He *would* kill Gavrill Kogan tonight.

The walk-in closet-cum-bedroom was the best spot to do it. Confined. Nothing within reach to grab in defence. Not visible through the unshuttered street-facing windows in the common area.

Oleksiy waited behind the door, checked whether the boxing wraps under his leather gloves were secure, then wound the ends of a fishline around his knuckles and gave it a sharp tug that made it go *twang*.

The evening wore on, one excruciating second at a time. More and more party-goers, not yet fully drunk, passed by the building, dance music blared somewhere in the distance and the occasional solitary firecracker slowly became the deafening standard.

The scratch of Oleksiy's wig—thinner and floppier than the one he wore to Saks Fifth—and matching goatee was interminable, and his palpitations became increasingly vehement with every explosion outside. What if Kogan wasn't coming? What if Al Thahouri had told him everything? What if the Berezivkas were waiting outside to gun Oleksiy down? Worse, what if he had to make good on his threat and rat Mrs. Al Thahouri out to the Emirati consulate?

Heavy footsteps, followed by the telltale jangle of a key entering a lock hit the brakes on his spiralling thoughts.

The main door squealed open. A switch clicked and light from the common area poured past the half-open bedroom door.

Oleksiy tightened the fishline's bind around his knuckles.

This was it.

Showtime.

A gruff, long drawn sigh sounded on the other side of the wall. Footsteps. Another door opening, then shutting. The toilet flushed, water faucet turned on and off. More footsteps.

'Yeah, *lialechka,* where are you?' Kogan's deep, booming voice made Oleksiy jump out of his skin. 'Yeah, yeah, I get that it's New Year's, but I'm here 'cause you asked me to. I'm a busy man. The least you can do is make your appointment on time … okay, okay, just hurry up and get here. You can repay me in several installments. And *lialechka*? I'm gonna have to enforce a no-clothes policy.' He chuckled. 'All right, see you.'

So Mrs Al Thahouri had made good on her end of the bargain. Oleksiy elongated his inhales and exhales to get his racing heart under control. Now to make good on his part.

Glass clinking. Liquid pouring. More footsteps. The TV switching on.

Buzzing with adrenaline, Oleksiy bounced on the balls of his feet.

Come on, come on, come on.

Then, despite all the time he'd laid in wait, despite his desire to get things over and done with, the footsteps crossed the bedroom's threshold all too soon, and the embedded lights overhead flicked on.

The briefest glimpse over the edge of the blocked door put Kogan to the far side of the closet-bedroom, pulling out a hanger from one of the recesses to drape his suit jacket over. His back was turned to Oleksiy.

No more time to think. Gingerly nudging the door out of his way, Oleksiy closed the distance to Kogan with one long, stealthy stride, then leaped up to lasso the fishline around his wide, brawny neck and yanked. Hard.

Kogan's rasps and gurgles reverberated through the resilient metal wire as Oleksiy gave its ends another twirl around his padded knuckles, then another sharp yank. Clawing at his neck and at Oleksiy's balled fists, Kogan bent over to throw him off. Not ceding control over the fishline at any cost, Oleksiy's heels lifted off the ground, forcing him to shadow Kogan's thrashing form on the tips of his toes.

He was a tall man, Oleksiy, but Kogan had three or four inches on him, and at least seventy more pounds in muscle. Planting his feet firmly on the floor with a mustering growl, bending Kogan backwards by the neck, Oleksiy drove his knees into the backs of his.

Garbled screams spilled from Kogan's crushed airways. He dropped to half his height, and Oleksiy, bolder, more bloodthirsty, made an anvil of Kogan's tailbone, slamming it with his knee again and again and again until his cries overpowered the steady drone of the TV outside and the fireworks further beyond.

'Not so tough without your underlings, are you?' Oleksiy spat, lips drawn thin, eyes crazed.

His purpled face awash with tears, Kogan uttered a shrill, slobbery growl, caught hold of Oleksiy's jacket and flipped him headlong into the wall.

The fishline slipped off and the petrifying sound of dry coughs filled the room.

Skull throbbing, stars skittering across his eyes, Oleksiy shook the fishline from his fingers. Reached for the serrated knife he had tucked away in his boot before rolling onto his side—

A white spark. An ear-splitting *bang*. A second sooner and it would have got him squarely in the abdomen.

But for better or worse, it was just a mosquito-bite sting in his right ankle, and he didn't have the luxury of time to worry about that.

Kogan shot again, this time missing, taking out a chunk of closet.

Oleksiy's boot flooded with blood. His ankle ground to a powder with every step. He grabbed Kogan's wrist, raised it over their heads. Then sliced into his torso.

The gun dropped from Kogan's clutch. His forehead came crashing into Oleksiy's nose.

Oleksiy fought the haze, ignored the torrents of wet warmth spilling down his face, the pain throbbing everywhere. He let go of Kogan to take up an unsteady boxing stance. Punched with one fist, stabbed with the other. Got knocked in the head, knuckled in the chin, kneed in the side.

A few seconds perhaps. A torturous eternity all the same.

Kogan stopped Oleksiy's blade a hair's breadth away from his jugular, bared his lower teeth as Oleksiy pressed closer, almost puncturing flesh.

Unable to take the shift in weight, Oleksiy's slippery and crumbling foot gave out. Granting Kogan the upper hand—literally—as he twisted Oleksiy's arm behind his back. Slammed him, face-first, into the wall. Squeezed his hand till his fingers went slack and the knife clattered to the floor.

The adrenaline drained from Oleksiy's body. The pain was unbearable without it. As was the abject shame of defeat.

His face left a gruesome trail of blood on the wall as he sank to his knees, not a drop of fight left in him.

Kogan wrenched his head back to look him in his bleary eyes. 'Who sent you?'

Oleksiy's head was sent careening into the wall.

Again, Kogan's hand reeled him back. 'Tell me and I'll kill you nice and quick.'

Oleksiy's eyes were too swollen, his sense of time too warped by pain to differentiate between the present and sixteen years ago. Nothing had changed. He was still that scared, naïve kid getting the shit beaten out of him.

Only this time he wouldn't get away with a broken arm.

This time it was certain, humiliating death.

And Payal . . .

Swaying on his knees, doing his best to train his dimming gaze on Kogan's, Oleksiy slurred, 'Likho.'

'Likho?' Kogan barked. 'The fuck is that?'

Blood sputtered from Oleksiy's lips as he chuckled. 'Your mama never tell you about Likho, the bringer of bad luck? Makes sense, I guess. Why else would you turn out such a miserable fuck?'

His head met the wall again, this time accompanied by a *crack*.

Payal.

She was a few paces ahead of him on the Riegelmann Boardwalk, her rich brown skin sparkling in the late summer sun, the ocean breeze whipping her hair across her face.

Crash.

He was on the precipice of the all-consuming dark—that last black whirlpool.

Crash.

She thought he hated her, and now he was going to die without ever telling her.

Crash.

Payal, I'm sorry.

Crash.

Payal, I love you.

Another gunshot. To finish the job, he supposed.

Light fled his consciousness, abandoning him to boundless darkness.

His last breath he devoted to two syllables—

Payal.

Sixteen

COLOURFUL RIBBONS OF GLITTERING LIGHT shot up into the sky. Blooming and withering in fleeting constellations, lighting up the darkened room Payal watched from as her parents slept upstairs.

Strange. So much had happened, yet this New Year's Eve was no different from the one last year. Or the year before it. Time seemed to march forward for everyone besides her.

Her phone's rhythmic buzz snapped her out of her dejection.

'Mykola?' she frowned, reading the name aloud.

Bitter as their fallout had been, Oleksiy hadn't reneged on the terms of their agreement. Mykola was at campus, waiting for her every day she had class, shadowing her until she went home. On the rare occasion Nasir couldn't come pick her up, Mykola accompanied her back to Scarsdale and stood watch until she was inside the house. Then, when classes let out for winter break, he told her he'd be on leave till the new year—which was expected, but that didn't mean he had to report back for duty the second the clock struck midnight.

'Hi Mykola,' she answered, summoning the patient elder-sister tone she always used with him. 'Happy New Year.'

'Uh yeah, Happy New Year, Payal. Listen, I can't get a hold of the boss.' His voice dropped. 'What do you want me to do with ... the package?'

'I'm ... not sure what you're talking about.'

'You know. The package. The one I've been guarding and feeding this past week.'

Did Oleksiy get a pet? Why was Mykola looking after it? Was he out of town? Had he decided to take that trip to Vermont they talked about? Did he go with someone? Maybe Alice?

She shook her head. 'Okay, now I really don't know what you're talking about.'

'The package,' Mykola clicked his tongue, as if repeating the word again and again was enough by way of explanation. 'Boss said to wait on his call, then drop it off at the spot, but I've been waiting here all night, and his phone's going straight to voicemail.'

'Mykola, I really don't know what this is about.' Payal's temples began to throb. Cryptic phone calls. Packages. Drop-offs. At this time of the night? 'Isn't there someone else who can help? Someone at Channel Fitness? Marisha or Grigori or—or the vor?'

'No, no, no, Boss said this can't get out. And the only person I report to besides him is you.' Panic stretched his voice thin, injected it with an undercurrent of fear that sent a chill up Payal's spine. 'So tell me what I gotta do.'

'Mykola, Oleksiy and I … we're not together anymore,' Payal offered apologetically. 'Even if I did know what's going on, I'm not in a position to make decisions for him.'

She could hear Mykola sucking his teeth on the other side of the line.

'Just … hang in there, okay?' she said feebly. 'I'm sure he'll get back to you as soon as he can.'

'Yeah, fine,' he said testily and hung up.

Mystified, Payal pulled herself away from the bay window and headed upstairs to get ready for bed. The throbbing at her temples intensified the more she dissected the exchange. Something was wrong. Very, very wrong. And the unease that slowly took hold of her thawed whatever resolve she had to sever all ties with Oleksiy. She shouldn't have been so quick to refuse Mykola. She should've plied him with questions until she knew what the hell was going on.

Her phone lit up just as she was about to call Mykola again.

It was an unknown number.

Oleksiy.

Her heart skipped a beat at the chance of hearing his voice again.

'Hello?'

'Payal? It's Grigori.'

Her feet turned ice-cold before Marisha's husband uttered another word.

'I need you to get to the emergency ward at Mount Sinai West up on 10th as fast as you can.'

Oleksiy's parents, Marisha, and Grigori were huddled in a corner of Mount Sinai West's waiting area when Payal arrived.

Oleksiy was in surgery. For a gunshot wound to the foot and severe head trauma.

Hospital authorities didn't know who had attacked him or who had brought him in. All they had was a scrap of paper with Grigori's name and number on it.

It was like the floor had crumbled beneath Payal's feet.

How is he now? Who did this? When did this happen? Why would anyone do this to him? How long is the surgery? When can we see him?

Is he going to live?

She was too petrified to voice a single one of those questions.

Not that it mattered. No one had any answers. Kotovsk guards were patrolling the hospital's perimeter. Tato and Grigori had mobilised their intelligence network to find out if Oleksiy was having trouble with anyone, or if a rival bratva had put out a hit on him to make a point. Apart from that, there was nothing to do but wait.

The hours wore on. Once everyone's heightened emotions seemed to have levelled, Grigori took Payal aside.

'Sestra.' His voice was a disdainful whisper, his eyes a clear, unsettling blue against his pale, sickly skin. 'Did Oleksiy ever say anything to you? Anything. Could be money troubles or someone with a personal vendetta.'

Payal shook her head. 'I haven't … we're not … I've been at my parents' since before Thanksgiving. I don't know what could—'

Her breath caught.

'Unless—' she looked up at Grigori in horror. 'Kogan. Oh, god ... '

Grigori considered her with unnerving calm. 'You told him about the hit Kogan put out on you.'

Payal stumbled back, too weary to look surprised. Her palms unconsciously splayed across her abdomen. 'You knew.'

'Oleksiy's not privy to all Kotovsk intel, but yes, we knew.' The cold, sterile crispness of his words made Payal's skin crawl. 'We always have. The vor wouldn't have sanctioned your union without a thorough background check. We also knew telling Oleksiy the whole truth would've dragged things out longer than necessary, and neither party could afford to delay the exchange of assets. Now, you can say telling him once the ink had dried was an option, but seeing where it's got him now, it was probably best we hadn't.'

That last part sounded an awful lot like a rebuke. Payal glowered at him. They had known. Oleksiy's own family had known all along and chosen to keep it from him. All so he'd marry her in time to pay off their arrears with her father's money.

Oleksiy had every right to be furious, every right to be paranoid. He'd been lied to, manipulated and betrayed by everyone he had ever held dear. His best friend. His own blood. His wife.

And now he was fighting for his life.

Grigori's hard expression warned her that he was the Kotovsk's second-in-command—he wasn't going to tolerate an incensed outburst from her. Not now. Not ever. His nostrils flared in exasperation. 'If this *does* have something to do with Kogan, our dearest, most upstanding Prince Oleksiy might've just triggered a full-blown war with the Berezivkas.'

Purple fury thrummed through his cadaver-like veneer as he drove a bony fist into the nearest wall, hissing profanities under his breath. Then, without a parting word, he stormed off.

Payal stayed rooted where he left her, shivering with rage and regret and, above all, fear. She didn't care about some far-flung turf war. The whole of Brighton Beach could go up in flames for all she cared.

She just needed to know if Oleksiy would be okay.

Kogan was dead.

Shot with his own gun during a botched burglary. The APB out on the two suspects didn't include any physical details matching Oleksiy's appearance. Oleksiy's accomplice—presumably the man who'd brought him to the hospital—was as much of a mystery to the Kotovsk as he was to the police, giving rise to tacit concerns he'd someday leverage Oleksiy's transgression for malicious purposes. Other than that, save for some stirrings of a power struggle within the Berezivkas, there was nothing to indicate that Grigori's predicted turf war would come to pass.

None of this brought Payal any relief.

Oleksiy's foot was on the mend, though doctors warned he'd likely have a permanent limp. They were less forthright about his head injury. He was under a drug-induced coma to curb the swelling in his brain and reduce risk of seizures. Whether his brain activity would return to normal when he awoke was anyone's guess.

Visitor restrictions meant the ICU couldn't be secured. So, with some help from Papa's desi doctor connections, Tato had Oleksiy moved to a private room rigged with ICU facilities. Two guards were posted outside the door, and a family member in protective mask and smock watched over him at all times. Payal did nights so Oleksiy's mama and Marisha could get some much-deserved rest.

She was dozing one night, head fogged, eyelids heavy. Oleksiy's vitals sounded steady.

The emergency lights had come on at some point, bathing the room in a dim neon blue glow.

A dark figure loomed over the foot of Oleksiy's bed.

Payal sat bolt upright, clutching the sides of her chair for support.

The intruder wore nurse's scrubs over a plain grey full-sleeved shirt. He wasn't particularly tall, but that didn't make him any less imposing. His biceps must have been as wide as Payal's head, and his thighs looked powerful enough to crack her skull between them.

'Always did tell him to shield that pretty nose o' his.' His voice was gruff, his tone light. Sentimental, even. With a throaty chuckle, he gripped his own large, kinked nose. 'But hey, can't say a broken nose don't got its charms.'

Payal's eyes flitted to the door. Ajar. Dim neon lights glowing in the corridor as well. Guards and attending nurse gone.

Leaping across the room, she threw herself across Oleksiy in a futile attempt to shield him. 'Get away from him!'

'Hey, hey, take it easy, all right? Wouldn'ta gone to the trouble of saving him if I was gonna smother him in his sleep. I just wanna talk.'

'Who are you? What have you done with the guards?'

'Coffee from the cafeteria mighta given them a little diarrhea. Nothing serious. Should be back in a bit, so we gotta make this quick.'

Payal considered stalling until they came back. *If* they came back. But she was too jittery to think straight. 'W-what do you want?'

'Al Thahouri,' he said. 'The Emiratis are starting to ask questions. I'm gonna need you to let him go.'

Payal looked at him as if he was speaking gibberish. 'I'm sorry, I don't know who that is.'

'His wife was having an affair with Kogan. Oleksiy picked him up to blackmail her to get to Kogan.'

What do you want me to do with the package?

This had to be what Mykola was talking about that night. The reason she hadn't seen or heard from him since.

'Sounds like none of my business,' Payal said.

Her impertinence didn't seem to bother him. 'I'd say it's more your business than calling the FBI on the Povnokrovnyy.'

Payal's breath caught in her throat.

'But look, that's not why I'm here, all right? I just need you to get Majid Al Thahouri back to his wife.'

Payal had trouble finding her voice. 'What makes you think I'd know how to do that?'

'Well, 'cause Lucky C here's my boy, my brother. The guy's a piece of shit for going after Kogan himself, but he'd never risk getting in too deep with the brotherhood. He'd have covered his tracks, and the smartest thing he coulda done was leave you and only you in charge in case things headed south.'

Payal narrowed her eyes in her study of the stranger. Of his dark hair, cropped at the sides, bristly and mussed at the crown. Of his nose, broken many times over. Of the ruggedness he exuded, like he made his own furniture and knew his way around an engine. Of his eyes, which looked impish now, but seemed like they could turn murderous in a blink.

The nickname, Lucky C, he used for Oleksiy ricocheted between each observation like a pinball till it punched a hole through to a memory from a lifetime ago—of a cold, rainy night. Of Oleksiy asking her to hold her in bed . . .

... of him telling her about a boy named Ruslan.

'*Your boy?*' Payal fumed with indignation. 'You broke your best friend's arm to get in with Berezivkas. Why should I do anything you tell me to?'

'How about 'cause I saved his life?' Ruslan's easy-going façade slipped a hair as he licked his lips and threw a quick glance over his shoulder. 'And if the Emiratis go to the police, it's all our asses on the line. Not just my guys, the Kotovsks too.'

'Why?' Payal tilted her chin up in defiance. 'It was a Berezivka having the affair. If Oleksiy did as good a job covering his tracks as you say he did, the only direction the trail's going to lead is to you.'

'Oy vey,' he hissed, scrubbing a palm down his face. 'Look, a woman's life is on the line.'

'As is my husband's!'

'Fuck, you're really gonna make me do it, aren't you?' He shook his head, chuckling grimly. 'All right, fine. If you don't do this, I'm gonna pull your immunity.'

'My … immunity?'

'What, you think that baby-faced teenager's gonna save you if the Berezivkas want at you? They don't touch you because I don't let 'em.'

'But'—Payal knew what she'd heard, but she couldn't begin to process it—'why?'

Ruslan came closer. Took her hand in his. 'I told you, he's like a brother to me. And I owed him one. So whaddaya say?'

He held her gaze, the intensity of the moment, of the revelation he'd just shared making her eyes sting.

She nodded.

'Atta girl.' He gave her hand a pat, then gently pulled her surgical mask down for a proper look at her. 'Yeah,' he grinned. 'I'd get my head smashed in for this face too.'

Payal burst into blubbering laughter in spite of herself.

'Do what you gotta do,' Ruslan said huskily, surprising her with a kiss on her cheek. He paused on his way out of the room. 'And uh … take good care of him, all right?'

The normal lights came back on shortly after he left. As did the Kotovsk guards, a little worse for wear and extremely apologetic for leaving their posts. When they asked if everything was all right, Payal didn't know the answer.

She had immunity from the Berezivkas.

She didn't need a bodyguard. She didn't need the Karmazin family's name.

I want you gone. Out of here. Now.

Letting out a shaky breath, Payal daintily caressed Oleksiy's battered face. His hair had been shorn off for treatment, and his mother had insisted his face be kept clean-shaven as well. He looked years younger as a result. Payal felt like she could've been speaking to the fifteen-year-old boy who'd fallen prey to the Berezivkas.

'Oleksiy? Jaan?' She choked on her words. 'We've all done you dirty. And I know what it's like to feel like you don't have any control over anything, and nobody deserves to go through life like that. Least of all you. But . . . but I'm going to fix it. I'm going to call Mykola, and I'm going to hand the reins back to you, okay? I'm going to get out of your life for good. And then you can go on and live the life you've always wanted.

'But you have to do your part and get nice and healed up, okay? Because I can walk away, but I can't live out this life knowing that you never got your happy ending.'

Seventeen

THERE WERE MURMURS IN THE WHISTLING whirlpool. More distinct than they'd ever been in his time there.

Light as a feather, a spirit without a physical body, Oleksiy continued drifting in the dark. His attention gravitated towards a familiar strain his mind, blunt from disuse, had trouble naming. It was of muscles expanding laboriously. In his chest. To let a trickle of cold air flow through.

It was the strain of breathing.

Aches from a million different directions flooded his consciousness as he took a sharper drag. Then another and another. His buoyant spirit turned leaden, sending him plummeting into the bottomless blackness. His heart skittered in his throat. He had fingers and toes he could feel. The murmurs became more distinct. And overhead, the all-consuming dark lightened to a bleary grey.

The bottom flew up to meet him, and his eyes parted a sliver on impact.

It hurt like a son of a bitch, keeping his eyes open, breathing. And Jesus, why did his right foot feel like a slab of concrete?

'Oleksiy?'

The voice belonged to a woman in a white lab coat. Behind her stood two hazy silhouettes he would recognise anywhere: Mama and Tato.

He'd been here before.

Except his right arm wasn't strapped to his chest like he remembered, and this excruciating headache was unlike anything he'd ever suffered.

'Oleksiy, I'm Dr Maggie Lo,' the stranger said. 'You're at Mount Sinai West Hospital. Can you tell me if you can understand me?'

The inside of his mouth was horribly stiff and dry. 'Yeah,' he groaned, eliciting teary sighs of relief from his parents. 'Why—what happened?'

'You were shot in the foot, and sustained severe blunt force trauma to the head.'

'That all?' he grimaced, shifting to relieve the cramped muscles in his back and shoulders, testing the mobility of his right leg.

'Oh, sarcasm,' Dr Lo remarked, flashing his parents a reassuring smile over her shoulder. 'That's a good sign. Can you tell me who these lovely people here with me are?'

'My mom and dad.'

'Excellent. Do you feel good to sit up for a bit? Maybe try a few cognitive tests and get some solids in you?'

Dr Lo inclined the head of Oleksiy's bed. The lights, purposely dimmed as they were, sent searing flashes of pain radiating from the bridge of his nose, through his eye sockets, across the entire expanse of his skull. Following in its heels came a violent wave of nausea. Empty as his stomach was, there was no mess. But the dry retching twisted and stabbed at his idle muscles, exacerbated the throbbing in his head, and his right foot . . . fuck, he felt it now—the tight joints, the creak of bones precariously held in place.

Grasping the bedrails, Oleksiy trained his swollen eyes on his parents and focused his energy on steadying his breath.

'You're doing great.' Dr Lo set up a tablet computer on the overbed table and opened it to a screen with a bunch of blank squares on it. 'Let's try a sip of water first, and then we'll get started, okay?'

The first exercise was simple enough: a different pattern would briefly appear in each box. Once all the boxes were blank again, a pattern would appear at the centre of the screen and Oleksiy had to match it with its box.

When Dr Lo began testing Oleksiy's ability to process conflicting information, Mama dipped out of the room and returned with a woman in tow.

'Here she is,' Mama said, exhausted but radiant. She nudged the stiff, impassive woman forward, caressing her hair like she would Oleksiy's or Marisha's. 'Silly girl was about to leave because she didn't want to be a bother. Can you believe it? After the huge support she's been these past few days!'

Cognitive test forgotten, Oleksiy stared at the two women. His family's social circle wasn't exactly the most diverse, so seeing Mama fawn over someone of South Asian descent was jarring in itself. But more so was the knee-jerk the woman elicited from him. Her dark skin looked wan to his hazy eyes. Hair frizzy and untidily braided over her shoulder, and figure obscured by a heavy-duty winter coat.

Somehow, his mind could fill in details with the utmost clarity. Like her large, half-lidded, almond-shaped eyes, or her plump, purple-brown lips, or her long, sinewy limbs, and soft, smooth skin that sparkled like gold in the summer sun.

A vision of her in a white top and a wide-brimmed sun hat flashed before his eyes, so vivid he could feel the brush of her arm against his. Echoes of things said and unsaid droned in his ears, too faint now, too far from his reach to make any sense of them.

'Hi,' the woman said, worrying her fingers.

'I … ' Clearing his throat, Oleksiy looked at her harder. 'I know you.'

'Oh, don't tease the poor girl, *sonechko,*' Mama reproached. 'Payal's been through enough as it is.'

'No, Mama, I don't—' He drew a deep breath and did his darnedest to look the woman squarely in the eye. 'A-are we dating?'

'Dating?' Mama remarked incredulously, looking from Dr Lo to Tato. 'Oleksiy, this is Payal. Your wife.'

'My—'

The sudden rounding of his eyes skewered his skull with a blinding bolt of pain. He clamped them shut, made to pinch the bridge of his nose, then jumped at a second jolt of pain from that.

Something deep in his subconscious clicked into place, though, and the next time he locked his gaze with the woman, his voice was laced with an embarrassingly juvenile sense of wonder. 'I … I'm married?'

His supposed wife didn't answer. Her face didn't betray a single emotion. Still, even with the distance separating them, Oleksiy could *feel* the shudder coursing through her.

'Oleksiy,' Dr Lo said gently. 'Can you tell me how old you are right now?'

'Twenty-seven,' he answered readily, looking at his parents and his wife—wait, he had a wife!?—for confirmation. 'I'm twenty-seven. Right?'

Going by the alarmed look on everyone's face, he was very, very wrong.

Payal didn't know why she felt like she'd been backhanded across the face. This was what she'd promised Oleksiy—a clean break. From his contractual obligations. From her. But losing five years' worth of memories meant she didn't even exist to him anymore.

She was ready to accept this was for the best, that providence was on his side. Ready to cut all ties with the Karmazins. Ready to leave. But Oleksiy's parents, and then Oleksiy himself had insisted she stay on the off chance it might jog his memory.

So she had.

At the far end of the room. In absolute silence. Pretending to be immersed in a book. Ignoring the weight of his gaze on her.

It was unbearable.

'Hey, you. You're finally awake,' she remarked when she couldn't take it anymore. 'Can I get you anything?'

He averted his eyes, clearing his throat. 'Yeah, um, maybe help me sit up so I can stretch out my back a little?'

'Sure.'

At his side, Payal reached for the bed's control buttons.

'No.' Oleksiy braced his hands on the guardrails. 'I want to do it on my own.'

'Oh, okay.'

Payal wasn't sure how to be of use. She slid an unsteady hand under his head as he levered himself upright, and cradled it until the worst of the dizziness from the change in posture passed. She winced along with him, caressed his back and cooed for him not to overdo it as he rolled the kinks from his joints and stretched the stiffness from his muscles. He was frustrated and out of breath by the end of it. Easing him back down against the inclined bed, Payal prayed the fatigue from the physical exertion would lull him to sleep.

'No, wait,' he said, patting the space beside him when she made to go back to her seat across the room.

Payal looked at him hesitantly. 'You sure?'

'Yeah.'

She lowered the guardrail and perched one glute on the edge of the bed.

Even with a broken nose and a face battered black and blue, Oleksiy's grin still made her heart flutter. 'I thought I was supposed to be the bashful one, meeting my wife for the first time. Come on, scooch closer. Lemme get a good look at you.'

Payal climbed onto the bed with a resigned sigh. Her breath faltered at the fleeting graze of their fingertips. Oleksiy mirrored her as she folded her hands on her lap, his smug grin never entirely leaving his face.

Payal looked away. 'You know, you're taking this whole amnesia thing astonishingly well. A lesser man would've been ready to throw hands if he woke up married to a woman he didn't know.'

'Yeah? Maybe. I just—' The bed reverberated with his embarrassed chuckle. 'I'd always kinda wondered who I'd end up marrying, you know? Where she was, what she was doing, who she was with, how I'd find her. And then, today, I wake up—I've got a bullet in my foot, my nose is broken, apparently Channel Fitness is up and running completely independent of the bratva and, on top of all of that, I've got you.'

Payal tried to appear amused in spite of the sharp constriction in her chest. 'So did you always think about honeymooning at the Ben & Jerry's factory?'

'We didn't!' Oleksiy gasped, trying his hardest to mask his pride for his future self. 'Oh man, for some reason I thought we'd gone to see the Taj Mahal.'

'We didn't go on a honeymoon.' A clean break. She had promised. Best to rip the band-aid off before he presumed theirs was some kind of a sweeping love story. 'It wasn't that kind of a marriage. Our marriage was arranged by our fathers. It was bratva-ordained.'

Brows pulling together, Oleksiy shook his head. 'But I remember. I have these snatches ... of a bar. I was taking you home, but we wound up hooking up in the car.'

So it was all still there, his memories. Jumbled, but still there. Bound to piece themselves together sooner or later. And when they did, he'd go back to seeing her as the embodiment of everything that made him sick. She had to do it, she had to cut the cord.

She looked him in the eye, her demeanour matter-of-fact. 'No, that's not how it happened.'

Oleksiy stared into the distance, nostrils flaring, mouth pressed into a thin line, muscles in his jaw twitching. After a long spell of silence, his voice raspy, he asked, 'Were you forced to marry me against your will?'

'No.'

'Was I good to you?'

Payal flashed him a compassionate smile. 'I wouldn't be here if you weren't.'

Oleksiy slumped against the bed, a long sigh of relief pouring from his lips. Without warning, he took her hand—eliciting an undignified squeak from her—and gave it a pleading shake. 'Give it to me straight. From the top.'

Payal told him everything. From her tipping off the FBI about the Povnokrovnyy Club, to how she had married him for protection after the Berezivkas put a hit out on her, to how he had gone after Kogan and how Ruslan had saved him and guaranteed her future immunity from the Berezivkas if she let Oleksiy's hostage go.

She left out the little things. Their camaraderie. Their growing attraction to each other. The plans they'd started making for their future. None of that mattered anymore.

'You're saying Gavrill Kogan's dead,' Oleksiy said, stunned. Bitterness twisted his mouth. 'And Ruslan's the one who put me here?'

'He didn't do this to you,' Payal clarified, motioning at Oleksiy's face. 'At least, I don't think he did. But he did bring you in for treatment.'

Oleksiy grew deathly quiet.

Payal drew circles on his hand with her thumb. 'You okay?'

'I don't know,' he replied brusquely, eyes welling with tears. His agitation grew more pronounced with every word. 'I've got a bullet in my foot, a broken nose, a business I can't begin to fathom running and—'

He cut himself off, though the brief glimpse he chanced at Payal betrayed his abject disappointment with her. Roughly scrubbing a hand over his stubbled head, he said, 'And my hair's gone!' His breaths came out in erratic huffs. 'Payal, I think ... I think I might be starting to freak out now.'

'Okay, okay, that's totally normal. Oleksiy, look at me.' The vulnerability in his pitch-black eyes dealt a sharp blow to her chest. 'Your hair's going to grow back. As for everything else, your memory's not that far gone. You *will* figure this out and get back on your feet. Literally and figuratively.'

Oleksiy suppressed the impulse to laugh dismissively.

'Oleksiy, you are the most optimistic and driven person I have ever met. If there's anyone who can make it out of these woods, it's you. A-and you won't have to do it on your own. Mama and Tato and Marisha and the whole of Brighton Beach is going to have your back.'

'And you,' Oleksiy said, cracking a smile.

'Mhm.' Payal bobbed her head guiltily. She tried extricating herself from his side before he demanded anything else she couldn't give.

'No,' Oleksiy mumbled, firming his grip on her hand. The rapid rise and fall of his chest had mellowed out to a slow and steady rhythm. 'Hold me? Just a little longer.'

Damn you, Oleksiy.

Payal acquiesced, even though the dying embers of their marriage maimed her with the ferocity of a brush fire. She held his hand until he fell asleep.

Eighteen

OLEKSIY'S DREAMS WERE PLAGUED WITH torrid streams of rainbow-coloured, bubblegum-scented froth. Yet, somehow, his waking hours made even less sense. Kogan was dead. Ruslan had allegedly saved his life. And the business he'd been struggling to get off the ground without bratva interference had somehow become a thriving enterprise overnight.

An entire lifetime had passed Oleksiy by and it all meant diddly-squat.

Where was the closure? What was he supposed to aspire to now?

He also had a wife now. A wife!

Sure, it smarted to learn that he hadn't completely evaded the bratva's clutches, but knowing it'd been in service of giving a hearty 'fuck you!' to the Berezivkas helped dull the sting a bit. Okay, a lot.

And if he was being completely honest with himself, Payal was a cut above the girls he'd been hooking up with. Maybe several. She could be a little too reticent at times, but she was mostly charming and kind and smart and funny. Not to mention a total knockout. She shared a genuine bond with his family despite the cultural differences and their being bratva. His own mama had never achieved that with Tato's family, and Grigori certainly hadn't managed it with his parents.

Oleksiy counted the minutes till she arrived every evening. There was no explaining the tug he felt towards her, the need to have her close. He didn't know her and she'd never said or done anything to suggest their relationship had progressed to anything romantic. A cynic might have written it off as patient transference, but Oleksiy knew it in his bones—their relationship ran much, much deeper.

Mama and Payal took Oleksiy to his parents' penthouse after the hospital discharged him. His apartment building didn't have an elevator, and he still had a way to go before he could manage stairs again.

Liza welcomed him home in the same deferential but coddling tone as she'd used since he was a boy. Later, she went about her housework, quiet as mouse.

Just as Oleksiy remembered.

His childhood home looked as he'd remembered too. But the longer he looked, the more changes he noticed. A new frame for the painting here, a reupholstered chair there, a new home entertainment system, a bunch of figurines missing from the showcase—each one a glaring reminder of all the time he'd lost.

Since waking up, he'd picked up scraps of news from political and cultural spheres that sounded like stuff ripped out of a bad improv sketch. None of it made any goddamn sense! And, somehow, he was supposed to catch up with it all *and* run a business *and* figure out how to be husband.

He ate lunch in silence, consumed by existential dread.

Payal cleared her throat after dessert. 'Okay, well, I guess I'll get going, then.'

'Going?' Oleksiy's head snapped up. 'Where to?'

'Home,' she said with a practiced smile.

'You're not staying?'

'Oh, I don't think I'll be much use now that you're home,' Payal said, her cheer tottering, voice fading.

'You measure all your relationships based on utility? You're my wife. You stay wherever I do.' He looked at Mama like a kid begging to have a friend sleep over. 'Right?'

'Of course.' Mama finished off her coffee. 'I thought that went without saying. This is your home too, Payal.'

'But Mumma and Papa are expecting me back home.'

All the way up in Scarsdale.

'No,' Oleksiy blurted, his heart scampering at the idea of being without her for a night. 'Stay. Please.'

Payal pursed her lips and tried to hold onto her resolve. Captive to his dogged gaze, however, she eventually relented with a sigh. 'I mean … I guess I could stay in Marisha's room.'

'Marisha's room?' Mama frowned.

'Well, we don't actually—' Payal gestured at Oleksiy and herself. 'You know.'

'Oh,' Mama said, visibly taken aback. It took her a moment to find her words. 'Right, of course. Yes, Liza can have it ready for you.'

That night, Payal went to bed straight after dinner, effectively putting an end to her nighttime vigils over Oleksiy. He did consider sneaking into her room for a clandestine rendezvous, but his stabilising boot and crutches made so much noise, any 'sneaking' on his part was bound to wake Mama and Tato up and open the floor to a slew of embarrassing questions.

So much for having a girl over.

Payal left for class bright and early the next morning. A burly, baby-faced kid by the name of Mykola with the most grating voice arrived later in the day with a box of Oleksiy's belongings from their apartment, chief among them his phone and laptop. His passwords had, mercifully, retained a predictable pattern and his recordkeeping and filing systems their consistency. Piecing together his professional life in the last five years would be difficult, but it was doable.

His phone's camera roll was packed with photos of sunsets, cityscapes and food, a lot of it home-cooked. There were a few group photos of the whole family at his parents'—for Tato's name day, by the looks of it. A few candids of Payal out on walks, studying, or lying on the couch, wrapped in a quilt like a burrito. Also a bunch of selfies of the two of them together, making silly faces in a few, beaming ear to ear in the rest.

Oleksiy didn't know what to make of them. They definitely looked couple-y, but maybe that was years of heteronormative conditioning talking. Maybe they were just really good friends.

Good friends messaged each other, though. They exchanged memes and called each other to make plans.

Oleksiy's phone didn't carry any sign of communication with Payal. He didn't even have her number.

Oleksiy was winded from the labourious climb down the basement stairs. He and Mykola followed Mama down a narrow aisle between floor-to-ceiling metal mesh lockers. As vor of the Kotovsk and owner of the building's penthouse, Tato had three extra-large lockers. At the very front of the farthest one stood a mountain of wrapped presents.

'It's gonna get pretty cluttered in here,' Oleksiy said to Mykola as Mama unlocked the locker door. 'Why don't you go up and get some fresh air?'

'That's okay.' The kid flicked his shaggy hair off his eyes and unfolded the chair he'd brought for Oleksiy. 'I don't mind.'

'Kid, get outta here,' Oleksiy said, his patience wearing thin. Balancing his weight on his good leg, he pulled a twenty out of his wallet. 'Here, get yourself a latte or a candy bar or somethin'.'

'Okay, jeez.' Mykola took the money, grumbling, 'Just trying to help.'

Mama waited until his clumsy stomps faded up the stairs. 'Want to tell me why you want to look through your wedding presents all of a sudden?'

'What?' Oleksiy levered himself around her with his crutches for a better look. His interest fizzled once it dawned on him how many presents there were to get through. 'I thought you'd be happy to have your locker cleared out.'

'Ecstatic. I'd been pestering Payal to do it for months. But why now? Are you ... ' she modulated her voice so she didn't sound too hopeful. 'Are you remembering something?'

'I dunno. There are these flashes in my head. These voices—they keep saying stuff like I've got enough money to be ambitious, and I oughta go through these so I don't end up buying stuff I've already got.'

He left out the part about the accompanying headaches, and the part about needing something to do besides obsess over why Payal was avoiding him.

Oleksiy grabbed a box at random and sat down. 'Weird, huh?' he said, chuckling to ease Mama's worry. 'Seeing how I don't even know what I've got in my apartment.'

With the exception of a few cringe-inducing showpieces and some crystalware better suited for larger homes, most of the presents were appropriate for a newly-wed couple living in a two-bedroom apartment in Brooklyn: table and bed linens, candlesticks, an espresso machine, tea sets, non-stick cookware, designer kitchen utensils, silverware, serving platters, a meat thermometer . . .

Oleksiy felt another headache coming. 'Hey, what did we do for Thanksgiving last year?'

'Liza made turkey dinner like she does every year.' Mama gave a silver tray a few flicks to test its quality. 'You couldn't make it, though. Said you were meeting with an investor.'

Huh. There his subconscious was again, planting bogus memories of turkey dinners in his head.

'And Payal?'

'She'd gone home to spend the weekend with her parents and Saira.'

Oleksiy nodded, turning the meat thermometer in his hand. 'Mama?'

'Yes, *sonechko*.'

Heat crept up his neck and flooded his cheeks. 'What were we like before, Payal and I?'

A melancholy shadow descended on Mama's face. Planting her hands on her hips, she shook her head at the clanging pipes overhead. 'I don't know. I thought you two were happy. That you'd gotten over your hang-ups about the marriage. Marisha was convinced you were madly in love. But I suppose it was all an act. I should be proud, really.' She drew a sharp, rueful breath. 'At how well you minded your duty to the family.'

I don't care what understanding the two of you come to, came a distant, distorted voice. *In public, you'll be expected to keep up appearances.*

Oleksiy's skull felt like it was going to squeeze his eyeballs from their sockets. He looked away to hide his wince from Mama. Weighing the thermometer box in his palm one last time, he tossed it in the 'keep' pile. Maybe his broken mind *was* misinterpreting pretense for genuine affection, but, for some inexplicable reason, he refused to give up the hope he might cook a whole turkey someday.

On the eve of Valentine's Day, Oleksiy decided to take charge of the situation with Payal.

He made her a card with an ink sketch of the Manhattan skyline as seen from Brooklyn. Inside, he scribbled a note asking her out to dinner at seven. No mention of Valentine's Day, of course—he was not a child. Slipping it into a drawstring pouch with some chocolates, he hung it on her doorknob after everyone went to bed.

He didn't wake up to a note turning him down the next morning, which was encouraging.

Didn't mean she couldn't stand him up.

Would she do that, though? She didn't seem like the type to be so cruel.

How would he know? He barely knew her and he couldn't be sure of what was real or not.

Anticipation and doubt ate away at him all day. Come sundown, he was ready to throw up and throw in the towel.

But she came. Cheeks flushed and nose a little runny from her walk over from the subway station, securely bundled in a classic black coat, a thick maroon scarf and a patterned knit hat with a pom-pom on the top.

'You ready?' she asked, depositing her backpack by the door.

After all that waiting, Oleksiy didn't have the presence of mind to form a coherent answer.

A car from the rental service took them to a Uyghur restaurant Oleksiy loved for its lamb ribs. It was a brightly lit establishment whose baby pink walls were covered in Uyghur paintings, scarves and decorative plates. Tables were draped with traditionally woven runners and furnished with glossy antique-looking chairs.

'I know it's not fancy,' Oleksiy said as they settled into a corner table, 'but the food here's amazing.'

'I know.' Payal pulled her hat off. Smoothing out the static in her hair, she unspooled her scarf from around her neck. 'We eat here all the time.'

'Oh. We do?'

'Yeah, it's a really short walk from our apartment.' There was laughter in her voice. A humming undercurrent that made her glow with warmth and comfort. Like a kitten's purr. *A pussycat.* 'I remember thinking it was hilarious they called their samosas samsas, but it turned out they had more in common with patties than samosas. Still meat stuffed in some form of pastry, though. So what if one's baked and one's deep-fried? I think it's amazing how things travel across cultures.' She drew a deep breath. 'And I'm rambling. I'll stop now.'

'No, please. I've missed listening to you.'

Her gaze dropped to the menu. Sucking on her bottom lip, she tucked her hair behind her ears. 'Should we order?'

A platter of dumplings and piping hot bowl of lamb broth lowered her defences. She was decisive about what she wanted, and ate it with abandon. No first-date fussing. Then again, why would there be? This wasn't a date. And this wasn't the first time they'd gone out.

'I loved your card,' she said between spoonfuls of noodle soup. 'Guess that bump on the head didn't wreck your artistic skills.'

Oleksiy snorted. '"Skill" might be a bit of an exaggeration.'

'No, seriously. I've got one of your skyline paintings hanging over my bed.'

A vision of her flashed before his eyes. In a hallway. Against a door. Her great almond eyes resolutely fixed on his, erratic huffs of her warm breath ghosting over his face.

I never got the hang of drawing fabrics right. The human form, though—a woman's—that's much easier.

'I ... paint.'

'Yeah, you do. You started out wanting to draw comics, but it turned out your strengths lay in still life and portraiture and cityscapes. Oh my God, Oleksiy, you're amazing. I'll have Mykola bring your sketchbooks over from the apartment tomorrow.'

Oleksiy's fists balled and eyelids fluttered upon recalling a nude portrait. He cleared his throat. 'Have I ever drawn you?'

'You have,' Payal said, more wistful than embarrassed.

Frowning, Oleksiy absentmindedly scooped and poured his rice back onto his plate. Smooth, sinewy, bare slopes flashed before his eyes. He'd drawn them. Maybe even kissed and caressed them.

'Can I ask you something? And I want you to be brutally honest. Was I really different before the'—he mimicked hammering himself in the head—'you know?'

Payal considered her answer a beat. 'Not really.'

Huh. Oleksiy slipped into a brooding daze for the rest of the meal.

There was no way they were *just* good friends. Why would Payal pose nude for him if he was just some guy—

descended from the bratva no less—she'd married out of convenience? Shit, why would he keep pictures of her watching TV wrapped in a quilt if he didn't think it was the cutest fucking thing in the whole world? She said it herself: he was still the same guy. And dammit, that photo was the most adorable thing he'd ever seen!

After dinner, back at the condominium's reception, Oleksiy pressed the 'up' button on the elevator and swayed back and forth on his crutches.

'Hey, Payal?' That tug he'd felt since he first laid eyes on her, that most tangible anchor to the time he'd lost, it reeled him to her on unsteady legs. Drove him to thread his fingers through her hair, and lower his lips to hers. 'Happy Valentine's Day.'

'Oleksiy'—Payal turned her head away, pressing a hand to his chest—'we can't.'

His heart plummeted. In a low voice, he asked, 'Is there someone else?'

'No.'

A nervous chuckle escaped his throat to offset his mortification. 'Is it my broken nose?'

'No, of course not.' Catching herself stroking the lapel of his coat, she snatched her hand away. Her voice was barely audible. 'It's you. You've got someone.' A shuddering, bracing breath. 'Her name's Alice. Alice Brisset. She's an installation artist and she's amazing and she knows Lady Gaga and you two are madly in love.'

Hurt and confused, Oleksiy sneered. 'Yeah? Well, where is she?'

'I don't know. It was before we got married, but you were very forthright about what she meant to you and I respected—I still respect your wishes. You and I—'

Don't say it.

'—we're just friends. Two contract partners with a deep respect for each other.'

The elevator doors slid open with a mocking *ding*.

'I see.' Oleksiy gritted his teeth. Extracting his fingers from her hair, he levered himself into the metal box. Thoroughly humiliated, but no less incredulous. 'I'm sorry.'

They rode up to the penthouse and branched off to their rooms without another word. Oleksiy fell back onto his bed with an exhausted sigh, glad to relinquish control to his nonsensical, rainbow-frothed dreams.

Nineteen

ALICE BRISSET'S NUMBER HE DID HAVE. Along with texts signing off with 'love you'. She'd decided what they did, when and where, always outside Brighton Beach. She'd probably never met Marisha or his parents, same as all his other exes. An internet search revealed that she was indeed 'amazing', with an impressive list of achievements, accolades and high-profile appearances to her name. She was also stunning. Having had the hugest crush on Jean Grey from the X-Men through his teens, it made sense he'd fall for someone like her.

Their text thread hadn't been active in eighteen months.

Payal had Mykola bring over Oleksiy's artwork and supplies as promised. Lots of sketches—some of them done in ink, some of them coloured in pencils, pastels, or markers—of cityscapes and strangers around the city. He broke into a nervous sweat as he flipped through them. There was no way he could make these now. No way he could achieve such detail with such skill. No way he could ever pick up a pencil again.

One of the sketchbooks produced a photo strip of him and Alice Brisset. Their hands and mouths were all over each other. A well-matched pair. Happy and carefree. Very much in love. But the images left Oleksiy cold and frustrated. Inadequate, most of all. Like he was desperately trying to be something he wasn't for validation that never came. Did his relationship with this woman sour? Was that why they hadn't been in contact for eighteen months? Was it over before he got married, or did they break up *because* of his marriage? Did he hold any of this against Payal?

Maybe.

Payal wasn't around to answer any of these questions. She had excused herself from the penthouse on grounds that she'd be keeping odd hours with mid-terms coming up. A flimsy excuse, but Oleksiy didn't protest. If she needed space after his embarrassing attempt at a kiss, it was the least he could do.

He busied himself getting reoriented with his businesses. He and his parents had decided early on to restrict news of his amnesia to their immediate circle so no one tried fleecing him. Mykola became a constant companion at the penthouse, announcing staff members' names when they delivered paperwork, sitting off-camera during virtual meetings, signalling or passing him notes if he sounded off. Once Oleksiy had a grasp on the basics, he braved going to Channel Fitness in person. He still had too many doctors' appointments to work full-time, but it was progress.

When he wasn't working, in spite of his trepidations, he picked up the pencil again.

To his immense relief, his hands still knew how to capture what he saw on paper.

His musings were never far from Payal. His pencil gave his dreams and memories of her solid edges, more definition, sometimes even slivers of context.

He had once drawn her at a festival of some kind, where the venue was decorated with colourful streamers and twinkle lights. Beads glimmered on her bodice. Her skirt was blue with flowers on it. And when she danced, it swirled around her like a butterfly's wings. Was this at their wedding?

The album Mama showed him said no. Payal had worn a blushing pink get-up encrusted with mirrors that day. Oleksiy couldn't get over how practiced and stiff they both looked. Now these were two parties meeting at a reluctant compromise, faking amity for the cameras. Somewhere between these photos and the ones on his camera reel, they'd struck a bond with each other.

Of deep respect.

Of friendship.

Of love.

No matter what Payal said, it was love that had kept her returning to his bedside all those nights at the hospital. That kept his thoughts circling back to her. Even five years wiser, he couldn't have been a good enough actor to fool Marisha *and* Mama.

If they'd thought he was in love, it must have been so.

If he woke up locking onto their bond despite losing five years of memories, it must have been so.

After spending mid-terms living at their apartment, Payal went to Scarsdale for spring break, which protracted from the standard one week to two. Before two weeks turned to three, Oleksiy decided to move back home.

The apartment bore no resemblance to where he used to live. His beloved stained and creaky futon had been replaced, for one. And the living room now had a proper entertainment unit, which meant the floors weren't littered with wires and extension sockets anymore. There wasn't a single delivery or pizza box in plain sight, and the walls were cream instead of blue.

'You had this exact reaction the day you first brought me here,' Payal chuckled, the sound music to his ears.

She helped him settle in as someone would a visiting relative or a friend: with immense kindness and grace. Oleksiy fell in step with her daily routine, making himself as useful as he was able, taking care not to bring up Valentine's Day or anything that might drive her away again.

If they'd found their way to each other once, they could do it again. All he needed to do was be patient.

Sadly, he saw more of Mykola than he did Payal. Now familiar with the bulk of his professional responsibilities, Oleksiy kept the kid around to run errands and help him up and down the stairs. Payal had also charged Oleksiy with helping him study for his GED test, which was fast approaching—a task that, like Payal and the dastardly stairs, required him to have the patience of a monk.

The menace of stairs and Mykola's incapacity for rudimentary algebra aside, immersion in his old routine and environment jogged his muscle and sensory memories.

When the Lohani family's chauffeur delivered a three-tiered hot box in the middle of the week and Oleksiy saw the first two tiers held vegetables and chicken, he knew the very bottom tier carried raw, rolled out dough before lifting its lid. Chapatis. The kind made from whole wheat, not pearl millet. They had to be roasted on a cast iron tawa, but a non-stick frypan worked just fine too.

Come laundry day, his gut told him to use the laundromat next door. Maybe because there was a problem with the machines in the basement. Whatever the reason, he was happy not to have to climb down an additional flight of stairs.

The exquisite nude portrait of Payal he remembered was gathering dust at the back of their storage closet, and he wasn't its maker. His portrayal of her was much more kosher. It held a prime spot on the wall by the entertainment unit. And in the entertainment unit itself sat a photograph of the two of them on their wedding day.

His credit card records corroborated that he'd bought the silver frame engraved with their names and wedding date. Weird thing for a man in love with another woman to do.

Sometimes he used Payal's bathroom when she wasn't home. To trigger more memories. Smell his fill of her honey-and-peach scent. Feel closer to her. He didn't baulk at the watering can beside the toilet—it was for washing up after doing your business, of course. He knew the colourful balls in the jar by the tub would explode into unicorn vomit once it hit water. He remembered soaking his feet in the unicorn vomit with Payal once, sipping champagne. She'd been wearing shorts and a baggy T-shirt, but her hair had been in a fancy updo, the red flower in it sagging because of the steam in the air.

And sometimes he ventured into Payal's room. The painting over her bed—another of his creations—always elicited a rancid reflex from him. *Pedestrian. Derivative.* What more could a boy raised among criminals possibly be capable of? Maybe Alice had strung him along anyway, taken him up as a charitable cause, probably in the hope she could 'fix' him.

He'd burrowed under the comforter in this room. With Payal. Thunder rumbling outside. He'd bared his soul to her, sought comfort in her arms.

It must have been so.

He had a nagging feeling when he cooked the Croatian shrimp recipe that he could prepare in his sleep. It tasted how it always did, and was a hit with Payal like it was with most of the ladies he'd cooked it for. Still—

'Have I ever thickened the sauce with parmesan instead of bread crumbs?' he asked mid-meal, wrinkling his nose at the blasphemous thought.

Payal's hand shot up to her mouth to keep her food from falling out as she giggled. 'I keep badgering you to do it, but you never listen.'

I'm here. At your service anytime, anywhere.

Bristling, Oleksiy blinked rapidly to fend off visions of Payal underneath him, draped over . . . what was that? The hood of a car? Countertop? Library carrel?

'Yes, yes, I know,' Payal rolled her eyes. 'Very "American" of me. But I never actually insisted you do it. I just like annoying you every once in a while.'

Her smile faltered. She dropped her gaze as if she'd said too much.

I want you to use me and only me, you got that?

Oleksiy rolled his right shoulder and lifted the corner of his mouth in a polite smile.

If annoying him had been such a frequent thing, why didn't she do it anymore?

Coney Island Beach in the dead of night. His breath misted in front of him, dissipating into the pale starlit night. He watched the wintry waves crash into the shore and recede, crash and recede, crash and recede. Not a care in the world. Nowhere to be. This was his night on the town.

He lay down on one of the benches overlooking the water. Let the crash of waves lull him to sleep.

Rough hands lifted him by the collar of his shirt, threw a bag over his head and tossed him someplace hard. Cracked, vicious adolescent laughter filled his ears. The ground reverberated with an engine's growl, bounced him off one kick-ready leg to another.

When the covering was snatched from his head, he was in an alley. Facing off a posse of rangy, pimply, patch-bearded, gum-chewing boys. Ruslan was among them. And standing at their fore was Kogan, too weathered, too brawny, too suited up and too balding to be hanging out with a bunch of kids.

Oleksiy rose to his feet.

'Whoa, whoa, whoa, Your Highness.' Kogan stayed him with a smack to the chest as he tried to pass. 'Where do you think you're going?'

To a chorus of the others' cheers, he shoved Oleksiy to the ground, rammed his foot into Oleksiy's ribs.

Oleksiy curled into himself to shield against the blow. His hand brushed against a knife handle tucked in his boot. Unsheathing it, he stood. Instead of the alley, he was in crammed bedroom. Instead of an entire gang, there was only Kogan.

He had a smoking gun pointed at him.

Oleksiy launched himself at him, squeezed the gun out of his hand, inched the knife towards Kogan's jugular.

'Oleksiy,' came a distorted voice.

Kogan's armed hand fell slack.

'Hey, hey, Lucky C. No, no, wake up.'

There was another man in the room. Oleksiy was too close to sinking his blade into Kogan's throat to get distracted.

'Oleksiy, wake up.'

'No, no, no, don't you die on me, C.'

Almost there.

'Oleksiy!'

A ginger brush of a hand on his shoulder snapped his concentration. Kogan knocked the knife from his grip.

Roaring out in fury, Oleksiy grabbed his throat and squeezed with everything he had.

'Oleksiy!' a woman shrieked.

His eyes shot open. His fingers squeezed harder.

'Oleksiy'—Payal clawed at the hand coiled around her throat—'Oleksiy, it's me.'

Twenty

'LEKH-SIY!' PAYAL GASPED. HER VISION blurred from want for air. Oleksiy had her pinned to the bed, legs thrashing under him. She dug her nails into his arm to pry him off of her. 'Leg gho!'

Oleksiy stared at her, frozen. His hand tightened around her neck, even as the horror of what was happening—what *he* was doing—sank in.

Paralysed, panicked, powerless, Payal twisted and squirmed in his grip until a voice in her head screamed that she had the training she needed to get out of this.

Defending yourself under professional guidance at a dojo wasn't the same as actually doing it under duress, though.

Still, she needed to get a move on.

Wriggling her feet to plant them on either side of his leg, locking the arm choking her against her torso, she thrust up into a bridge and swung him off of her. Sending him tumbling off the bed with a resounding *crash*.

She flipped onto her elbows and knees, heaving. Her airways were crushed too tight to handle the sting of oxygen. Bout after bout of agonising, nail-on-chalkboard-shrill coughs racked her frame. All while an excruciating stiffness claimed her neck and her pulse felt primed to explode.

'P-Payal?' came Oleksiy's voice, trembling, small and scared. 'Oh god. Oh god, I'm—I'm so—I didn't—I'm sorry—I didn't mean—'

Payal waved feebly to let him know she'd be okay.

'No, no, no, no, no,' he panted, a sob caught in his throat. Even in the dark, Payal could make out the strain in his face, the veins protruding from his neck and forehead. Kneeling beside the bed, he hovered his hands over her, too afraid to touch her. 'No, please, I didn't mean it. I'm not like this. I would never'—he struggled to breathe in between sobs—'I've never … never ever, ever … I'm sorry, I'm sorry, I'm sorry.'

'It's okay,' Payal croaked out. She reached out to calm him. 'I get them too. The nightmares.'

'No.' Shaking his head vehemently, he fell back and scrambled away, backing up against the closet door. 'No, no, no, no.' He carried on shaking his head, dropping it into his hands, agitatedly running his palms over it. A violent quake felled him sideways into fetal position. 'It's not okay,' he wept into his chest. 'I don't—I'm not like this.'

'Of course you're not,' Payal coughed. She slid onto the floor and crawled over to him on unsteady limbs. He was shaking all over, drenched in cold sweat, struggling to breathe. 'Jaan,' she caressed, then cradled his head. 'Look at me, I'm fine. Everything's fine.'

'No, it's not.' Another breathless, violent sob racked his broad frame.

'Sh, sh, shh.' Enveloping him in her arms, she scooped him upright. 'Breathe with me,' she murmured. 'Slowly. Before you give yourself a headache.'

Hit by a fresh wave of heaving sobs, Oleksiy tried to duck away from her.

'Jaan, no, it's okay. I'm not mad at you. Saira used to buck me like a dressage horse when I'd wake her up for school. Next time, I … I'll swat you with a towel or throw a book at you or something.' She wiped the tears from his face. 'Please don't cry.'

Unspooling herself from him, she hurried to the kitchen, wincing as she downed a glass of water. Then brought him a glass, which he accepted reluctantly.

'Breathe,' Payal repeated.

'I'm sorry,' he hiccupped, slumping against the closet door, gaze downcast.

'Apology accepted.' She ran the back of her fingers up and down his cheek. 'How's your head feeling?'

'No worse than usual.'

A squeeze to his right thigh. 'And your foot?'

Releasing an impertinent huff, Oleksiy banged his casted foot on the floor. Repeatedly.

'Shh. Neighbours.' Payal squeezed his leg again. 'You good to get up?'

She helped him back to the edge of the bed, then got a damp cloth from the bathroom. His pitch-black eyes were unwavering in their scrutiny of her as she dabbed his face clean, so spellbinding they blurred everything else out, wrapping the two of them in a vacuum where it was just the sound of his ragged breaths slowing to match hers. A vacuum where the pounding of her heart rose to explosive decibels when his head dropped to her stomach and his arms circled her thighs.

No, she couldn't do this. She had a promise to keep.

But she didn't have the fortitude to leave him like this, riddled with guilt, hurting, vulnerable.

She didn't have the fortitude to extricate herself from his touch.

Slowly, she lowered a hand to his luscious black hair. Almost back to its normal length, it swallowed her fingers, coaxing her to caress it again and again.

The relief in his responding sigh gave her butterflies.

'You ... must be drained,' she said, her capacity to resist touching him dwindling rapidly. 'Try and get some sleep.'

His arms tightened around her. 'No.'

Even as her eyes darted about the room for an escape, her treacherous body shifted closer and hugged him to her firmly. Her promise to Oleksiy blared on a loop in her head, while her mouth, with the utmost tenderness, said, 'Do you want me to stay with you?'

He nodded into her stomach, razing the remnants of her defenses.

He needed to heal first. Without that, her promise was pointless.

Surely she could withstand being this close to him till then.

He refused to let go of her, even to climb into bed. Awkwardly pitching the damp cloth into the bathroom, Payal twisted in his embrace to lie back and brought him down on top of her. He burrowed his head into her chest, raised her thigh over his and clasped it there for good measure. A couple more hiccups and tremors, and he was soon out cold.

Payal nuzzled him, drinking in that cocoa-orange zest scent she'd been deprived of so long, moulding herself flush against that familiar, giddying warmth.

She had every intention of returning to her room. She really did. But for the first time in months, she felt like she was home.

Just a little longer.

Her eyelids drooped. Before she knew it, she sank into a deep, cozy, contented sleep.

Force of habit had Payal reaching for Oleksiy when she stirred. His side of the bed was empty.

Luxuriating in his scent while grumbling about his absence, it took her a few beats to remember she wasn't supposed to be in his bed.

She bolted upright. The room was shrouded in pale grey darkness. It was drizzling outside, and not early like she'd presumed. The clock on Oleksiy's bedside table said it was 10.07 a.m.

Shit. She wasn't going to make it to her morning class.

Throwing off the comforter in a huff, she padded out to her bathroom in the corridor. The kitchen and living room were both empty.

'Oleksiy?'

He wasn't in her bedroom either. His stabilising boot, crutches and coat were gone. Wallet, keys and cell phone were still on his desk. Payal knew he didn't have a doctor's appointment scheduled. He wasn't anywhere within view of their balcony, nor was he anywhere in the building.

She called Mykola, then Oleksiy's mama, then Marisha. None of them had seen or heard from him. Telling Mama and Marisha she'd keep them posted, she told Mykola to search the neighbourhood and set out in the rain to do the same.

She checked every café, bakery and grocery store flanking Brighton Beach Avenue, of which there were many. At the intersection between Brighton Beach Avenue and Ocean Parkway, she started towards Neptune Avenue. On second thought, she headed south to the Riegelmann Boardwalk.

Blustering winds sprayed her with rainfall. The planked path was deserted with the exception of the odd jogger and teenagers playing hooky—no witnesses if someone from a rival bratva spotted her and took her hostage. She batted the thought away along with the water in her eyes.

Past the aquarium, she saw him. A speck of a man. On the sand, wobbling on his crutches, staring out at the thrashing grey waves like a lighthouse keeper forlornly awaiting his mermaid lover.

'Oleksiy!' The wind carried her voice in the wrong direction. She cut across the sand and punched him in the arm. 'What the hell's the matter with you? I've been worried sick!'

Face spattered in rain, he didn't take his eyes off the waves. 'It's a miracle none of us got frostbite.'

'What?' Payal bellowed.

'That's what you said.' He turned to fix her with an expectant gaze. His excitement mounted with every word. 'We were here once, on a wild night on the town, and we got drunk and got kicked off the D. And instead of going home we came here and huddled together on one of these benches because it was late and cold. And when we woke up in the morning, you said, "It's a miracle none of us got frostbite," and I said, "We're lucky we didn't get—"'

'"—picked up by the bratva."' Payal finished.

'So it happened,' Oleksiy's voice pitched high with hope, his black eyes sparkling. 'It really happened. I'm not—I'm not just imagining this stuff. Everything I have going on up here, these are real memories that really happened.'

His face darkened at her pregnant pause.

'What? They're real, right?'

'You did say I was lucky,' Payal said slowly, 'but that wasn't you and me who fell asleep on the bench. That was a story I told you about me and my friends during undergrad.'

Groaning in defeat, Oleksiy pivoted on his good foot and stomped away.

'Oleksiy, this is good,' Payal called after him. 'You're remembering. You're making progress.'

'It's not progress if half the shit I remember is made up.'

'It's not made up! You're just confusing different memories.'

A thunderclap-like growl ripped through Oleksiy's chest as he flung one of his crutches at the water.

'Oleksiy!' Payal cried out, shocked, then livid.

The crutch missed the water by a few feet. By the time she retrieved it, Oleksiy had sunk to his haunches wearing a look of abject despair.

'Get up,' Payal seethed with chilling composure. She dropped the crutch within his reach, and pulled out her phone to call a car. 'We're going home.'

Back at the apartment, straining to contain her anger, she made calls to Mykola and her mother-in-law to let them know she'd found Oleksiy. Oleksiy, in the meantime, plodded over to the couch, stabilising boot and crutches tracking sand everywhere, and sat his sand-dusted behind down.

Payal's right eye twitched. She held out the phone to him. 'Mama wants to speak you.'

'Not now,' he said irritably.

Eyes narrowing, jaw locking, Payal forced a sunny tone. 'Hi, Mama? Yeah, he's wiped out. Can I get him to call you back? Great. Talk to you later. Bye.'

She strummed her fingers on the breakfast counter, waiting for him to deign to look at her. Briefly considered walking away, waiting for this mood of his to blow over. Paced the kitchen, hands palming her face, drawing long, deep breaths.

'You cannot,' she said as evenly as she was able, 'just up and leave like that without telling me.'

'No one asked you to come after me.'

The absolute nerve!

'Oleksiy, you could've fallen down the stairs! Tripped on the street, hit your head again, blacked out, had a goddamn seizure! And Coney Island? Someone from the Berezivka could've seen you. Do you think you could've defended yourself? We wouldn't have had a clue! Why? Why would you do that? How irresponsible do you have to be to leave without taking your phone or your keys or your ID?'

'You got my number?' he asked.

'What?'

'You wanna know where I am at all times, but do you have my number?'

She glared at him. 'I would've had someone call you.'

'Right, well'—with a dour chuckle, he levered himself up onto his feet, spreading more sand on the floor with every tap of his boot and crutches—'everyone in this neighbourhood knows who I am. If something had happened to me, you'da found out soon enough. But as it so happens, I'm doing peachy, so everyone can cool it with the incessant babying.'

'Babying?' Payal snarled.

He ignored her and headed down the corridor to his room.

'Oleksiy!' Payal called after him angrily. Then, huffing out a sigh, she softened her voice. 'Look, I know how hard this is for you. I've been there. I get it. You are an extremely proud and ambitious and independent man, and I get how frustrating it is to be stuck at home like this, to be in pain, all these doctors' appointments and having to rely on others, but—'

'No,' he cut her off, his voice hollow. 'The only thing that frustrates me about any of this is that the woman I'm married to—my wife—doesn't have my phone number.' He gestured at himself with a spiteful smirk. 'And vice versa!'

Lips parted, Payal stared at him.

'How?' he asked, his eyes growing impossibly black.

'How … what?'

'How did we manage to live under the same roof without exchanging numbers?'

Good question. Payal wished she had a satisfactory answer. 'I guess … we just never got to it.'

'How?' Oleksiy pressed, stomping his crutches on the floor, speckling the floor with more sand and catapulting Payal's heart into her throat.

'I don't know! I told you, we don't—our relationship—it's not—*we're* not married like that. We're not a couple that does regular couple-y things.'

'Yeah,' Oleksiy smiled mirthlessly, his gaze so piercing she felt he could see through her, 'that's what you keep telling me. You pull away any time I try to get close and somehow, you're still etched into every fiber of my being. Somehow, I still know you. I—I know your moods, I know the different sounds you make, I know that you wanted to get stars tattooed on your foot, and I know all this sand on the floor is driving you insane, but I can't for the life of me remember why.

'And you keep telling me we're not together like that, and I'm hearing what you're saying, but it's not clicking up here.' Unsteady on his feet, bulging eyes welling, he jabbed at his temple, then his heart. 'And it sure as hell ain't clicking here. Do you have any idea how that makes me feel?'

His lips quivered as he spoke and his control over his crutches faltered. Payal couldn't bear to see him like this, but she was at a loss for what to do.

'You think I don't know "no" means "no"? That I want to be some sick lowlife who strong-arms a woman into saying "yes"? You think I like going through your stuff when you're not around, touching and smelling it like some pervert? You think I like waking up from the most vivid dreams of holding you in my arms when you keep telling me we're not a couple?

'I feel'—he shook his head, voice cracking with shame—'entitled. I need to be yours and you to be mine, and it's eating me alive and I've had it! I'm tired of being this—this reprobate, this monster.'

'No,' Payal gasped in dismay. 'Oleksiy … '

He turned his back to her, shrugged away her consoling touch. Swerving around him, she blocked the way to his room and cupped his face.

'Oleksiy, if anyone's been strong-armed, it's you. You had nothing to gain from this marriage. You were in love with another woman, but you still welcomed me into your home and took care of me and saw to my every need and comfort. And your outlook on the world—Oleksiy, the hope that guides all your art and your work … you inspire me to be better.'

Oleksiy scoffed.

'No, really, you convinced me I could and should do so much more. You, Oleksiy Karmazin, are the sweetest, most wonderful man. You're kind, considerate, compassionate and brave.' Tilting his head up, she looked him in his red-rimmed eyes. 'You are the farthest thing there is to a monster.'

'Says the woman I nearly strangled,' he grimaced.

'That was an accident. I know you'd never hurt me on purpose.'

Oleksiy wasn't convinced. The muscles in his jaw twitched as he studied her long and hard over his nose. Then, just as Payal settled into the quiet stillness between them, he swooped down and claimed her mouth.

His crutches clattered to the floor somewhere. Payal was too stunned, too high-strung, too starved for his touch to tell where. His long, rough fingers seared a trail across her scalp, tugging her hair for better access to her lips. And she arched into him, clasping his face tighter, greedily accepting whatever he had to give. She acquiesced to her mouth being pried open. Waited with tremulous breaths for their kiss to deepen.

He sank his teeth into her bottom lip with a low growl, instead, jolting her, unleashing pieces of herself she'd so laboriously tucked away to the fringes to be ignored and forgotten.

'Still think I'm not a monster?' Oleksiy challenged.

She pressed her lips together, willing the sting of his bite away, but it settled inside her like a steady thrum, a quiet song in the dark, heralding the hope of something a long time coming.

'No,' she whispered, her head swimming.

His mouth was on her again, swallowing her moans, sliding his tongue along hers. He dragged it down her chin to the column of her neck, kissing, licking, sucking and scraping his teeth along the flesh bruised raw by his fingers the night before, heightening her pleasure with tiny bursts of pain, soaking her panties.

'Stop me, Payal. Tell me I'm a disgusting brute. That you never want to see me again.'

The mere suggestion of stopping made her want to weep. Why would he want her to say that? Why wasn't she supposed to be doing this, again? She couldn't remember.

'Do you want to stop?' she panted, blinking rapidly to orient herself.

He gingerly brushed a strand of hair off her face. 'Do you?'

She went still for a long beat. Letting what was happening sink in. Failing to fathom its weight.

Then she answered. With a kiss.

It didn't have to be the final word. She could have changed her mind at any moment. Like when she led him by the hand to his bedroom. Or when he pulled his shirt over his head, and she hers. Or as they pressed their bare chests together in an unhurried hug, drunkenly skimming their fingers over the other's dips and swells and plains and ridges. Or as he nuzzled her hair, and she listened to the rapturous beating of his heart.

Every act was a choice, and the opportunities to stop were endless. But with Oleksiy, here, now, for evermore, backing out seemed inconceivable.

His molten black gaze transfixed her as he grazed his fingertips down the slopes of her neck to her breasts, cupped them, and rolled and plucked her nipples to stiff peaks. He bent down to kiss them, but snapped back up with a sharp inhale and pained wince.

'You okay?' Payal asked, squeezing his shoulders.

'Yeah, fine.' He pulled her toward the bed. 'Too much strain on the foot, is all.'

An anxious squeak escaped Payal as he made to sit on the bed. He caught himself just in time, though. Flashing her a knowing grin, he pulled his sandy sweats down before touching the bed linens. He took off his boot with her help, freed the pants from his casted foot, and pulled her in to stand between his legs.

Payal held her breath as he took in the jagged skin over her stomach. She wasn't self-conscious about her scars. She knew she didn't have to be, not around him. She knew the protectiveness that would flash across his eyes when he saw them up close, knew the tenderness with which he would trace them and kiss them. But knowing didn't make the sensation any less overwhelming. How was it like this? How was his response to her unchanged, even though he'd lost his memories of her?

Kissing the sensitive spot under her navel, he hooked his fingers through the waistbands of her bottoms and pulled them down, running his fingers along her inner thighs on his way up, smirking at how incredibly wet she was. Filling his palms with her butt cheeks, he scooped her onto his lap to kiss her again, flooding her mouth with his breathy moans as she ground herself against his hard length.

He rolled her onto her back. Nipped at her earlobes. Pressed wet, open-mouthed kisses into the crook of her neck. Lapped at her nipples and slid a hand between her legs.

Payal palmed his erection. Reached into his boxers to free it.

'No.' Kissing the back of the offending hand, he set it above her head. His lopsided smirk crinkled the corners of his eyes as if he was staring at the sun. 'I want to learn you first.'

Payal felt as if she was levitating. She bit down on her bottom lip and arched off the crumpled sheets in offering, bucking into his hand as he spread her arousal over her sex, slipped one, then two fingers inside her, and pressed the heel of his palm into her clit.

He didn't need to learn how to pleasure her. He didn't have to remember. He just knew. Because their bond was etched into their souls. Because she was his, and he was hers.

The immensity of that thought did as much to unravel her as his practiced fingers. She curled into his body as the liquid tremors seized her, panted and cried out into his mouth, sank her nails into his flesh and crushed him to her like she would a life jacket in choppy waters.

Reeling him in between her legs, she hummed at the feel of his weight on top of her.

'You okay?' she sighed, ghosting her fingers over the faint bruises around his nose. 'Nothing hurting anywhere?'

'Nah,' he said cockily, enclosing her head between his forearms and bending down to nibble her earlobe.

Payal pushed his boxers down with her toes and snaked her hands between them.

He pulled away abruptly. 'Condom.'

'It's okay,' she cooed, stroking his length. 'I'm on the pill.'

'But I—' His breath faltered as he momentarily lost his train of thought. 'I don't know if I—'

'You don't have anything. Neither of us do.'

His features hardened. 'It's just been you, hasn't it?'

Payal stilled, heart thundering in her ears.

His hand was at her throat again, pressing a thumb into the underside of her chin, giving her nowhere to look but at his formidable, bottomless glower. 'Payal.'

A tear slipped from the corner of her eye. Nearly inaudible, she confessed, 'Yes.'

He thrust into her and kissed her in tandem, the force of his movements knocking the wind from her lungs, the feel of his palpitating muscles on and inside her fanning the heat within.

'Why didn't you tell me?' he groaned into her skin. 'Why are you hiding from me?'

I'm going to get out of your life for good.

Payal's eyes flew open. Her heart plummeted to her stomach, hitting rock bottom with a nauseating *thud*.

And then you can go on and live the life you've always wanted.

She clung to him, burying her face in the crook of his neck, and let him propel her to a second peak. And when he quaked and cried out with his own release, when all his weight collapsed on top of her, she clung even tighter, never wanting to let go.

But she'd made a promise. To a man who deserved better. To the man she loved.

Every act was a choice.

And it was high time she made the right one.

Twenty-One

THERE WAS NO CONTAINING THE blissed-out grin plastered across Oleksiy's face. Crushing Payal to him, he flipped onto his back and planted an effusive, lingering kiss on her forehead.

It was real. Them. Together. All those waking and dreaming visions he'd been having—they weren't fantasies spun from a portrait. Those encounters, those seismic, life-altering feelings that constantly tugged at him—they were memories.

He peered down at Payal. Head laid on his chest, exactly as it should be, she drew absentminded circles on his shoulder. He stroked the damp hair from her face and splayed his palm over her side, feeling the expansion and contraction of her ribs as she breathed.

Her honey-peach scent took him back to a book-flanked corner in a long, dank room where the tiniest *clip-clop* of rickety furniture blared as loud as a police siren.

Seems like living on the wrong side of the law suits you just fine.

Oleksiy bit back a chuckle. 'Did we ever … do it in a public library?'

'Mmm,' Payal purred, the delicious sound reverberating through his chest. 'The Butler Stacks.'

Grin widening further, he kissed each of her fingers and entwined them with his.

'I can't stay,' Payal said after a while.

Oleksiy hugged her tighter, nuzzled deeper into her hair. 'Just a few more minutes. Or hours.'

'No, after finals … I have to leave Brighton Beach.' She propped her chin on his chest, eyes cast down. 'I don't have anything lined up for the summer, so I'll head to my parents' first, look for something closer to school for the fall.'

'Your parents?' Oleksiy frowned. 'Why? Wh—what's wrong with Brighton Beach?'

'Oleksiy.' The solemnity and remorse imbued in his name shot him with cold dread. 'This wasn't supposed to happen.'

'What? Us? No, of course it was. This is the first thing about us that makes any sense. Look, I know you're trying to protect me. I know you don't want to spring a marriage on a guy who doesn't remember getting married, but I *am* remembering and I'm not afraid of being married. Not when it's to you.' He cupped her face, imploring her to meet his gaze. 'We're compatible. We like each other'—major understatement—'you're a saint to me and I promise—'

'Oleksiy, please,' Payal sighed, shrinking from his touch, nudging his arm to let her go.

'—to be the man you deserve.'

'I can't.' Breaking free from his embrace, she slid out of bed and started pulling her clothes back on. 'We can't. We've been down this road before, and you nearly died because of it.'

'I was looking out for you.' Oleksiy dragged himself across the bed and sat up.

'No. You got sucked into the world of thieves. After dodging it your entire life, marrying me threw you straight into the deep end—spying, kidnapping, attempting murder.'

'All for good reason! Look, none of that matters anymore.'

'It mattered to the man I married.'

'Well, fuck that guy. He's not here.'

'But he is.' Insinuating herself back between his legs, she squeezed his shoulders. 'Oleksiy, you're still the same guy with the same heart and the same principles.'

Oleksiy shook his head vehemently.

'You are,' Payal insisted softly. 'You'll see when you get your memories back. And I can't give you a reason to resent me when you do.'

Oleksiy squeezed her hands. 'I could never do that.'

'Sure you can.' Her melancholy smile speared his heart. 'And you will.' She drew a shuddering breath. 'And I'd like to be spared that a second time.'

Her words were like a punch to the gut. They sent him toppling into a crater. A grave. This wasn't a black whirlpool that stripped him of his agency. No, he was free to roam and bury and exhume as he pleased. But he was frozen in the dark. Struck with fear so paralysing, his mouth forgot how to form words.

What had he done for it to come to this?

'Besides,' Payal said with an airy note, 'it doesn't make sense for us to stay married anymore. Kogan's gone and Ruslan gave me full immunity from the Berezivkas.'

'Payal, no, please.' He tightened his grasp when she began to withdraw. 'You can't leave. I'll never get a handle on the time I lost. And what about my family, huh? They've been good to you, haven't they? They love you.' *I love you.* 'And Mykola? You know I can't get that kid ready for the GED all by myself.'

'I'm not leaving this instant, silly. I'm going to get everything in order, make this as easy for you as possible.' Her easy-going façade slipped a hair, betraying her inner conflict. 'But I agreed to honour your wishes, and I intend to keep my word.'

'No.'

'You're going to be fine, Oleksiy. Better than fine. And you're going to carve out the life you always wanted for yourself, free of any bratva entanglement, helping people rise above their circumstances, breaking the endless cycle of discrimination and poverty and crime. You're going to make the world a better place.'

Not without you!

'Now, you put some clothes on.' With a final boop to his nose, she pulled her hands free and padded out the door. 'And help me figure out what to do for lunch. I'm starving.'

Oleksiy stared after her at the empty doorway, skull throbbing, expression vacant.

He was going to lose her and it was all his fault.

God, he *was* a monster.

He had to exhume what was in that crater. He had to remember.

He had to fix this.

Oleksiy knew what it was like to come home to an empty apartment. He remembered the way his lungs and heels burned as he sprinted home in the chilly rain, desperation mounting with every utterance of Payal's name that went unanswered.

The excavation was an infuriatingly stagnant process. He'd uncover the occasional superfluous detail, but most days he didn't even manage that.

There was one memory that kept calling to him. A memory buried deep in his subconscious, under a foreboding mound of hubris and shame. He dwelled on it for hours, searching for pressure points that could crack its rock-hard crust. If only he could blow it to smithereens. But explosions needed triggers, and he didn't know the first place to start looking for one.

He started keeping meticulous journals. Plied Mykola with questions about the days leading up to New Year's Eve. Once the weather and his mobility improved, he ventured out on long, solitary walks around the city, often stopping to draw in a sketchpad he kept on hand. It became something of a coping mechanism as Payal's finals drew closer.

He entertained guilt-tripping her into staying, convincing her he wasn't mentally or physically fit to be left alone by himself. She did say she would make this as easy for him as possible. But he was done being a monster. He didn't want a nurse, he wanted his wife. The only way he was going to get her to stay was by making her want to stay. By convincing her that he was worth staying with.

He was replenishing his art supplies at a place on Flatbush Avenue one afternoon when the poster tubes caught his eye. Did Payal know what she was going to do with her portrait in their storage closet? It wasn't exactly something she could dispose of, and there was no way she was taking it to her parents' mounted in its frame.

That's when it hit him in earnest: he wasn't going to make it in time. Payal really was going to leave Brighton Beach, and the life he'd woken up to, the one he'd accepted, dauntless and without question—the very fabric of his reality was going to splinter beyond repair.

Worst of all, he caught himself reaching for a poster tube. A part of him had already accepted defeat.

Snatching his hand away, he hobbled over to the pencil display and appraised different grades of pencils with a sense of purpose. The tubes lurked in the periphery of his vision, though, watching him, beckoning to him, urging him to give up.

Another customer stepped up beside him, mercifully blocking the tubes from view. Able to hear his thoughts again, Oleksiy made quick work of pulling the pencils he used most often from their respective slots.

'Argh, I never did get these numbers on the pencils,' the customer said, leaning in a little too close for Oleksiy's comfort. The guy was heavyset, maybe a half-foot shorter than him. 'Do they get darker or lighter the higher the number?'

'Erm.' Oleksiy put some distance between them. 'Grades tell you how soft the graphite is. The Bs get softer and darker the higher the number, and Hs get harder and lighter.'

'Sweet.'

Forcing a polite smile, Oleksiy manoeuvered his basket and crutches toward the sketchbooks. The guy followed him. Then stopped when he did.

Last time that had happened, he'd ended up in a van with a bag over his head.

Heart in his throat, he took stock of how many other people there were in the store and how far he was from the exit. Not that any of that mattered. He was on crutches. Even if he managed to get out, there was no way he could outrun this guy.

Of all the days not to bring Mykola along.

He took another few steps toward the sketchbooks. No footfalls trailed him this time.

Oh, thank Jesus. He was just being paranoid. Still, he sneaked a peak over his shoulder to make sure.

The guy was still looking at him, a clownish smirk tilting his hideous bushy mustache sideways. Sliding his oversized '80s-style glasses down his broad, many-a-time-broken nose, he waggled his eyebrows suggestively.

'What the ... ?' Oleksiy steered himself around and narrowed his eyes at the man.

The robust mustache was offset by baldness at the crown of his head. Wispy hair around the sides were gathered in a low ('ponytail' was too generous) rat tail. Under a puffy, faux-fur-collared corduroy jacket, he wore baggy denim overalls stained with grease. Add those glasses to the mix and he looked as sleazy as they came, someone whose presence didn't surprise anyone but spurred everyone to avoid eye contact and pick up their pace. It was the perfect disguise to get around New York City unnoticed.

The nose was a dead giveaway, though. As was the impish twinkle in his eyes.

'Are you following me?' Oleksiy hissed, closing the distance between them.

'Nah, don't flatter yourself.' Ruslan sucked in his bottom lip to suppress his glee. 'Had business in the neighbourhood, and thought I'd come by to pick up a few things.'

'Yeah? The hell's a man like you need from a place like this?'

Ruslan held up a Bob Ross colouring book like a debutante would a hand fan. 'Yoga instructor I was seeing turned me onto them,' he offered in answer to Oleksiy's bemusement. 'It's therapeutic and it hones my aesthetic sensibilities.'

'You're dressed like a vintage porn star crossed with a trucker,' Oleksiy remarked drily.

'Why, thank you.' Ruslan gave his shrivelled rat tail a proud flick. 'Lotta care went into curating this here ensemble.'

Oleksiy struggled to keep a straight face. It'd always been like this with Ruslan: clowning around, laughing at the dumbest things till they were on the verge of tears. Then the son of a bitch had to go sell him out to the Berezivkas. He had no right to make Oleksiy want to laugh.

His old friend's nose looked even more mangled than he remembered. 'I see you've been following your own advice.'

'You and me both, brother. Though, I gotta say'—drawing closer, Ruslan studied Oleksiy's nose from every possible angle—'you got off pretty easy.'

'Yeah, just your run-of-the-mill gunshot wound and near-fatal head trauma. No biggie.'

'Eh,' Ruslan shrugged. 'What's a near-death experience when you get to go on being pretty? Now come on, help me pick out some colouring pencils. I got a pack from the dollar store, and they keep breaking on me.'

Oleksiy considered not obliging. He'd spent years hating this man, refusing to see his side of things, believing he was unworthy of forgiveness. But seeing him again now, speaking to him, he struggled to remember why.

He begrudgingly followed Ruslan to the colour pencil aisle and found him a twelve-pack.

Ruslan whistled when he checked the sticker at the back. 'At this price, they break and I'll sue.' He nodded at Oleksiy's basket. 'Got everything you need?'

Those damn poster tubes were back in Oleksiy's line of vision, peering over Ruslan's shoulder like Victorian waifs from a horror movie. Turning on his good heel, he scurried to the sketchbook aisle.

At the cash counter, Ruslan slid his colouring book and pencils over to the cashier as she processed Oleksiy's purchases. Ignoring Oleksiy's indignant scowl, he flashed her what he must have considered a suave grin. 'These too.'

'Would you like them in a separate bag?' Her voice was pitched lower than when she'd acknowledged Oleksiy.

Ruslan leaned his forearms on the counter. 'Only if it's not too much trouble.'

Biting her bottom lip, the cashier ducked her head to hide her blush.

Seriously? With the glasses and the rat tail and the greasy overalls?

Then again, Oleksiy was no authority on what women wanted. His wife wouldn't be leaving him if he was.

'Right, so … ' he started once they left the store. 'We got what we came for.'

'Sure did,' Ruslan said brightly.

Awkwardly, they headed in the same direction. Oleksiy opened his mouth on several occasions to declare an end to their chance encounter, but stopped himself every time. He could tell Ruslan sensed how conflicted he was. He probably even relished it. What else could explain the aggressively smug spring to his strut?

Then, without a word, he disappeared into a gated garden at the end of the block. Oleksiy stayed standing on the sidewalk, staring at the iron gateway. Maybe the whole situation with Payal was messing with his judgement, or maybe he was still a fifteen-year-old kid at heart, but he was a little crestfallen it was already over.

He missed being around his best friend.

A few moments passed and Ruslan popped his head back out. 'What's the hold up?'

Beaming on the inside, Oleksiy stepped through the gate. A brick path wound around the vacant garden in an irregular loop, flanked by every vibrant spring bloom imaginable. New leaves sprouted on the branches overhead, casting swaying, delicately patterned shadows pierced by sparkling sunshine on the lush foliage below. Ruslan led him to a semi-circular extension of the path. A brick-backed bench traced its curve, and a pine oak and silver maple tree by the iron fencing kept it hidden from passers-by on the street.

Oleksiy eyed the spot, then Ruslan, then the rest of the garden for signs of suspicious movement.

'Relax.' Ruslan got comfortable on the bench, splaying an arm over its back. 'Nobody's out to nab you.'

Oleksiy remained standing, swaying back and forth on his crutches.

'So, how's it going?' Ruslan asked. 'You look good. Up and about, hair growing back in—lemme tell ya, bald was not a good look on you.'

Said the man sporting a rat tail with a combover.

'Hey,' Oleksiy said, suddenly keen to pick a fight. 'You broke my arm.'

'Ugh, this again.' Ruslan rolled his eyes. 'Yeah, what about it? If I'd shown up so much as two seconds later on New Year's Eve, they'da been scraping your brains off of Kogan's wall. Face it, C, I saved your life. I put a bullet in him for you. I cleaned up after you. If anyone's keeping score, you're the one who owes me, not the other way around.'

'So, what, I'm supposed to pay you back in colouring books now?' The words made Oleksiy cringe before they finished leaving his mouth.

Snickering, Ruslan cocked his head to the side in mock-contemplation. 'I mean, you're not exactly good for much else, what with your commitment to staying on the right side of the law.' He waited for his laughter to subside before adding, 'But, hey, seriously, I'm not expecting any favours. Anything I do for you, I do it 'cause you're a brother.'

'Oh right, a brother,' Oleksiy said sarcastically. 'Because that's what brothers do, watch you get the shit kicked out of you, six to one, then join in to get in with the cool kids.'

'Please,' Ruslan snorted. 'Like you'da done it any different.'

'I'd have stood up for you. I'd have put my neck on the line defending you.'

'Not in my shoes you wouldn't.' Ruslan leaned forward to rest his elbows on his knees. 'My dad's not a vor, C. I couldn't afford to have your morals. Still can't, most days.'

You can't imagine . . .

Payal's face drifted before his eyes, raising her head up from his chest, smiling.

You're so privileged . . .

She stood before him, her glistening eyes imploring, lips quivering, breaths coming out in hiccups. Her hurt morphing into anger in a blink.

But you never stop to think about the dumb luck letting you make your choices.

'Most of us are just doing what we gotta do, you know. To survive,' Ruslan continued, oblivious to the colour draining from Oleksiy's face. 'Working a crooked system to our advantage.'

Steadying his balance, Oleksiy blinked rapidly to dull the throbbing around his eye sockets. 'Doing a whole lot better than getting by, from what I hear.'

'Yeah, it took a good few years, but I've carved out a place for myself. Gotten a good bit easier to manage, too, since Kogan.'

'You're welcome,' Oleksiy said haughtily.

'No, *you're* welcome, smart-ass.'

Alice never lied to me, Oleksiy heard himself roar, *She didn't work for the enemy. She never lured me to bed to get to my family.*

A ruthless lightning bolt tore through him, striking the impenetrable mound inside him, hitting him with a violent wave of nausea.

'Whoa, whoa.' Ruslan sprang to his feet to catch Oleksiy before he lost his balance. 'You okay?'

Oleksiy allowed himself to be led to the bench. 'Fine. Just a headache. Been getting a lot of them since I came to.'

'You got anything for it?'

Oleksiy shook his head, then winced at the spike in pain the tiny motion triggered. 'Too many painkillers risk more headaches from withdrawal. Doctor said to just ride it out.'

'Ah, all right.'

The peaceful silence that followed, accompanied by the twitter of birds and the steady whirr of passing cars, was the antithesis of the hell waging inside Oleksiy. The mound was crumbling, suffocating his senses with noxious fumes, laying bare the hideous thing that resided within.

It was a fossil, a creature long dead. An abomination. Even in its miserable, rotting, lifeless state, the heinous things he'd said to Payal—things he'd since regretted—still secreted poison.

As though hearing the train of his thoughts, Ruslan asked, 'So how's the old lady?'

Oleksiy could have screamed in agony. 'Don't think she's gonna stay my old lady much longer.'

It wasn't conjecture anymore. It was plain fact.

'Why's that?'

Oleksiy let his head fall back with a resigned sigh. 'Some jackass gave her immunity from the thing she needed me to protect her from.'

'No,' Ruslan remarked in disbelief. 'Well, shit, man, say the word and I'll take it back. Not that that makes any sense. Last I saw her, sis was ready to take a bullet for you.'

Oleksiy whipped his head around, paying no heed to the skewering pain that ensued. 'You pointed a gun at her?'

'No, of course not! But she'da done it all the same. Girl like that's not just in it for the perks.'

I want you gone. Out of here. Now.

Bile rose up Oleksiy's throat. He shuttered his eyes, begging for some relief from both the blinding pain and shame. 'I might notta been the man she deserved.'

'So be him now,' Ruslan said, simply.

Through narrow, twitching eyes, Oleksiy fixed him with a murderous glower.

Ruslan shrugged. 'Hey, all I'm saying is, if you find someone who gets you, someone who sticks by you and accepts you for everything you are, no matter how fucked up, ah … that shit's for keeps, man. I'd suck it up and do whatever it takes to make her stay. Girls like yours, they don't come in large supply. Believe me, I've looked.'

'What, little miss yogi-who-likes-to-colour didn't cut it?'

'Naw, man,' Ruslan said with a heavy sigh. 'You can't mindfully breathe your way through the shit I deal with. Need someone who'll just ... be there, you know. I dunno, sometimes I'm not even sure I have a family on my cards. This world of thieves, it's not safe for innocents. But it sure does get lonely.'

'Yeah.'

A comfortable silence filled the space between them. Oleksiy was familiar with the faraway look in Ruslan's eyes, the plaintive note in his words. They'd often spoken of similar things when they were kids, sharing their hopes, frustrations and fears. Amazing how much time had passed, but they'd still managed to pick up where they left off.

'I do get why you did it, by the way,' Oleksiy eventually said. 'That day in the alley. I didn't want to admit it because I'd lost my best friend and I wanted to make it about me, but I do. I get it.'

Ruslan waved him off.

'And thank you,' Oleksiy added. 'For saving my life.'

Later, after making plans to meet again and parting ways, Oleksiy returned to the art supplies store for the poster tube. He was ready to do as Ruslan said, ready to do what he had to. But not to make Payal stay. He had no right to expect that any longer. Some things, once said out loud, were simply too unforgivable to let bygones be bygones.

He was ready to give her the last word, ready to accept whatever fate she dealt him.

Twenty-Two

PAYAL STEPPED ASIDE TO LET MYKOLA PASS with a stack of dessert bowls and spoons, then continued hovering by the doorway, watching his mama and teenage sister manoeuvering around each other in their sliver of a kitchen as they cleared away dishes and plated dessert.

Mykola had passed the GED. By a whopping one point. It wasn't anything to write home about by Payal and Oleksiy's standards, but it was enough for a certificate which was enough to enroll in community college. His mama, Alla, was over the moon, and had invited them over for a celebratory dinner.

'I wish you'd let me help,' Payal said from the kitchen's threshold. She didn't want to enter the narrow space without express invitation for fear of being more of a nuisance than of assistance.

'Nonsense, you're our guest,' Alla said. 'Everything's under control here.'

Arms fidgeting at her sides, Payal ambled about their modest living room. At the dining table, Oleksiy angled himself sideways to stretch his legs. She caught him following her movements, but rather than look away, he flashed her a warm smile, his gaze steadfast.

Something had come over him since he got her the poster tube for her portrait, the act in itself catching her off guard. The unrelenting exasperation he'd radiated since she'd decided to leave had quieted and seemingly given way to acceptance and peace. Maybe he'd realised his attachment to her had more to do with his reluctance to endure modern dating again than it did with having actual feelings for her.

If that was the case, Payal wished she could convince herself of the same. With only two days left before she moved out, the reality of life without Oleksiy was only just beginning to set in. It made her antsy, borderline desperate. She leaped at every opportunity to bask in his steady, sturdy presence, to be the reason the corners of his eyes creased, to get one last hit of his scent . . .

... to press her arm flush against his as they all squeezed around the compact garden table shouldering a dinner for five.

She scavenged them all, stowing them away for the many rainy days she knew were ahead.

Mykola's sister, Inessa, served everyone a slice of almond peach cake. Alla poured out the fruit tea, then tried some of the shrikhand Payal had made for the occasion.

'Mmm,' she remarked, contemplatively swirling her spoon in the creamy dessert. Payal had coloured it pink with a dollop of Rooh Afza. 'It's a sort of nutty cheesecake.'

Well, she wasn't wrong. Payal had used cream cheese instead of hung curd and Rooh Afza instead of saffron. Her ancestors must've been rolling in their graves. 'Kind of, yeah. With cardamom powder for aroma instead lemon zest.'

'We have something similar.' Alla helped herself to some more. 'Syrnyk. It's goat cheese, sugar and eggs, and then we bake it, exactly like New York cheesecake. Do you enjoy cooking or do you prefer takeout?'

'We get takeout sometimes, yeah,' Oleksiy said, briefly glancing at Payal. 'But Payal's mama sends us a week's worth of home-cooked food at the beginning of every week.'

'And Oleksiy's an excellent cook too.' Payal's heart fluttered at the shift of Oleksiy's arm as he drew a breath.

'Oh, that's very good. That's how it should be, husbands and wives sharing this kind of work.'

Payal sensed Alla's words were more for her children's benefit than hers and Oleksiy's.

'You take care of the home,' Alla continued, 'and you take care of each other. And when you do that you have the peace of the mind, and that's happiness, I think. Not money, not fancy cars or Rolexes or property in the Hamptons, no, no, no.'

Mykola rolled his eyes and muffled his groan with a forkful of cake.

'Mrs Karmazin,' Inessa piped up. 'When did you start studying for the SATs?'

Earlier in the evening, Alla had mentioned Inessa was getting decent grades at school and that she'd developed a liking for geography and math. But despite several prompts from her mother, the teenager had been too shy to speak to Payal until now.

Payal nearly choked on her cake. 'Please call me Payal. And I don't know, I think I did two practice tests before giving the test. Got a really bad score, then studied really hard for about three months and took the test again.'

Inessa's face darkened with a dismayed frown. 'But a test's like, fifty bucks a pop.'

'Right.' *Way to flaunt your privilege, Payal.* Mortified, she clasped the closest thing her hand could find. 'Which is exactly why you shouldn't do what I did. You're a sophomore, right? This summer would be the best time to start. Trust me, don't leave it till the school year starts. You're never going to get four-hour stretches to practice. Tell you what, why don't I order the books so you can get started as soon as school's out for the summer? Yeah, that's what we should do.'

'Oh, Payal, no,' Alla said. 'You and Oleksiy have already done so much for Mykola. We cannot accept.'

'No, please, it'd be my pleasure.' Payal smiled at Inessa. 'And you can come to me if you ever have any questions about the test or about college or looking for scholarships and internships. Anything. No such thing as a stupid question.'

And Payal sincerely hoped she took her up on the offer. It was only a matter of time before Inessa grew into her rangy frame and sharp features. Pretty, impressionable girls were always going to be at high risk in a neighbourhood teeming with thieves. Payal had no doubt Mykola and Alla and maybe even Oleksiy would look out for her, but she could still help. Show her what was out there, keep her on course for a better future.

'How's she supposed to do that if you're gone?' Mykola asked sourly.

'It's not like I'm moving to another country. I—' Glancing down, Payal realised she'd been gripping Oleksiy's hand this entire time. And he'd been holding it back, rubbing circles on the back of her palm with his thumb. He loosened his grip before she tried to tug free, allowing her to discretely slide her hand down to her lap. 'I'll only be a short train ride away. And there's always e-mail and phone.'

A quiet, close-lipped chuckle escaped Oleksiy.

'You're moving?' Alla's brows furrowed. 'But Mykola didn't mention anything. Where to?'

Oleksiy's parents, gracious as they had been in accepting her decision, felt it best she left quietly. There would be speculation about her prolonged absence, of course, but the Karmazin family would be spared the embarrassment associated with divorce. With enough time, Brighton Beach would forget there had ever been an Indian girl called Payal who was married to the Kotovsk's prince. The mere notion would seem preposterous.

'I haven't decided yet,' Payal replied. 'But most probably somewhere on the Upper West Side, to be closer to school. I'm expecting a more difficult course load next semester so a short commute would save me a lot of time.'

'It'll be a long commute for you, though, to get to Channel Fitness,' Alla said to Oleksiy, impressed. 'It's very good of you, putting your wife's studies before your own convenience.'

'I, uh ... ' Oleksiy shifted in his seat. 'I won't be going with her.'

'Oh. Two apartments. In New York. Oh, my.' To Payal, she asked, 'And how many years until your graduation?'

'One year.'

'Oh!' Alla breathed a sigh of relief. 'Then you'll be back home in Brighton Beach before you know it.'

'Ugh, Mama!' Mykola's fist slammed onto the table.

Stilling the rattling table, Alla shot her son a reproachful glare. 'Get up,' she hissed. 'Get the *podarunok* from my room.'

Mykola pushed away from the table with a petulant huff and stomped down the corridor.

'Your cake's lovely, Alla,' Payal said to fill the awkward silence. 'I adore peach.'

That amused Oleksiy for some reason. She could feel him smiling his lopsided little smile beside her.

Mykola returned with a large, flat, gift-wrapped box. He held it out to his mother, who exasperatedly gestured for him to give it to Payal.

'A little thank you present,' Alla explained, 'for all that you've done for my son.'

'Oh, Alla,' Payal said, picking the tape off the wrapping paper. 'You shouldn't have gone to the trouble.'

Inside the box lay a ceramic decorative plate. Painted on it was a nest of fern leaves in which two little birds sat on either side of a flower the colour of flames.

'Wow!' Payal handed Oleksiy the plate to appreciate. 'This is gorgeous! Thank you.'

'The fern flower is very difficult to find, you see,' Alla said. 'It only blooms once a year at a very specific time. We have a saying that the couple who finds it will be showered in an abundance of riches. You two are a strange, unusual match. Like the fern flower, you've been a blessing to everyone around you, truly. It's my prayer that you stay like this, beautiful and healthy and happy together so you can keep watching over the rest of us.'

Hands trembling, with a sob caught in her throat, Payal returned the plate to its box.

'Thank you, Alla,' Oleksiy said, his voice hoarse. 'You give us too much credit.'

Payal and Oleksiy walked home at a glacial pace that night, even though they were both naturally brisk walkers. It wasn't on account of Oleksiy's foot, which was mostly healed and only necessitated crutches on uneven terrain. Nor was it the weather, which was finally getting warmer after a few false starts. They did it because this was it. Every step they took together was one step closer to their last.

Their living room was cluttered with moving boxes. Payal hadn't planned on taking anything other than her suitcases and books, but Oleksiy insisted she go through their wedding presents and pack whatever she'd need for her apartment.

'Why waste money on buying stuff you've already got, right?' he'd said.

Smart man.

Payal removed Alla's present from its box. It had a cavity at the back so it could be hung from a nail.

Rounding the moving boxes, she took down Oleksiy's sketch of her on the wall and replaced it with the plate.

'There.' Feeling Oleksiy's eyes on her, she asked, 'What do you think?'

'Alla meant for you to have it.'

'She gave it to you too. It should be here where you can see it. So you remember why you do what you do. How important it is and how loved and revered you are because of it.'

She flashed him a warm smile, then looked down at the framed sketch of her. 'Mind if I keep this?'

He didn't answer. She slipped it into a box anyway. Then, planting her hands on her hips for strength, she turned her back to him and surveyed the entertainment unit for anything left to pack.

Their wedding portrait stared back at her. The photo was inconsequential—she had them all backed up on a hard drive—but the frame Oleksiy had gone out of his way to engrave with their names, fooling her into thinking, if only for a few blissful days, that they were meant to be . . .

'I'll keep that one.' Oleksiy was at her side. 'If that's all right with you.' He removed the frame from her grasp and put it back. Then, moved closer. 'In case the plate's not enough of a reminder.'

Payal's eyelashes fluttered at the feel of his breath against her face. The depth of his voice and the heat rolling off of him reeled her in towards him. It *was* rare—what they had. And she was nowhere near the same vicinity of being prepared to sever the cord connecting them.

She could never get enough of him, never stop needing him.

Just one last whiff of his scent, one last brush of his fingertips, one last kiss.

'Payal ... '

His proximity stole her breath away, made her burn for his touch, and his pitch-black eyes invited her to spend the rest of eternity in their oblivion.

He waited, unmoving. What happened next was up to her. Her choice.

And she'd promised the man she married she'd make the right one.

'No, of course, it's all right.' Pulling away, she sidestepped `him and marched to her room. 'Goodnight, Oleksiy.'

Twenty-Three

PAYAL TOOK IN THE LIVING ROOM FROM HER perch at the breakfast counter. The space looked a whole lot bigger without the moving boxes and her desk.

Moving day. Well, evening. Nasir had arrived to pick her up hours ago, but she had to return her keys and Oleksiy still wasn't back from work.

She also had to give him the thick manila envelope carrying their divorce papers.

But mostly she just wanted to see him one last time. Say goodbye.

Her phone vibrated.

'Hi Mumma,' Payal answered.

'Hi, how far have you reached?'

'Oh, umm, I'm still at Brighton Beach,' Payal said guiltily.

'You haven't—? But Nasir set out a long time ago. Everything all right?'

'No, no, everything's fine. I just need to give Oleksiy the keys.'

'Okay, well, don't take too long. You'll be late for dinner.'

'Yeah, sorry, I'll be on my way soon.' Payal rubbed her brow. 'See you in a bit. Bye.'

Hanging up, she checked the time. He should've been home two hours ago.

Another fifteen minutes passed.

Maybe he wasn't running late. Maybe staying away was his way of saying goodbye. It was a kindness, really. For their mutual dignity.

She left the envelope on the breakfast counter, switched off all the lights and locked up. The keys could be mailed later. Downstairs, Nasir sprang out of her parents' car and held the door open for her.

'Payal!'

She whirled around.

There he was, tall and elegant and handsome as ever, striding up the street in one of his impeccably tailored charcoal suits and a maroon tie. His eyes glimmered like black gems, bathing her in warmth, filling her heart to the point of bursting.

'Payal, hey,' he said softly, timidly. He drank her in, mouth frozen in a half smile. 'Gonna be real weird, not saying your name.'

Heart pounding feverishly, Payal blinked to break the spell he cast on her. 'You came.'

'Yeah, sorry, I thought I'd wait until after rush hour.'

Payal's brows pulled together in confusion. What did rush hour have to do with him walking three blocks? Had he gone to meet a client somewhere?

It didn't matter. She had to get away from him before her brittle resolve gave way.

'Here.' She handed him the keys to their—no, his—apartment. 'And—uh—there's an envelope on the counter. It's stamped and addressed, so if you could just sign it, we can … you know … '

'Gotcha.'

'Okay, then, I guess I'll just … ' She anxiously tucked her hair behind both her ears. 'Good luck, Oleksiy. With everything. I wish the world for you, every happiness, every dream you've ever had. Take care of yourself and umm … try staying out of any more life-threatening situations.'

'Afraid I can't promise that, Payal,' Oleksiy said with a roll of his shoulder, smirking at how her face fell. 'Comes with the territory. But hey, how 'bout we go somewhere, hm? One last hurrah before bringing the curtains down on … us.'

Yes, please.

Payal drew away, shaking her head. 'I really should get going.'

'Come on.' Moving closer, he bowed his head to be at eye level with her. 'Give me a reason to say your name a couple more times. Your parents mind if we take their car?'

'Their car? Wh-where … ?'

'You'll see,' he said with a mischievous wink. 'Come on.'

Once inside the car, he told Nasir to head for the Battery Tunnel.

'Sir said to bring Apa home,' Nasir said brusquely.

Payal looked from Nasir's disapproving eyes in the rear-view mirror to Oleksiy and back. 'Go. I'll let Papa know we'll be late.'

'You know,' she said to Oleksiy, tapping out a text to her parents. 'It'd be easier explaining this to them if you told me where we were going.'

'I know. But then it won't be a surprise.'

Payal smiled in spite of herself. This was infinitely worse than if he hadn't shown up. Parting ways was going to be agonising now. Why was he so intent on making this so difficult for her?

Once out of the tunnel, Nasir took them up FDR Drive. More and more of the East River whipped past them, yet Oleksiy refused to share which exit to take. Payal began to suspect there was no destination, that they were still headed to Scarsdale, but by a roundabout route so he could steal a few more moments with her.

Then he undid his tie and shuffled closer.

'Okay,' he raised the tie to her eyes. 'Put this on.'

'What?' She swatted at his hand. 'Why?'

Oleksiy smoothed the cool fabric over her eyes. 'You'll see soon enough.' Reinforcing it with a knot at the back of her head, he asked, 'How many fingers am I holding up?'

'How would I know?'

'Perfect.'

He told Nasir to take the next exit and became more forthright with directions from thereon. Payal should have been able piece together where they were headed, but the lack of visual cues made it exasperatingly difficult.

She made to pull the blindfold off when Nasir parked the car.

Oleksiy stilled her hand. 'Not yet.'

'Oleksiy … '

Sounds of a busy city street flooded the car as Oleksiy got out.

'Oleksiy!'

The door on her side opened. Oleksiy took her hand and guided her out. 'I got you.'

Reluctantly allowing herself to be led, she frantically pawed about with her free hand for something—a wall, maybe, or a guardrail—to hold on to, inadvertently smacking someone in the face. 'Oh! Oh God, I'm so sorry!'

'It's okay, it's okay.' Oleksiy came up behind her like a turtle shell, shielding her from passing pedestrians and steering her with light squeezes to her arm and nudges to her back.

He pressed closer to reach for something in front of her—a door . . . that revolved. A burst of cool air and they were inside a lobby of some kind. With high ceilings, judging by the echoes. Oleksiy exchanged pleasantries with someone. Then, after some more steering, he came to a halt. There were people around them speaking a myriad of languages.

'Can I take this off now?'

Oleksiy gave her shoulders a gentle squeeze. 'Just a bit longer.'

The firm breadth of his chest brushed her back. Yeah, she could do with a bit longer. Angling her head over her shoulder, she sank further back into his warmth, wanting to be held closer, to feel his nose trace up the slope of her neck till his lips found hers, to twist in his embrace till they were flush against each another . . .

Snapping back to her senses in the nick of time, she gasped, 'Oleksiy, your crutches!'

The close-mouthed chuckle in her ear seeped into her bloodstream like warm, decadent syrup. 'I'm good.' Enveloping her in his arms properly, he said, 'I got all the support I'll ever need.'

An elevator's melodious *ding* bounced off the high walls. Doors slid open and people shuffled around them in a hurry. Oleksiy manoeuvered Payal around the others. His embrace was unyielding the entirety of the lengthy ride up.

'Okay, watch your step now,' he said once they finally got out.

'Oleksiy, where—?' Icy wind whipped at her, knocking the air from her lungs. She backed into him and clutched his arms. They were out in the open. Exposed. Maybe unsafe? And why did she feel short of breath? 'What's going on? Where are we?'

'Just a few steps this way, and—' Unwinding his arms, he thrust her into a world of panic by stepping out of her reach. 'Okay, you can look now.'

Payal yanked the tie from her eyes. Spun around to lock on to Oleksiy. Then registered the dazzling bird's-eye view of the city behind him.

They were on a brick walkway flanked on one side by a parapet made taller with metal fencing. Payal had never come here in person, but she'd seen it and its coin binoculars in countless movies and TV shows. Lost for words, she stumbled towards the parapet, then turned her back to the city to peer up at the brightly-lit spire that rose several more storeys from the observation deck's centre.

Oleksiy had brought her to the Empire State Building.

He offered her half a shrug and a rueful grin. 'Figured we could make good on at least one of our plans.'

'You … ' Payal blinked away the sting in her eyes, swallowed the lump rising up her throat. 'You remember.'

Oleksiy nodded. A long beat later, he added, 'Everything.'

Payal drew a sharp breath and nodded in one final, humiliating admission of defeat. *Everything.* The word hit her like a ton of bricks. Good thing then, that she was leaving when she was.

'You were right about me,' Oleksiy said. 'I *am* a clown.'

Pursing her lips to quell their trembling, Payal frowned.

'But not because I kept coming back to you. No.' Oleksiy drew closer. 'Never that. Those horrible, despicable, unforgivable things I said to you that night—the night we—that I found out about Kogan's hit on you … I should've been there for you, supported you, held you and loved you and promised to protect you. But, instead, I—' He winced in anguish, his voice so hoarse, Payal could barely hear it. 'There's no excuse for the things I said that night. I was the cowardliest of cowards. An egotistical asshole. And I'm ashamed of myself, and you're completely right to leave, but God, it kills me that I'm never gonna make up for it.'

'Oleksiy, you don't have to make up for anything,' Payal said. 'I shouldn't have kept those things from you. It was your life too, and you had every right to know.' She cupped one side of his face. 'I'm not leaving to punish you. I'm doing it so you can have your agency back. So you can decide your future for yourself, be with someone who's not bratva-chosen, build a life where you're not answerable to the bratva in any way.'

'And what if I told you that's never going to happen?' he asked, his pitch-black eyes wide and glistening. 'What if there's no scenario where I'll ever be fully free from the bratva, even with you gone?

'Payal.' He turned his face into her palm to kiss it. 'Payal, Payal, Payal, Payal, Payal.' He reverently drew both her hands to his heart. 'I'd fooled myself into thinking I was better than everyone else for helping out. That a clean break would give me the moral high ground. But my work isn't about proving myself. It's about helping others. I was an idiot to think I could cut the bratva out of my life. I'd tried doing it with Alice, but no matter how rotten the roots, I can't deny who I am. And I don't want to. Because doing that discounts my purpose. And it discounts everyone who's ever helped me get to where I am today. And you were right. The world of thieves might be a cesspit of crime and violence, but I've had the privilege of knowing everything that's good in it, the biggest of them being my wife.

'Payal.' Her name carried in the wind like anklet bells chiming in an empty hall. 'You say I inspire you, but you, Payal—you inspire *me*. To stay fearless and kind and generous in the face of adversity. To do the right thing, no matter how ugly the consequences. To *choose* to make the best of what we've got, every time, every day. It shoulda been a no-brainer, but I was a clown. You're the one, Payal. My anchor, my guiding light, the embodiment of all my dreams. I was just too proud to admit it.

'I love you, Payal. I've loved you since that sweaty afternoon we stuffed our faces with hot dogs at the beach. And I woke up from that coma remembering nothing except that I love you. I know I don't deserve to be forgiven for what I said that night, but I need you to know that, from the bottom of my heart, I'm sorry. I was out of line, and if I could, I'd go after a hundred other Kogans—'

'No.' Payal shook her head.

'—if it meant I could take it back.'

'No, no, Oleksiy stop. I don't want that.' Payal shook him by his lapel. 'I can't see you get hurt again. Don't you ever do something that stupid again. Promise me. Please?'

Oleksiy looked down at their hands joined atop his chest. 'I want you to be happy, Payal. So I'm just going to ask you this one last time.' Releasing her hands, he took a step back and straightened to his full height, as though waiting his turn at the gallows. 'I'll accept your answer, whatever it is.'

The loss of his touch left her legs feeling unsteady. She stared at him with bated breath.

His voice cracked. 'Stay?'

Payal bit back the reply that sprang to the tip of her tongue, instead asking, 'Is that what the Oleksiy I married wants? No takebacks.'

'No takebacks.'

Too afraid it was all a dream to crack a smile, Payal dipped her chin in something akin to a nod.

Oleksiy's shoulders slumped with relief. 'Yes?'

'Yes,' Payal sobbed, throwing herself at him and showering his face with kisses. 'Yes, yes, yes!'

Oleksiy folded her in his arms as he kissed her back, every press of his lips more effusive than the last.

'No more secrets,' Payal promised.

'No more secrets,' Oleksiy hummed, coming back for a deep, unhurried kiss. 'And no more using Mykola as a carrier pigeon. We text each other like normal couples from now on.'

Payal giggled into his mouth. 'Deal.'

They lost themselves in each other's arms, unperturbed by the looks tourists shot their way. It never had mattered what others thought about them. Theirs was a match everyone had believed was a bad idea from the start. But time and again, they'd defied the odds. The rarest flowers did bear the greatest fortune, after all.

When they eventually came up for air, Payal lazily nuzzled Oleksiy's nose, basking in being held by him again. 'I love you.'

Grinning that grin that creased the corners of his eyes, Oleksiy tucked her hair behind her ears and kissed her forehead. 'I'll be worthy of it. I promise.'

Epilogue

A Year and A Half Later

THE CHATTER OF THE GUESTS IN THE LIVING room receded to the fringes of Oleksiy's attention. Meat thermometer in hand, he stood at the ready as Payal lowered the oven door and pulled out the rack holding their Thanksgiving turkey. The bird was cooked to a glossy reddish brown, its rich juices sizzling and giving off a mouth-watering, citrusy aroma of sweet maple. Resisting the urge to burn his finger for a taste, Oleksiy skewered the thermometer's needle into the turkey's breast.

'Don't let it touch the bone,' Payal said, clumsily removing the aluminum foil they'd tented over the legs with a knife and a pair of tongs.

She was on edge, hair frizzed and T-zone coated in a thin film of sweat, even though she'd planned every last detail down to the tee. Try as Oleksiy did to assure her everything would be all right, he also gave her a wide enough berth to go through the motions. Dissuaded by the demands of her dissertation and course load the year before, this was their first time hosting a proper joint family dinner. They were serving a spread neither of them had any experience cooking, and Payal's mumma believed so little in their combined culinary skills that she'd brought along four casserole dishes of food, 'just in case.' The nerves were warranted.

Oleksiy squatted low and tilted his head sideways to read the temperature. 'One-fifty, fifty-five, sixty-four, sixty-seven and … one seventy-one.'

'And the thigh?'

He stuck the thermometer into the thigh. 'One ... seventy—no, eighty-two.'

'Yeah, that's done.'

Donning oven mitts, Oleksiy took the turkey out and set it aside to rest. Payal readjusted the racks, moved the mac and cheese to the top and slid the pan of seasonal vegetables to roast in the bottom. On the stove, a pot of butternut squash soup and a smaller pot of mushroom gravy were set over low flames. Oleksiy suspected Payal intended to stand watch and stir till they came to a simmer.

'Can't forget our guests, pussycat.' He pried the wooden spoons from her hands and gently extricated her from the kitchen. 'Come on.'

Saira rose from her seat between Payal's mumma and Marisha. She'd put on *Miss Congeniality* to tide the two families through awkward lulls in the conversation. 'You guys want some apple cider?'

'Yeah, that'd be great.' Oleksiy caressed the small of Payal's back, entreating her to sit. 'Thanks, Saira.'

'Turkey looks good,' Marisha remarked, heading to the kitchen to admire their handiwork. '*Smells* incredible.'

'Yeah, well.' Oleksiy raised the glass Saira handed him in a toast. 'Here's hoping it's edible. Though I expect glowing reviews from everyone even if it isn't.'

The entertainment unit was decked in fall leaves, acorns, hand-sized pumpkins and bouquets of wheat stems for the occasion. Oleksiy righted the photo frames nestled among them—their wedding portrait and a photo from their honeymoon in Granada the summer before last—on his way to join Tato and Payal's papa at the far end of the room. Grigori was out on the balcony taking a call.

'Payal's tato was just saying there's a property over at Bath Beach you might be interested in,' Tato said before Oleksiy could sit himself down.

'Oh.' Taking a chug of his cider, Oleksiy nodded at Payal's papa with feigned interest. 'That's a great neighbourhood. But I'm gonna hold off launching another Channel Fitness branch for the time being. I've already got my hands full with the Sheepshead Bay launch, and with Payal working such long hours, I don't want to spend any more time apart than we already do.'

The Center for an Urban Future had recruited Payal in her final semester at graduate school. She and her team were currently hard at work supplying legislators with statistical evidence proving that the New York Power Authority could directly power all state- and municipal-owned properties and public transport with renewable energy within a few short years. She was also developing models to explore the long-term cost reductions and societal benefits that could result from low-income neighbourhoods transitioning to renewables.

She was Oleksiy's pride and joy, living up to her full potential just as he strived to live up to his. And though there were days he wished their schedules weren't so gruelling, days he dreamed about spending entire mornings and afternoons lounging about the apartment, holding her in his arms, he wouldn't have had it any other way. Their work could make a difference. However small, it was important.

'It's your life.' Tato shrugged as if he'd expected Oleksiy to brush him off. 'Still, the property's coming cheap and, depending on what your long-term expansion strategy is, it would be the next logical step.'

Oleksiy's long-term plans were more concerned with welfare than profit. He wasn't interested in owning an expansive chain of fitness centres. Doing so would draw precious time, energy and resources away from what he really wanted to do, which was saving people from the bratva. He had to diversify his ventures, create more opportunities for the residents of Brighton Beach and its neighbouring areas. The security firm was picking up steam, having acquired a few medium-term contracts in the Garment and Financial Districts over the last year. He and Payal were also looking into starting a scholarship fund and collaborating with mentorship programmes for at-risk youth. Tiny steps. Nothing too drastic. Persistent in their efforts till the changes stuck.

'I'll have a think about it,' he said, hopefully laying the matter to rest for the time being.

The downstair door's buzzer went off, rescuing him from any more unsolicited advice.

Then again, a little unsolicited advice was preferable to Tato and Grigori never speaking to him again, which could very well happen after tonight.

Oleksiy catapulted himself off his seat, tripping over his own feet as he reached to press the door release button.

'Careful, Oleksiy,' Mama chided.

'Come on up,' Oleksiy said into the microphone, holding the button down for a long moment.

Ignoring Grigori's re-appearance in the living room, he made a show of checking on the soup and gravy.

Payal appeared at his side, whispering, 'It's going to be fine.'

'Yeah. Fine.' He pulled her face in for a desperate, steeling kiss. 'We got this.'

'Eh,' she shrugged, unconvinced.

Oleksiy shook his head wryly. 'Terrible.'

'The absolute worst.'

A knock at the door startled them both. On the other side stood Ruslan, out of disguise, as his strapping, debonair self; bearing a pie box in one hand and a reversible jacket in the other. He launched into his charm offensive without missing a beat, kissing Payal a little too close to her mouth. 'Hey there, Payal. Happy Thanksgiving.'

'Happy Thanksgiving, Ruslan,' Payal said, smitten. 'Here, let me get your coat.'

He impishly sucked on his bottom lip as he turned to Oleksiy. 'Happy Thanksgiving, C.'

Sighing in good-humoured exasperation, Oleksiy bumped fists with him and drew him in for a one-armed hug. His arm stayed around him as he led him to the living room. 'Everyone, this is my old friend, Ruslan.'

A frigid stillness gripped the room. Sandra Bullock and Michael Caine's banter on TV exacerbated the torturous seconds during which nobody dared utter a peep. Mama fixed Oleksiy with a weary look. Grigori's ghoulish blue eyes turned murderous, and Marisha shuffled closer to set a quelling hand on her husband's thigh. Tato assessed the situation calmly, ankle crossed over knee, elbow on armrest, finger pensively tracing his mouth.

Then there was Saira. Eyes flitting around the room to gauge if it was okay to ogle the new arrival.

Ruslan showed everyone the pie box. 'I, uh, got pecan pie.'

'Aw, my favourite!' Saira said gleefully. She sprang up to her feet to take the box from him. 'Can I get you some cider?'

'Oh, yeah, I'd love some. Thanks,' Ruslan said with a knowing grin. 'Good to see you all. Marisha. Vor Karmazin. Mrs Karmazin. Grigori.'

Nostrils flaring in indignation, Grigori acknowledged him with a tight nod.

'Right, then.' Awkwardly gesturing over his shoulder at Payal, he backed himself into the kitchen and whispered, 'Please tell me there's something I can do to avoid being social.'

'Hmm, I dunno,' Payal said, giving the soup one last stir before switching the stove off. 'How's your hand-eye coordination? Can I trust you to pour the soup into the tureen?'

'Please,' Ruslan scoffed cockily. 'Mastering the borsch ladle's a prerequisite to handling a gun for us thieves.'

Payal arched an incredulous brow, then shrugged. 'Okay. Saira can get the gravy in the boat.'

She and Oleksiy, in the meantime, tended to the precarious task of transferring the turkey onto a serving platter.

'Bold of you,' Oleksiy teased, so quietly it was only meant for her ears, 'trusting him around Saira, knowing the effect he has on women.'

Payal's harried glare had him biting back laughter.

'Do you children need any help?' Payal's mumma called from the living room.

'No,' the four of them replied in unison.

Dinner was served buffet style on the breakfast counter around a candelabra they'd received as a wedding gift. The tension of Ruslan's arrival eased a hair as everyone marvelled at the spread.

'Should we go around and share what we're all thankful for?' Payal asked with a laugh.

The consensus was a gruff, fervent and borderline appalled, 'No!'

Rolling her eyes like she wasn't at all surprised, Payal handed Oleksiy the carving knife and prongs to do the honours.

The thief prince sliced into the meat, thus starting what would hopefully become a longstanding tradition with the people he cherished most—people, who up until this day, he'd never imagined seeing in a room together.

He had a lot to be grateful for. And as he fumbled with his cutting implements, making mince out of their beautifully cooked turkey, he looked up at the person who'd helped him see how much he had, the person who'd helped him accept who he was, the person without whom none of this would've been possible:

His wife.

Acknowledgements

WHEN I STARTED WRITING *THE THIEF PRINCE'S WIFE* back in the summer of 2021, it was purely for my own amusement. A year later, I was very apologetic to my agent, Mita Kapur for sending her a book with such a silly premise, but she put me at ease, assuring me it was a fun read. I am immensely grateful to her for championing my work.

A big thank you to the team at Westland Books, especially Sanghamitra Biswas for acquiring the book, and Sanjana T for her meticulous and thoughtful edits.

Lastly, I'd like to thank my family and friends, especially my parents (who aren't allowed to read this book) for their unconditional love and support. I wouldn't be the author and person that I am without them.